"[A] heart-stealing opener to the Chicago Rebels sports contemporary series. . . . The mix of sexual tension and emotional decisions will lead Meader's series launch to many a keeper shelf."

—*Publishers Weekly* (starred review)

"Meader's writing is always impeccable, but she outdoes herself with this stellar contemporary romance. Flawless from start to finish, with smart dialogue, sizzling sex scenes, and the perfect amount of sweet moments."

—Lauren Layne, *New York Times* bestselling author

"Meader's signature firefighter heat transfers flawlessly to the world of high-stakes ice hockey in her hot-as-sin Chicago Rebels series."

—Gina Maxwell, *New York Times* bestselling author

PRAISE FOR
THE HOT IN CHICAGO SERIES

SPARKING THE FIRE

"The many instances of a family sticking together through it all are more than enough to tug on the heartstrings, but the steamy sex and sentimental pillow talk make this book a must-read."

—*RT Book Reviews*

"WOW . . . Amazing, beautiful, and tissue-worthy. That is what this book is."

—*Harlequin Junkie*

PLAYING WITH FIRE

Winner of the RT Book Reviewers' 2015 Award for Best Contemporary Love & Laughter

A *Publishers Weekly* Best Book of 2015

A *Washington Post* Best Romance of 2015

"Meader packs the flawless second Hot in Chicago romance with superb relationship development and profane but note-perfect dialogue."

—*Publishers Weekly* (starred review)

"Steamy sex scenes, colorful characters, and riveting dialogue . . . a real page-turner."

—*RT Book Reviews* (Top Pick Gold)

"A smart, sexy book."

—Sarah MacLean, *The Washington Post*

FLIRTING WITH FIRE

"Sexy and sassy . . . I love this book!"

—Jude Deveraux, #1 *New York Times* bestselling author

"Get your fire extinguisher ready—*Flirting with Fire* is HOT and satisfying!"

—Jennifer Probst, *New York Times* bestselling author

"This book is everything you want in a romance: excellent writing, strong characters, and a sizzling plot that keeps the pace up throughout the story."

—*RT Book Reviews* (Top Pick)

BOOKS BY KATE MEADER

The Chicago Rebels Series

In Skates Trouble
Irresistible You
So Over You
Undone by You

The Hot in Chicago Series

Rekindle the Flame
Flirting with Fire
Melting Point
Playing with Fire
Sparking the Fire

Hooked on You

KATE MEADER

Pocket Books

New York   London   Toronto   Sydney   New Delhi

Pocket Books
An Imprint of Simon & Schuster, Inc.
1230 Avenue of the Americas
New York, NY 10020

This book is a work of fiction. Any references to historical events, real people, or real places are used fictitiously. Other names, characters, places, and events are products of the author's imagination, and any resemblance to actual events or places or persons, living or dead, is entirely coincidental.

First Pocket Books paperback edition June 2018

POCKET and colophon are registered trademarks of
Simon & Schuster, Inc.

For information about special discounts for bulk purchases, please contact Simon & Schuster Special Sales at 1-866-506-1949
or business@simonandschuster.com.

The Simon & Schuster Speakers Bureau can bring authors to your live event. For more information or to book an event, contact the Simon & Schuster Speakers Bureau at 1-866-248-3049 or visit our website at www.simonspeakers.com.

Interior design by Alison Cnockaert

Manufactured in the United States of America

10   9   8   7   6   5   4   3   2   1

ISBN 978-1-5011-8090-3
ISBN 978-1-5011-6857-4 (ebook)

To all the women who were warned, silenced,
and dismissed, yet still persisted

You miss 100 percent of the shots you don't take.

—Wayne Gretzky, NHL Hall of Famer

I am not throwing away my shot.

—*Hamilton: An American Musical*

PROLOGUE

She needed a drink.

And while Violet Vasquez wasn't big on boozing before five, she figured that now might be as good a time as any to start. Neither was she big on signs, but the one that had caught her attention *had* to be the universe telling her something.

The bar, called the Empty Net, had two hockey sticks crossed like cutlasses over the door.

Yeah, someone was screwing with her, she thought as she exited the cab on the main drag in Riverbrook, thirty miles north of downtown Chicago—and she had an idea who. But she wasn't one to back down from a challenge. Day drinking would commence in three, two, one . . .

Pulling the heavy oak door open, Violet walked out of the sun and into a bar fight.

On closer inspection, this was pretty tame as bar fights went. It had the makings of a doozy, though, because at the center of it was a hulk. A long-haired, bearded, fuck-with-me-if-you-don't-want-to-live behemoth. Three guys with a death wish and/or shit for brains surrounded him, all but begging to be crushed.

One of them was right up in his face, his spittle-flecked lips working soundlessly, his fists clenched at his sides. Another had the hulk boxed in on the shorter end of the L-shaped bar with a pool cue in his hand. And number three? This joker was clearly the spokesman, and right now he was getting something off his chest.

"You're a lowlife, St. James," the leader spat out. "You haven't had a good season in years. You got some nerve showing your face around here."

St. James—which was sort of ironic, because this guy looked like he rode with the devil instead of the angels—didn't defend himself. Just held himself taut, ready.

"Better not be any trouble," a female voice called out. The bartender. Violet, familiar with the undercurrents of drunk drama from her nights tending bar at Rusty's Biker Emporium in Reno, recognized the thread of concern in her voice. She was staffing the place alone in the middle of the afternoon. Maybe they had security at night, but right now this woman was helpless to break up a fight with anything but diplomacy.

"There'll be no trouble," the hulk said, and though he was responding to the bartender, the message was for the Three Stooges in front of him. There was also something odd about his voice: deep, resonant, and . . . Irish?

As the guy with the pool cue moved closer, the bartender caught Violet's eye, her expression one of mild panic. Violet shook her head slightly. She trusted that the hulk had this under control, that he could defuse the situation.

"You don't want to do that," he said to Pool Cue.

"I'm calling the police," the bartender said.

Nope. Not helping.

"No police" was the hulk's response, but he said it like *pole-is*. Now Violet heard it more clearly—she'd watched enough *Outlander* episodes to recognize a Scottish accent.

No sooner had he affirmed that the law was not needed than the idiots surrounding him burst into action. Clenched Fists raised his right hand, only to have the Scot react with lightning speed and cover it with one king-sized paw. At the same time, he grabbed the cue from the other guy's hand, smashed it against the bar, and held the splinter-topped weapon to Pool Cue's throat. Crushing a fist with one hand, threatening a jugular with another, he stared directly at the guy who had been mouthing off.

And raised a very expressive eyebrow.

Violet's entire body tingled and her heart thrashed about. Oh, the Scot was something else.

The lynch mob spokesman backed up, hands raised. "Got it. We're just talking."

"Go talk over there." A chin jerk from the Scot indicated another part of the bar. Rather charitably, to Violet's mind, he released the raised fist, then placed the shattered cue on the bar. The bar fight that had never quite started expired with a whimper as the men slunk away to lick their wounds.

Violet took a look at her surroundings. For early afternoon, the bar was surprisingly busy, with a few people playing darts and a couple of guys at a pool table. The TV screens blasted a hockey game, though it was mid-September and out of season—she knew that much. But the entertainment shouldn't have been all that surprising, given the bar's proximity to the arena of the local NHL franchise, the Chicago Rebels.

The team she now owned.

Violet stepped forward and picked up the other half of the cue. Carefully, she placed it with its soul mate on the bar.

The Scot didn't acknowledge that, as if he hadn't even noticed her, which was generally impossible because on a noticeability scale of one to ten, Violet usually landed at nine. But not today, because for this visit to Chicagoland, she'd gone conservative and changed her hair from magenta streaks to its original dark and dull brown. Damn her conforming hair color!

Mr. Surly took a seat and caught the eye of the bartender, who walked over, looking like she was *this* close to having a coronary.

"You okay?"

The Scot turned slightly, and Violet realized that the bartender was speaking to her.

"Oh, fine. Chivas rocks, please." She climbed onto a bar stool beside the Scot, who was frowning in a most attractive manner.

"Plenty of seats elsewhere," he muttered.

Oh, you old romantic you!

The barfly gods were shining on her, because at that moment, Violet's Chivas appeared. Extra tip for you, barkeep.

"Yeah, but my drink is right here."

Evidently unable to fault that logic, he spoke to the bartender. "My usual, Tina."

"Are you sure—?"

He cut off her question with a glare. "It's your funeral," she finished.

"Nicely handled," Violet said when Tina was out of earshot. "What's their problem, anyway?"

"Me."

"I got that." She imagined this guy would be a whole lot of problems, at least 75 percent of them sexy. "Why specifically did they want to rearrange your pretty face?"

He turned, eyes narrowing on her. "You don't recognize this pretty face?"

She looked more closely—not a chore in the slightest. She supposed he did look a little familiar, kind of like if Jason Momoa and Gerard Butler had gotten down and dirty and sweated out a big-shouldered beast-child.

While her body's tingles moved south, she reassessed the situation. Sports bar with hockey on TV, proximity to the Rebels arena, expectation of being recognized.

He must be one of the players.

She played dumb. "You owe them money?"

"Owe them something. Or they think I do."

Tina placed a shot of Johnnie Walker before the Scot and, with a *hmph*, moved off. Interesting.

Violet took a sip of her Chivas. The Scot had yet to lift his whisky. They sat in semicomfortable silence for a few moments while Violet thought this through.

The past eighteen months had been the road trip to hell, but Violet had made the return journey and now she tended to look at things from a different angle. "The Year of the V," she'd been calling her adjusted outlook. She was determined to try new things, step up and be counted, find out who Violet Vasquez was, for want of a less vomit-inducing phrase. Fear had a way of closing a person off, making the world a small and lonely place.

Fear could go fuck itself.

The next time she had sex would be the first time since the surgery, since she'd woken up bound like The Mummy, with new breasts to replace the diseased ones. A quickie in a bar restroom with a hot stranger would be the perfect way to jump back on the horse. Clothes would stay on, scars would stay hidden . . . the Scot would be strong enough to lift her against a wall and slide right in.

Then she'd be on a plane back to Reno, her pleasurable memories the best souvenir.

Before she could turn on her rusty wiles, the stranger spoke. "You disagreed with Tina. About calling the cops."

She liked it better when he called them the *pole-is*.

But the notion that he had been aware of her silent objection even while he had other things going on was a pleasant surprise.

"I've worked in bars, most of them not as nice as this one. The threat of cops, in my experience, usually escalates an already bad situation."

He studied her now, as if she had suddenly said something worth listening to. Those tingles started again, her body reflooding with sexual awareness. She was unable to look away, and it seemed he was in the same boat. Something charged, hot, and melty zinged between them. Her nerves were no longer tingling. Now they were shrieking.

"Whatever you're thinking," he murmured, "it's a bad idea."

Blood heated her cheeks. Was she so obvious? She picked up her drink and took a gulp. When she looked up again, he appeared closer. More dangerous.

"Season's about to begin so you thought you'd come in here and bag yourself a player?"

Now wait a second, who the fuck did this guy think he was? So maybe the idea of gracing him with the pleasure of giving her an orgasm had crossed her mind for a foolish moment, but what kind of asshole said that? As if she were some sex-crazed hockey groupie.

"Yep, that's exactly what I thought." And then she winked.

He laughed, and the sound gave her heart a hug. *Still got it, Vasquez.* The bartender shot them a glance, then peered curiously at Violet, Laugh Maker.

The Scot turned serious again, his blue-eyed gaze flicking to the untouched shot of whisky. "Go on home, lass, before you get hurt."

"By you?" She snorted. "I don't think you could hurt anyone." She'd seen how he handled those idiots. He could have done some real damage, but he chose to restrain himself. It would be fascinating to see him lose control.

He inhaled a weary breath. "That's where you're wrong. I have a tendency to destroy everything I touch." He raised his gaze to her, and what she saw there shocked her. A pain she recognized.

"I'm tougher than I look," she said, not quite willing to let this go, though common sense told her she should probably run back to Nevada as fast as her combat boots could carry her.

He stood. Loomed was more accurate, all six feet two inches of him, yet there was something both aggressive and tentative in his stance. Color flagged his cheekbones. Fire rimmed his eyes. Her own greedy gaze was drawn to his thick forearms, then continued on a trail down to his two clenched fists.

Was he angry? No. Or at least, not with her . . . oh, God.

He was using every ounce of his self-control trying not to touch her.

She had never wanted someone to lose a battle with his demons so much.

"You driving?" he managed in a harsh whisper.

"I came in a cab."

"Good. Make sure you go home in one." With his strong accent, it came out sounding like *guut*. He threw down a twenty and left without a backward glance, his shot of whisky still untouched on the bar.

The bartender—Tina—came over, her expression one of disapproval mixed with pity that Violet had been rejected. Not that Violet really saw it that way. What had happened between her and the Scot was far more thought provoking.

"Want that?" Tina asked, nodding at the shot glass.

"Nah. I don't drink swill."

Tina laughed appreciatively, picked up the glass, and poured the shot into the sink.

"So, who's been warming this bar stool beside me for the past ten minutes?"

"You really don't know him?"

Violet shook her head. "I'm new in town."

"That was Bren St. James, current captain of the Chicago Rebels, the local hockey team. Though whether he'll be captain for much longer is open to speculation."

No need to ask for details, because Tina was in full flight now.

"He showed up to one of the last games of the regular season drunk, and the way he'd been playing all year, it was clearly not the first time. Most people think he should've been cut long before that, and *some* people"— she jerked her chin in the direction of the troublemakers from earlier, who were now back to playing pool like nothing had happened—"think he needs to be taught a lesson. Folks are pretty crazy about hockey around here, and when your team is suffering through its longest-ever championship drought, it makes the fans loco. The players, too."

Sports people. Fucking nutjobs, the lot of them. Before Violet could inquire further, the bar's phone rang and Tina went to answer it while Violet was left to ponder Bren St. James, the grumpy Scot shrouded in mystery. A man with demons that needed soothing and sating. *O captain! My captain!*

The Year of the V had just become a lot more interesting.

ONE

Eight months later...

Bren sank his ass into one of those low-slung leather chairs specifically designed to make a man feel small. The last time he'd sat in this office he had left with orders to dry out or get out. Miraculously, he'd escaped with his job, if not with his dignity. Now he was back on a different mission of mercy.

The man he'd faced the last time was no longer in charge. Clifford Chase had finally choked on his own bile, and Bren didn't miss him. Harsh as it sounded, Cliff's death was the best thing that could've happened to the team, because in the eight months since he'd bought the farm, the Rebels had gone from zeroes to heroes.

This was largely due to the woman before him.

Harper Chase—all five feet one and a half inches of her—would probably not agree with Bren, but she was more like her father than she'd care to admit. A complete hard-ass, but unlike him, she had a gooey center, which was now on display.

"Bren, we're going to do everything in our power to

support you and your family. Now, how are the girls doing? This must be a shock for them."

"Aye." Bren rubbed his beard—a play-off beard because the Rebels were in the postseason for the first time in fifteen years—and thought about how much he wanted to share with his boss. But he and Harper went way back, and now wasn't the time for reticence, not when his ex-wife had screwed him over again.

"They've wanted to live with me for a while. It's just that the circumstances are not exactly ideal."

"I know you've missed them . . ." Harper said, leaving the rest unspoken.

What she probably wanted to say was, *I know you've missed them, but your ex-wife chose the worst fucking time to have a meltdown in the granola aisle at Whole Foods and then check herself into a clinic for a "rest."*

"The worst fucking time" being two days before the start of round one of the play-offs.

In Dallas.

Against the top-seeded team in the Western Conference.

"What about your in-laws?" Harper asked.

Bren's stomach churned at the mention of those vultures. Two days ago he'd received a call from Drew Cassidy, his ex-wife's current boyfriend. Kendra needed "space"—though the online pictures of the place where she was staying definitely put it in on the "spa" end of the spectrum—and had called her parents to care for the kids. Drew might be the guy who banged Bren's ex-wife while she was not-ex, but he wasn't a complete asshole.

"They're your kids, man, and I figure you should know. Kendra didn't want me to call you. She just wanted to let her parents handle it, but it doesn't seem right."

No, it did not.

Three hours later, Bren was in Atlanta and in a face-off with his in-laws, the Gordons, who had chartered a jet from LA to get there.

To steal his fucking kids.

"This is what Kendra wants, Brendan, and as the girls' primary caregiver in the divorce, her wishes should be obeyed. Caitriona and Franky are coming to LA with us."

Bren could have gone ballistic. Every cell in his body itched to. But that would've scared his girls and given grist to the Gordons' mill. Instead he'd called his lawyer, explained the situation, and then calmly told his in-laws what was going to happen.

The girls would live with him until Kendra was better.

The Gordons could visit, but not for a month, until the girls had settled in.

If they wanted to make a fuss, they'd better load up their guns, because Bren would never back down.

"Not an option," Bren now told Harper. "And you know I don't have any family nearby." His parents were long gone, and his stepmother in Winnipeg wouldn't be interested. Besides, the idea of sending his kids away was like stripping his skin to the bone. They'd lived with their mom for the last year and now he had them again. Shitty circumstances, but he had them.

This time, he wasn't letting go.

"We can arrange something through a service," Harper continued. "Nannies shouldn't be hard to find."

"I suppose," Bren said doubtfully. He'd need more than a nanny. How about a housekeeper? On top of that, a tutor would come in extra handy because there were two months left in the school year, and he'd had to pull them as soon as he heard what happened. So three different positions right there, because he doubted Mary Poppins actually existed.

"We'll all chip in and help, Bren," Harper said with a cheer that was starting to piss him off. "Until you find someone, they can stay with me during away games."

His head snapped back. "Harper, I can't let you do that."

Harper sat in the other leather armchair beside Bren, hands clasped in her lap, her petite stature making her sink even farther.

"We go back a long way, you and I," she said quietly.

"Aye, we do." He'd started with the Rebels feeder team in Rockford before his call-up to the majors eleven years ago. He'd had chances to leave, but he stuck around through the bad times and worse. One of them was finding Harper in the Rebels locker room, her lip bloody, another player looming over her and shaking out his fist. That bastard didn't remain on the Rebels much longer. Left a couple of teeth behind, too.

Harper might think Bren's defense of her created an obligation between them, but not as far as Bren was concerned. She had repaid him handsomely last year.

Instead of canning his ass when he showed up for a game drunk, she'd persuaded her father to give him another chance as long as he entered rehab.

He'd spent the past eleven months acting like a monk. No booze, no fighting, no sex.

Christ, he missed sex.

"You don't owe me this, Harper. I'll figure something out."

"What? We need you in Dallas when the team flies out tomorrow."

"The girls can travel with me."

"They're nine and eleven, Bren. You can't be dragging them all over the country. They need stability and we need you playing to the best of your ability and not worrying about who's looking after them. We'll work on hiring professional help, but for this first round of the play-offs, you're going to have to let us help you. The WAGs are on the case. Me, Addison, Isobel, and—"

"Not Violet."

He almost spat out her name, immediately regretting how much it revealed about his state of mind. What he didn't regret? How his mouth felt when shaping the word: *Vi-o-let*. It had a musical quality that had always appealed to him. Pity its owner was *far* too appealing.

Harper looked understandably taken aback. "Well, she's not a wife or girlfriend, but I'm sure she'd help out if asked. In fact, given that she doesn't have an official role in the organization—or an actual job—she could prove useful."

He snorted. What was wrong with him? Usually as stoic as they came, he found it near impossible to control himself whenever the youngest daughter of Clifford Chase was mentioned. Or came within earshot. Or was near enough to touch and taste and—

"She's sort of . . . flighty," he said, trying to sound reasonable, when his thoughts on Violet were anything but. "A party girl. This wouldn't interest her."

Caitriona and Franky had endured far too much insecurity, most of which was Bren's fault. They didn't need an unreliable slip of a girl like Violet who laughed too hard, flirted too much, and did an admirable job of getting under Bren's skin.

He wasn't fool enough to deny his attraction to her, but then he'd always been drawn to wild women, like his ex. And look how that turned out.

"My lawyer thinks I have a good chance at full custody, but I have to do this right. Dot the i's and cross the t's. Keep my head down and my nose clean." He let her infer the rest. He refused to give Kendra any extra ammunition, and that started with ensuring that his daughters' child-care arrangements were handled professionally.

Harper patted his arm as if his Violet objections were the most natural thing in the world. He felt a little guilty at painting her in a bad light, and even more so now that Harper seemed to readily understand.

"We'll figure it out, Bren. Let the girls stay at Chase Manor while you go to Dallas for the first two games. I'll work with an agency to set up some interviews for a more permanent position. I can even arrange to have someone open up your house and get it ready for the girls."

The house. He hadn't even thought about that. While his daughters usually stayed with him in his rented apartment when they came to visit once a month, they had all once lived together in the house on the lake. Being back on their old stomping ground might help them adjust to the big changes.

"That'd be great, Harper."

She squeezed his arm. "We old-timers have to stick together, Bren. It's also what family does. And the Rebels are family."

Violet had never been a fan of kids.

Okay, not exactly true. She wasn't a fan of the small, wrinkled, poopy ones. Ankle biters fared much better in her eyes when they developed personalities.

So, faced with the sight of two kids in the Rebels front office suite—girls of an indeterminate age because Violet could never guess these things—she was curious, because personality radiated from them. She'd seen St. James's daughters once before from a distance. Now, close up, she tried to determine if they looked like him. Both dark haired, one had a snooty air to her, while the other rocked a nerdy look with glasses. They sat in the chairs outside Dante's office, eyes glued to an iPad and a book respectively, looking a little lost.

Behind her, a deep voice rumbled, "They don't bite, y'know."

She turned to take in the hotness that was Dante Moretti, general manager of the Rebels. "Can you guarantee that?"

Dante shrugged one broad shoulder encased in a dove-gray designer suit. "These ones? No. I only have experience with a couple of mouthy Brooklyn chicks who would sell their souls for Taylor Swift tickets."

Violet laughed softly. "Your nieces sound adorable."

Perhaps sensing she was being studied, the girl who looked older—ten? fourteen?—squinted in suspicion at Violet. Reminded that she sported purple-streaked hair and was dressed in a denim mini that showcased her tattooed thighs, Violet offered a smile to affirm she was one of the good ones. Unimpressed Child returned to her tablet.

"You here to see Harper?" Dante asked.

"Yeah, we were going to do lunch."

"She's in my office with St. James."

Violet figured as much. She jerked her chin and walked down the corridor a ways so they were out of earshot.

"What's going on?"

Dante looked over his shoulder, his lake-blue eyes troubled. "The girls will be staying with their father for a while. Mom's checked in to some facility for a rest."

Code: rehab. Shit, the mom as well? Those poor kids couldn't catch a break.

Dante went on. "Harper's giving him the spiel about

how we've got his back, et cetera. Expect the Bat-Signal any minute now to get everyone on a baby-sitting roster."

That sounded like her oldest sister. Harper was a fixer, the kind of person who liked to run people's lives like a pro hockey team, which had worked peachy while she was trying to ignore her own needs.

Dante was eyeing her speculatively. "What?" she asked.

"So, what exactly do you do around here, Vasquez?"

Despite the affection she heard in the question, she bristled. So maybe she knew jack about hockey, unlike Harper and their sister Isobel. As in Isobel Chase, NCAA champion, Olympic silver medalist, and celebrated coach. Violet had only stuck around because dearest Dad's last will and testament required that all three sisters manage the team jointly, or it would be sold off. The team also had to make the play-offs—and now they had. Achievement unlocked, and her cut of the pie was definitely worth more now than when she'd first arrived.

To be honest, Violet didn't have any good reason for remaining in Chicago much longer. Her sisters would buy her out as soon as she asked. With that kind of money, she could travel. Get a college degree. Visit her mom in Puerto Rico. Anything.

And the way Dante was looking at her, she just might get cracking on that plan sooner rather than later.

"I mooch off the Chase family name. What do *you* do, Moretti?"

He smiled. So pretty. "Any good with kids?"

Nopeity-nope-nope. "You put those kids under my

care and they'll be pierced and tatted by the end of the week."

"As long as it's a Rebels tat, I don't have a problem with that."

"Like you said, there'll be plenty of WAGs dying to help out. Hell, you could flash a Nanny Wanted sign on the arena scoreboard and have them lining up around the block for a chance to polish Highlander's peen."

"Hmm" was all Dante had to say about that.

Before Violet could protest further, the door to his office opened and out came the man himself, wearing a tee with Scotland vs. Everyone emblazoned across his vast chest. Bren St. James, captain of the Rebels, aka Saint aka Highlander aka Nessie. Though only Violet called him that last one, and man-on-fire did it piss him off. His brutally handsome face would transform into a scowl that was probably the hottest thing Violet had ever seen.

So she'd say it again. *Nessie.*

Super scowl. Wet panties.

Today was no different. His midnight-blue eyes clashed with her green ones and she didn't even have to open her mouth. *Holy lip bite.* The scowl was already activated on sight and Violet's lady parts were already damp. The fact that this guy totally despised her was a bonus that revved her engine from zero to sixty in seconds flat. When they finally got it on, the sex would be spectacular.

Ha-ha, very funny, Vasquez. That would *so* not be happening. The Grumpster blew it that first day they met in the Empty Net.

"Dad!" The shorter girl with the glasses hopped up and hugged St. James as if it had been months since she'd seen him, instead of the hour max he'd spent in that meeting. "We have to get home to Gretzky. He doesn't do well alone."

The Scot's growly demeanor melted as he wrapped his big arms around his daughter. Meanwhile, more melting was happening in Violet's immediate vicinity, points south. Oh yeah. This guy would have zero problems finding child care.

"Franky, the dog is fine. I leave him alone all the time."

"Better he's alone so we don't have to smell his farts," said Tall Diva without even looking up from her tablet. Violet would bet her share of the Rebels this one took after her mom.

As soon as the thought formed, Violet mentally berated herself. She had no idea what St. James's ex was like. The woman was probably a saint for putting up with this brood monster for years before he finally hit rehab on orders from team management. Yet Violet couldn't help thinking there was more to Bren St. James beyond the bullet points splashed all over sports websites during his meltdown last year: *Washed-up alcoholic. Bad husband. Rotten father.*

Harper appeared behind the Scot, petite, blond, and perfectly put together.

"Hey, girls, so what do you say to a sleepover at my place?" she asked. "I have so much ice cream that I really need help getting through it."

Violet gave Dante a sidelong glance. "Are you kidding?"

"Probably practicing for when Remy knocks her up," Dante said under his breath, and Violet laughed.

The laugh focused St. James's attention on her. Or rather refocused it, because he'd definitely spotted her when he exited the office.

Time for her daily fun. "Nessie! How goes it?"

He inhaled deeply and ran a hand through his overlong dark hair, his irritation obvious. Ignoring her as usual, he addressed his girls. "So, you know the play-offs start the day after tomorrow? I have to go out of town for a few days, and you're going to stay with Harper."

The youngest girl—Franky—frowned but quickly adjusted it to a smile, first at her dad, then at Harper. Either a people pleaser or a master manipulator, she was one to watch.

"Caitriona?" St. James spoke to the older girl, still riveted to her iPad. "That okay with you?"

"Do I have a choice?"

"Nope," her father said, and his matter-of-fact manner made Violet laugh, then immediately stifle it when she felt Dante's gaze zero in on her. "I'll bring them over tomorrow morning before the bus leaves for the airport," Bren said to Harper. "Thanks again."

"Not a problem. Looking forward to it." And then to the girls, "Bring your appetites, ladies!"

With protective hands on his daughters' shoulders, Bren walked them toward the suite's exit, which meant he had to pass by Violet and Dante.

"What, no introductions, Nessie?"

Franky peered up at her. "Why does she call you that, Dad?"

"Because she's a bit cracked in the head, love."

Violet laughed again—a little too hard, if the weird looks Harper and Dante threw her way were any indication.

So, here was the deal: Violet found it virtually impossible to act like a sane female around St. James. There was something about his grumpy, beastly exterior that made her itch to provoke a reaction, and as the sullen Scot went out of his way *not* to talk to her, she could tell he was desperate to do it. Or maybe she hoped he was. Her efforts to provoke him couldn't be all for nothing, could they?

For the past few months, she'd been in a faux friends-with-bennies situation with Cade "Alamo" Burnett, a gay Rebels player in need of cover, which gave Violet the perfect opportunity to needle the team's captain. Whenever Bren was in earshot, Violet would laugh heartily at Cade's jokes, causing the hottie Texan to roll his eyes dramatically and grind out, *I'm not that funny.* Her response? Flutter her fingers on Cade's chest, bat her eyelashes vehemently, and giggle-gasp, *I know!* with an extrabig laugh to punctuate it. But Cade no longer needed her help since announcing to the world that he liked boys in general and Dante in particular. His secret was public and so, in a way, was hers.

Outed as a fraud who got her kicks from cock teasing an irascible, alcoholic Scotsman. *For shame, Vasquez.*

Violet tilted her head at Bren's youngest daughter. "You ever heard of the Loch Ness Monster?"

Franky nodded solemnly.

"That's why we call him Nessie. Because he's Scottish. Mysterious. Mythical."

"And a monster," the girl added, still solemn.

Oh dear, that wasn't Violet's intention at all. "Well, I wouldn't go that far."

Before she could assure the girl that her father wasn't *really* a monster, Franky broke into a huge grin that knocked the whole room sideways with its power. She peered owl-like at her father.

"Just kidding, Dad. You're not a monster, and you're *definitely* not mythical."

St. James appeared spectacularly resigned. "Sure I am. My skills are legendary." Seeming to realize that could be taken a number of ways, he reddened and added, "On the ice." He caught Violet's eye, his expression lovingly murderous at being drawn into this weird conversation.

Violet smiled evilly in return. "I meant the fictitious interpretation of mythical versus the one that implies you're a legend, Nessie. Let's not go overboard, 'kay?"

Was that a kick to the corner of his mouth? It was so hard to tell with that beard of awesome.

The older girl rolled her eyes. "Dad, we should go."

"Aye, we should." He turned to Harper. "Thanks again. I'll see you soon."

Franky smiled at Violet as she walked by. "I like your hair."

"Hey, thanks. I like your glasses."

With St. James and his brood gone, Dante split a

glance between Violet and Harper before finally settling on the woman in charge. There was a fair bit of twinkling going on in those Italian blues.

"Are you thinking what I'm thinking?"

Before her sister could respond, Violet jumped in. "Uh, I'm not baby-sitting. I've got too much going on. Redecorating the cottage. Working on my tan. Improv and flamenco classes."

"You'd be doing us a huge favor," Dante said.

"Actually," Harper said with a tight smile, "we won't need your help, Vi. I've got it all under control."

Violet tensed, realizing she'd protested too much. No way did she want people thinking she wasn't a team player. Although she pretty much refused to have anything to do with the business of running the team—and she spent most of her days taking fun classes and shopping—she knew the meaning of real work. After busting her balls for so long and going through a serious medical situation, the past few months had been the ultimate breather. Getting closer to the half sisters she'd never known up until eight months ago had been an unexpected bonus—not that she'd ever tell them. They weren't really that kind of family.

"I don't mind helping out. If you need me to drive them somewhere or supervise playdates . . ." She had no idea what kids that age needed. "Call on me."

Harper squeezed Violet's arm and Vi sensed—oh, God—*pity* in the gesture. "Sure, we know where to find you. Now, let's grab lunch."

TWO

A captain's band meant something. Responsibility, leadership, rock-solid strength. Bren had always thought he had these traits in spades.

Even when he was drinking a bottle of whiskey a day.

Even when his wife was fucking an NFL wide receiver.

Even when his problems started to sneak up on him, affecting his play.

Because even when all that shit was going down, he had his girls, his beautiful daughters for whom he would skate through fire. If someone told him he had to surrender his band to spend more time with them, he'd rip it off without question. If Coach Calhoun said he couldn't play in the finals and be a good father at the same time, there would be no contest. While Bren was a natural skater, he was a born father.

Fancy sentiments, for sure. They meant sweet fuck all without action.

His girls didn't like him much right now. Well,

Franky liked him fine, but then she was an eternal optimist. Caitriona wanted to believe. He saw it in her eyes, that quick spark of hope that would dull because he'd let her down. Chosen his love of the bottle over his love for her.

At the ripe old age of thirty-one, he had a second chance: the play-offs *and* his girls. Twelve years in this business and his first time in the postseason. Possibly his last time. He'd stayed in Chicago for Kendra, who liked living there until she didn't. Now he was damaged goods and no team but the Rebels would have him.

Sitting on the visitors' bench in the Dallas Steers FedEx Arena, Bren tried to focus on the game. One goal apiece, middle of the third. It might have been his imagination, but this level seemed faster, like moving from junior league to the farm team, from the minors to the NHL. Each new grade put you against bigger guys, faster skaters, blink-and-you-miss-it plays. The Rebels had played Dallas before, so it shouldn't be different. Yet it was.

Desperation tinged the air. It was a best-of-seven series and it felt like everything was riding on this first game.

"You're in, Highlander," Coach shouted to be heard above the crowd noise. But he needn't have bothered, because Bren would have heard a whisper if it told him it was his turn. This was what he lived for.

Remy came off and touched his arm, like a passing of the baton. They were both centers, so they rarely played on the same line unless Coach wanted to mix things up. No one experimented during the play-offs, so when Bren was on, Remy was off.

"*Allons-y*," the Cajun said. *Let's go.* All those Frenchisms used to annoy Bren—Remy used to annoy Bren—but not anymore. Remy was the reason the team had found its way back in the past eight months. The man stepped up when Bren couldn't, and the chatty charmer had become one of his closest friends.

Bren skated on, assessing everyone's position, figuring out the dynamic. Every team, game, and play had a different one. This minute, Callaghan was on the right, Petrov on his left. Bren was the traffic cop, making sure every pass got to where it needed to go. Block, intercept, push, retreat—it was all part of his repertoire and the reason people in the know considered him underrated. Solid and steady, never flashy. The wingers scored more, but that was as it should be. He wasn't one for the spotlight.

Where Bren excelled was in the face-off. He had a 58.6 percent record going into this game, and no way in hell was he letting that stat slip. After two minutes on the ice, they had the chance of a five-on-four power play, their best shot at pulling ahead.

Bren won the face-off and passed to Petrov, who took the puck and stuck with it down the line like it was Velcroed to his blade. Holstadt, one of the Dallas defenders, cross-checked him but didn't get called for a minor, probably because Petrov managed to get the puck back into Rebels possession.

Back onto Bren's blade.

In the attacking zone, Bren studied the placement of everyone. Some nights his mind operated with the vision of an overhead drone. God's view. This was one of those nights. He drew geometric lines in his head between each player, figuring out who would benefit most from his pass. Needing to think three moves ahead, he held the puck for an extra half second before flicking it behind him to Petrov and praying the Russian was paying attention. With a side step to reveal the opening, Bren moved and watched with satisfaction as Vadim slapped the shot and bulged the twine.

The goal-scoring buzzer was the sweetest sound imaginable. Well, almost as sweet as his girls' giggles.

"Hello, I'm Bren and I'm an alcoholic."

"Hi, Bren," a chorus of strangers' voices sang back at him.

The beauty of AA was that no matter what city you were in or the time of day, there was usually a meeting happening nearby. Dallas was no different. The Rebels had won the first game of the series last night, but that didn't stop the gnawing ache that threatened to eat Bren from the inside out. The team might be his brothers, but these strangers were his tribe.

Another day, another musty church basement. Damn, he could create a handy-dandy travel guide for church basements across North America.

Seattle: damp, smells of fish, excellent coffee.

Nashville: strains of country trickling in from the bar on the corner. Irony of meeting location noted.

Dallas: plentiful beef jerky and donuts. The same haunted faces as any other AA group.

Standing up and sharing was something Bren hadn't done much of since the earliest meetings after he exited rehab. Back then, it was a way to prove he was taking the process seriously. Now he was more likely to load up on caffeine, sit back, and listen. Chronically shy as a child, he'd used alcohol as a crutch and a way to connect with his equally reticent father, and without that lubricant, the talking refused to come easy to him. But today, he needed to be heard in an environment where no one judged.

He inhaled a shaky breath. "Last night, I took a step toward something that could amount to a career high if it all goes as planned." Getting specific wasn't necessary; sharing in AA was all about *emoting*. "Basically, I won something and if I keep on winning, it would mean the world to me, my team, a lot of people who care about what I do. For years, I've been used to losing. Losing suits the alcoholic. Losing suits me. When I lose, I have an excuse to drink. No one questions drinks downed in self-consolation."

A few in the group nodded in recognition.

"Things are looking up for me, though. My daughters are back in my life. My career is on an upswing. I'm not dating yet—still inside my year. Not that I'm counting down the days or anything."

Everyone chuckled at that. AA guidelines recom-

mended a twelve-month break from relationships, and
Bren had been using it as some sort of benchmark for
when his life truly would be back on track. *Follow the
rules. You do you.*

He'd woken up earlier at the team hotel with his
usual morning wood, and instead of tapping into his
mental spank bank of images, he'd gone for a run.
Been a while since he'd done that. Usually, his time at
the gym and on the ice kept him fit, but he'd forgotten
the satisfaction of pounding the pavement, Slipknot
screaming in his ears, sweat rolling off his body. He'd
run a lot after rehab because it was either that, drink,
or fuck.

Two of the three were now off the menu.

One year, four months, a week, and three days—
that's how long since he'd been inside a woman. Given
that his divorce was finalized nine months ago while
he was in rehab, he guessed he should be grateful that
he hadn't added infidelity to his list of sins. The last
woman he slept with was his wife, which was miracu-
lous, considering how much of his spare time was spent
wasted, bellied up to bars, with women crawling all over
him. Some kernel of decency deep inside him had prevented him from going full-grade assholic and cheating
on Kendra.

*Don't worry, man, you have a million other sins to atone
for.*

A saucy grin lighting up sparkling green eyes flashed
through his brain. Whenever he thought of sex—and
these days, that was nonstop—it was invariably Violet's

face he saw. Violet's body he imagined beneath his. Violet's moans he heard in his fevered fantasies.

He shook his head, recalling his current purpose. "So yeah, it's all good for now. My girls, my job, my band of brothers. I've been so used to losing I'd forgotten how good it feels to be on an upward trajectory. And, well, it fucking terrifies me."

More nods now. The tribe understood fear of all stripes: of failure, but mostly of success, because it left you waiting for the other shoe to drop. If he'd been talking this out with Remy or someone on the team, they'd be interjecting at this point, fobbing him off with the usual platitudes. But not in AA. "No cross talk, no interruptions" was one of the rules.

"No one in my life before I got clean would've ever questioned me knocking back one or ten when my team lost. Just as no one questioned it when we won. My life was a perfect setup to cover my alcoholism. It still is. I don't have a nine-to-five job. I'm on the road constantly in the company of hard-drinking men, most of them younger than me with sky-high tolerance and whip-fast metabolisms. I lose, I drink. I win, I drink."

"Drank," someone called out. Against the rules, but Bren didn't mind, because he needed to hear that. He nodded at the weathered-looking guy in the third row who had spoken.

"Drank." Bren affirmed the past tense with a half smile. "Every day I struggle to stay sober. It's been almost eleven months of cultivating new habits. The habit of self-respect and of fatherhood. The habit of drinking Coke without Jack. The habit of teamwork and pride in a job well done. I hope that eventually it'll include the habit of being a good enough man for a woman. I hope also to acquire the habit of success—and appreciation for it. I live in hope, I suppose."

He arced his gaze over the group, few of whom knew and none of whom cared that he was a pro athlete in the first round of a Stanley Cup run. Well, the guy in the Dallas Steers jersey sneering at him from the front row might care because his team had gotten their asses handed to them last night. *Sorry not sorry, brother.* AA cared nothing for wealth, status, the sins that had stained your life to this point. The only requirement for membership was a desire to stop drinking—and a high tolerance for musty church basements.

"Thanks for listening." Bren took a seat to the soundtrack of *thanks, Bren*, knocked back a mouthful of godawful coffee, and settled in for the next speaker.

THREE

Maldito, she was out of coffee.

Definitely a first world problem, because Violet happened to live on the grounds of Chase Manor. Not *in* Chase Manor itself—heaven forbid—but in the coach house at the end of the drive near the main entrance. Like where the horses were desaddled or something in olden times. That was the kind of life her sisters had growing up, a life Violet couldn't relate to at all.

Eleven years ago, when she was thirteen, Violet had found out about her father. Who he was (Clifford Chase, NHL Hall of Famer, three-time Stanley Cup winner). Who he didn't want to be (an actual parent to the messy result of his one-night stand). He might not have known immediately, but he'd eventually learned that her mom had left that restroom at Caesar's Casino in Vegas with a puck strike between the pipes: Cliffie-boy's sperm, meet Louisa's egg. Ding, ding, ding—jackpot!

Informed of his responsibility, he made a settlement, but never any effort to contact his daughter until much later. To have any influence in her life other than financial. It had hurt more than Violet would ever reveal. Still did.

His leaving her a one-third ownership of his beloved hockey franchise was odd, to say the least. It felt like a game. A trap. Or, as she swiftly learned, some sort of test for Harper, whom he didn't trust to lead, and Isobel, in whom he placed all his faith. As for why Violet was included in this cluster, she couldn't be sure. Why not give her a chunk of change and be done? Not even the letter he left behind addressed to her personally gave much away.

Violet,

*I haven't been much of a father to you, and when I
realized my error, you had already decided you were
better off without me. I won't apologize for how
I behaved. It is what it is. While you refused my
efforts to help you financially with your medical bills
while I was alive, it seems petty to refuse now that
I'm dead. But that's not all I'm hoping for. I haven't
done the best by Harper and Isobel. The competitor
in me wanted them to duke it out and show me
what they were made of. I think your injection into
the mix will shake things up, and getting to know
your sisters might answer some of the questions
you've had all these years.*

Clifford Chase

Apparently, Violet's role was to play umpire while her half sisters navigated the thorny paths of *their* relationship. What a crock!

She didn't have to stay. She could have demanded they sold there and then, taken her cut, and gone on her way. But then she had that strange run-in with a cantankerous Scotsman in a bar and Harper had offered her a place to live rent-free. A few months to catch her breath was all she needed while she figured out her purpose.

She wasn't here to please a dead man, that was for sure. She knew all she needed to know about her father, and every moment she spent with Harper and Isobel since had only confirmed her initial impressions: the guy was an out-and-out asshole. His daughters, however? Pretty awesome.

She sighed. It was much too early for this level of navel-gazing. Back to her coffee issue.

Just before 7 a.m., she headed out, trudging toward the big house like she was on a mission to the South Pole. A beautiful April day, the air was crisp, the sun watery bright and making the fluffy clouds glow. Lake Michigan lay silent behind her as she picked her way up the path to the stone and cedar mansion where Harper had grown up, living with her dipso mom after her parents divorced when she was six years old.

With the key Harper had given her the day Violet moved into the cottage eight months ago, she unlocked the kitchen door to the main house and slid in, early enough that there was a good chance her oldest sister was still asleep.

Bren St. James's kids were seated at the kitchen table, eating Cheerios.

Violet recalled the vibe in the Rebels HQ front office a few days ago. Harper didn't want her near these kids, and while she'd tried not to let it bother her, the itch had slid like a burr under her skin. They had been here for the past few days, and knowing this, Violet had stayed out of their way.

The chartered flight from Dallas would have arrived early this morning. She'd assumed—oh hell, she didn't know what she'd assumed. That they wouldn't still be here? That the Scot would have picked them up because he missed them?

Franky looked up. "Hey, Pink."

"Hey, there." Perhaps the kid was color-blind, because her highlights were most definitely purple.

"Did you know that some species of gastropod mollusk practice apophallation during mating?"

Violet was inordinately proud that she understood about half of those words. "I had no idea."

Her ignorance must have been written all over her face, because Franky patiently explained. "It's when a slug's penis gets bitten off by his partner—or sometimes himself."

Okay, Harper and Iz must be playing a prank on her.

"That's disgusting," Caitriona said. Beats headphones cradled her head, but apparently the dick-eating habits of slugs penetrated all.

"It's nature," Franky said. "They just need the slug penis once, but the male slug doesn't die." Said as if the now dickless slug should be grateful. "It switches genders and just goes on to produce more eggs. It's a more efficient allocation of resources."

Violet's mom and two aunts—or the Macbeth Witches, as her ex, Denny, used to call them—would have gotten a perverse pleasure out of this conversation. Man haters to the core, all of them.

"Just came in for some coffee," Violet said, feeling she should justify her presence. Nothing new there. "Harper around?"

"She's throwing up," the slug expert revealed.

"Excuse me?"

Franky blinked big behind her glasses. "She was making us scrambled eggs and then she got this look on her face. Kind of like Dad used to get in the morning. Then she ran out."

"Hungover," pronounced Caitriona without even looking up from her cereal bowl.

This seemed a bit of a stretch, but who was Violet to argue with the logic of children who'd witnessed their alcoholic father worshipping the porcelain god? Maybe the baby Gorgons had driven Harper to overimbibe last night.

She surveyed the kitchen CSI-style. Half-scrambled eggs in a pan, untoasted bread in the toaster, a full pot of freshly brewed coffee. Conclusion: someone had started breakfast and hadn't finished. *Astounding, Sherlock.* She grabbed a cup off the phallus-shaped mug tree, smiling in memory at this misbegotten product of one of the Chase sisters' awkward sister bonding nights, and poured herself a cup of joe.

"You guys watch the game last night?"

"Yeah," Franky said with a long-suffering sigh. "Dad didn't play as well as he did in the first game, but Remy and Cade were awesome."

Violet's thoughts exactly. St. James should have performed better, but he was in a weird spot in his life, worried about his ex and his kids. She should probably go check on Harper, but she felt odd about leaving the girls on their own. Maybe they were used to it. They seemed like self-sufficient humans.

"So, what did you do with Harper on your visit? Anything fun?"

"We watched *Wonder Woman*."

"Oh yeah?"

Franky had a curious smile on her face. "Harper said it had important lessons for female empowerment, but by the third viewing, she didn't seem so thrilled about it."

Violet couldn't help her laugh. "Strange."

"Yeah. Strange."

What a cool kid. Must have gotten it from her mom, because St. James had never demonstrated this level of personality.

The older girl, who Harper had said was eleven years old, was not as friendly as her sister. Maybe she just needed to be drawn out.

"So, Cat, whatcha listening to?"

No response.

Violet waved a hand in front of her face. Caitriona wrinkled her nose, looking like Violet had opened a

sewer in the kitchen, but because someone had taught
her manners, she turned off her music.

"Did you say something?" She had the St. James
scowl down pat.

"Just wondering what you're listening to."

Caitriona was clearly restraining herself from a mas-
sive eye roll that pronounced Violet an idiot.

"*Hamilton*," Franky said. "That's all she ever listens to."

"No, I don't. You don't know a thing about it."

"Hamilton had a big mouth. No wonder Burr shot
him."

"God, you're so stupid, Slug Girl."

"How am I stupid? You listen to the same music over
and over. That's stupid!"

"That's art!"

"Hey, girls," Violet cut in, feeling a smidge guilty for
upsetting the fragile ecosystem with her pesky questions.
"Let's chill. You're going to wake hungover Harper."

Oops. *So* not the right thing to say. These kids had
probably witnessed enough hangovers to last a lifetime.

"I suppose I'd better check on her." The kids were
unlikely to miss her, so Violet went on her way, coffee in
hand. No sign of Harper near the first-floor bathroom,
so she headed upstairs.

Sometimes Violet couldn't believe all this affluence
and beauty surrounding her. And in another few weeks,
she could take her share and do whatever she liked with
it. That knot behind her breastbone throbbed, the same
one that activated whenever Violet thought about her
inheritance or leaving.

"Hey, Harper?" Violet peered into Harper's bedroom, only to find her in PJs, sitting on the bed, and looking off into the middle distance.

On seeing Violet, she clutched her chest. "You scared me."

"Sorry. I called out." Harper looked pale and not her usual fresh-faced self. Witnessing her in anything less than the full bloom of health made Violet uneasy—it was a little too close to the memory of her own illness. "The girls seemed to think you were hurling your guts out."

"Well . . ."

Recognition dawned. "You're knocked up!"

"Yes. And this kid already hates me."

Setting her coffee down on the nightstand, Violet sat on the bed beside her sister. Should she put an arm around her? Harper wasn't really the touchy-feely type, but *what the hell*, Violet went for it anyway. When she felt Harper relax against her, she knew she'd made the right call.

"Other than the fact you're carrying a succubus, how do you feel about this? Does Remy know?"

"I'm . . ." She shook her head, a smile slowly creasing her perfect porcelain doll features. "Excited. Remy doesn't know yet, but he's going to be thrilled. You know it's exactly what he wants. But . . ."

"But what?"

"I want him to have the Cup first. And if we don't win it this year, I was going to convince him to stay on in the NHL, not retire like he'd planned. Now he'll feel extra pressure to get it done this time, and if we don't—"

"He's going to feel the pressure anyway. This is the first time in fifteen years the Rebels have even made the play-offs. You think every single one of them isn't feeling the pinch? If anything, this will spur him on. He'll want to get your kid baptized in that hardware."

Harper giggled, a sign she'd come a long way. The Harper Violet met eight months ago was not a giggler. "I know. He's going to make such a great father. You should see him with his nieces."

A tiny pang of envy seized Violet's heart for a moment, but she willed it away. Would she be here to see her new niece or nephew? Would her sisters want her to stick around if they knew she'd effectively stolen one-third of their inheritance when her mom baited the honey trap?

She swallowed around her discomfort. "Shouldn't Remy be home by now?"

"Yeah, but when he loses, he'd rather go home to his apartment. He worries about snapping at me." They shared a smirk of acknowledgment at that ridiculousness. Remy was so good-humored that his version of a bad mood probably involved a light scowl at a puppy.

"You have to tell him."

"Have to tell him what?"

Violet looked up, surprised to see Remy after Harper had so adamantly assured them he wouldn't be here. She squeezed Harper's hand in encouragement. *Tell him, it'll be okay.*

Harper squeezed her hand back, but nothing emerged from her mouth.

Remy tugged at his beard. Squinted. Assessed. With lightning-fast speed, he moved in, dropping to his knees before Harper. "*Minou*, what is it? You're not looking so well."

"Oh, it's nothing," Harper said overly brightly, blushing at Remy's term of endearment for her. It meant "kitten," but it also had a more X-rated meaning.

Violet opened her mouth to spill the beans, but Remy spoke first. "You're pregnant." He said it with such reverence Violet's heart almost cracked in half.

Harper's mouth wobbled and tears welled in those green eyes they'd all inherited from Papa Chase. "It's the worst timing! I'm so sorry. This is not what you should be thinking about right now."

His hand cupped her face. "Now, stow that attitude where it belongs—in some deep, dank place. We're having a baby and nothing could make me happier or prouder. Unless"—his blue eyes turned troubled—"you're not ready."

Now it was Harper's turn to put her partner at ease with a stroke of his face. Jesus. Violet's eyes stung like a mother. She needed a bucket of popcorn for this beautiful sapfest.

"I'm ready. I'm just not sure you are. By the time this Cajunette arrives, you're supposed to be retired and getting fitted for that BabyBjörn. You know I have an empire to run, honey."

"We'll figure it out. We've got an army of helpers and a lifetime of love ahead of us to figure it out."

Gah, that sweet-talking lug. For once in his life,

could he not come up with the perfect thing to say? Violet stood and retrieved her mug, not that anyone noticed. "Well, congratulations! I guess I'll be off then. I only stopped by for coffee."

"Sure," said Harper, not looking at her.

"Uh-huh," said Remy, his eyes still lovingly trained on his baby mama.

On leaving, Violet threw one last look over her shoulder to find Remy with his head resting against Harper's stomach, whispering something in French, whether to Harper or the baby she didn't know. The only thing that marred the scene is that Harper looked like she might throw up all over his head.

Still, pretty perfect. Taking her envy with her, Violet quietly left them to the joy of each other.

FOUR

Bren had always liked the house on the lake. Scratch that, he'd always *loved* it. Growing up with divorced parents and splitting his time between Scotland and Canada, he'd usually lived in small, pokey places. When he signed his first big contract with the Rebels, he bought a house. Even before he had a wife and family, he knew he wanted a place of his own.

While most of his childhood was spent with his mother in Glasgow, his summers were spent in Winnipeg with his father and cousins. No matter that the warmer months were out of hockey season, his crazy Canadian family took to the ice oval all year-round, and that's where he'd learned what he was fated to do. Learned to put away the bevvies like a champ, too. Back home in Scotland, a country with no ice hockey tradition, he'd practiced as best he could, but every year as summer approached, he knew that his destiny waited for him across the pond. Finally, when he was fifteen, his mother let him move to Winnipeg for good, just in time for him to get serious about making hockey his life. It was the only thing he was good at. The only thing that made sense to him. Until fatherhood.

This house—his dream house—overlooked Lake Michigan from the shores of Highland Park. Set back off Hazel Avenue, its solid red brick sheltering six thousand square feet represented his arrival. His achievement. Having a woman like Kendra show interest in him was the cherry on top, the validation that this scrappy Scot bruiser had made it big time. He'd had all the trappings: lucrative contract, fancy house, beautiful wife, and a growing family. But beneath the perfect surface, he was a mess of doubts about his right to be here. Was he good enough to sustain the life he'd built?

Apparently not.

When he and Kendra separated a year ago, and she moved with the girls to Atlanta to live with her new boyfriend, Bren had shut up the house. Turned out his dream was a nightmare without his girls in it.

His daughters jumped out of the car as soon as he hit the top of the drive. Even Caitriona was excited, the first time she'd shown enthusiasm for anything since she'd arrived in Chicago. He didn't understand her hostility. For months, the girls had been saying they wanted to live with him—a shock in itself given how he'd scared the hell out of them on his last drunken binge. Now that it was a reality, Franky was on board, but Caitriona was acting like he was the Antichrist. If this was how she was at the tender age of eleven, what kind of horror was in store when she hit puberty?

Don't even think about that.

"Dad, hurry!" Franky pushed her glasses up her nose. "Gretzky's hungry."

This was probably true, because Gretzky was always hungry. The big mutt bounded out of the car at the sound of his name, anxious for company after spending the past three days kenneled.

The front door opened, and for a second, Bren recoiled in expectation, then breathed out in relief. It wasn't Kendra standing in the doorway, but Harper.

"Hey, guys! Long time, no see, as of all of two hours ago."

"Hi, Harper!" Franky turned to Bren, wondering how long she had to be polite.

"Up you go and see if your rooms look the same," Bren said, but both of them were already off.

"Have I told you you're an absolute saint?" he asked as Harper grinned at the sight of his fast-disappearing children.

"No, but I wouldn't expect you to. This is going to get me through the pearly gates—purely ulterior motives." Abruptly, her face turned chalk white and she raised a finger of *just one moment*. She was gone so fast he would have thought his kids' vanishing act was contagious.

Almost better. He'd rather no one bore witness to his discomfort as he walked through the house for the first time in a year. Memories rose to haunt him, physically represented by framed family photos on the walls and one of Gretzky's chew toys discarded under a table in the foyer. Around each corner lay ghosts of his marriage, specters of the life he'd trashed. In the music room—Kendra's name for it—his heart swelled at the sight of the piano, which Caitriona had played since the age of six. Someone had polished it—the cleaning crew Harper had hired, no doubt. He'd expected the air in the house to be stale, but they'd obviously opened up the windows and removed all the dust, which was good, because Franky was allergic to everything except Gretzky.

Heading toward the kitchen, he heard music: Fleetwood Mac's "The Chain," the part where its bass progression builds to that famous outro. A flurry, as his Scottish granny would call it, trickled down his spine, a sign of something momentous on the horizon.

Such as Violet Vasquez's ass in tiny denim shorts.

That grade A rear stuck out of the fridge while she bent over, its perfect curve of butt cheek playing peek-a-boo through frayed hems. His eyes followed the shorts' seam along the cleft of her ass until it disappeared to that mouthwatering spot between her thighs. *Ker-ist.* The inviting accessibility of it hardened his cock in his jeans.

Sixteen months without sex. That's all it was. He was hard up, and his hard-on was making everything so fucking hard.

"Hey, Harpsichord, not sure you bought enough cheddar cheese. And that was sarcasm, by the way." Violet laughed at her joke, her voice a musical echo inside the fridge.

Backing up, she turned and frowned on seeing him ogling her so blatantly, as if her ass making him wild was *his* problem.

He couldn't help his grouchy reaction. "What the hell are you doing here?"

She stuck out her tongue. "Ingrate."

He curved his gaze around her, a lump forming in his throat at the sight of a full-to-the-freezer fridge.

"I—" He rubbed his mouth, feeling too warm and cock-dumb. "I didn't expect to see you."

Reaching up, she tightened the topknot that barely contained her lush waves of dark hair, which was now streaked with ribbons of pink instead of purple like the last time he'd seen her. She usually wore it down, unrestrained, a rebellious mass he longed to plow his fingers through.

His eyes were drawn behind her to one of the open cupboards and a bottle of Johnnie Walker Double Black, whose label he'd recognize from a hundred paces. First order of business: dump all the booze. There was an entire cabinet of liquor in the den, a bar in the living room, bottles stashed anywhere and everywhere because he could never risk going without.

While he was trying to recall where else he might have hidden one of his "friends," Violet walked over to the kitchen island, hit the screen on her phone to stop the music, and leaned her hip against the side. The stance drew his attention to her thighs, which were covered in a riotous garden of colorful blooms. Beautifully shaped, those thighs tapered to perfect, smooth golden calves and red Converse. Bren knew little about fashion, but he had enough wherewithal to recognize that Violet's style was definitely unique. Up top she wore a loose-fitting sweater, which couldn't help slipping off her body, revealing a wafer-thin blue bra strap bisecting one lovely mocha-skinned shoulder.

Christ, sobriety had turned him into a poet—and a horndog.

"Your girls with you, Scottie?"

"Aye, upstairs." *Where the bedrooms are. With beds. With my bed.*

The rapidity of his dirty thoughts seemed to have a direct correlation with how fast Violet's sweater slipped off her shoulder to reveal more skin, as if what was on display wasn't enough. He wanted to rip that sweater off with his teeth and lick his way down her lush body.

Instead of that he tried something even more dumb. Speaking. "So, you're here. Helping Harper out."

"I'm here to fill your fridge." She winked. "If ya know what I mean."

She leaned over on the island, her curves flowing with her. The sweater gaped now, giving him an entirely different vista to lust after. The dark shadow between her breasts made his mouth water.

Stop. Please fucking stop.

"Yeah, well, I'm sure you're busy." Annoyance at his reaction to her made him testier than usual.

"Nessie, Harper needed help and I offered my services. Calm down, I'm not here to corrupt you."

A strangled sound emerged from his throat. Dressed like that, she could corrupt the pope.

Her eyes widened, something like surprise—and desire?—in them. But, as it had been a long time since he'd seen a woman's eyes flare that way, he dismissed it as impossible. Violet wasn't attracted to him. Not really. She just liked to tease him, like she did the entire team.

He shoved his hands into his jeans pockets, frustration loosening his tongue. "You live to test me. Nothin' but trouble."

Unfortunately, he had a major thing for trouble.

No. He had a major thing for Violet.

"Well, Trouble's just bought and unpacked a shit-load of groceries, Scot. And it's made me oh so thirsty." She turned back to the fridge and opened the door, leaning in so her hips hinged and her ass popped up as if to say, "Wanna bite out of this, baby?" She rummaged within and called out softly, "Can I tempt you?"

"No," he lied as he moved behind the island. "Thank you for the groceries. That was very nice of you."

Suddenly, tiredness clobbered him over the head like a two-by-four. He'd not been able to sleep on the flight back from Dallas, but he would now for a few hours. He might even take himself in hand, imagining his tongue trailing down Violet's body to where she'd be soft, wet, and begging for his invasion. A harmless fantasy, surely.

She pivoted, a can of lemon LaCroix in her hand, and kicked the door shut with her foot. "So, I took a rummage through your closet, Scot."

"What?"

"Remember the bachelor auction at the Hockey for Everyone fund-raiser a few weeks ago?"

He did. He also remembered that she had joked about placing a bid on him. But he'd been in no mood to be viewed as a piece of man meat—his no-dating rules applied equally to charity stunts—so he'd not volunteered for the block. Instead, she'd bought a date with Erik Jorgenson, their Swedish goalie. In all the craziness of the past two weeks, he'd forgotten that.

Instead of asking if they'd gone on this date already, he went with: "What's the auction got to do with you ransacking my private property?"

"I was looking for a kilt. Did you think that not making yourself available for the bachelor auction—for a *children's hockey charity*, Mr. Scrooge—would get you out of our bet?"

"What bet?" He knew, but he looked forward to her take on it.

"I bet a hundred bucks I'd see you in a kilt by the end of the season."

"Season's over. You lost."

She leaned over, her perfect tits skimming the granite counter, her gorgeous ass shoved high in the air. Behind the island, the knuckle of his index finger pushed gently against his rock-hard cock, willing it to behave but only making it pulse harder.

"I think we can agree the postseason has extended the bet, Nessie."

"I don't own a kilt. This bet is already moot." He rubbed his beard, not even sure what the bet was exactly. "And my recollection is that I told you I didn't need the money and I'd think of something in kind."

"I don't really need the money, either," she murmured, and every word held dirty, delicious promise.

Christ. This conversation had veered way out of control.

He fumbled for something innocuous to temper it. "Right, the franchise gets more valuable with every game we win."

"Sure does. Keep it up so my share of the pie is bigger when I sell it to Harper and Isobel."

His heart jerked hard against his rib cage. "You're not going to continue to run the team?"

Her lips curved in amusement. "That's cute of you to include me in 'running' the team, St. James. We all know building team morale doesn't really count."

"What'll you do? Leave Chicago?" It came out scratchy, but she didn't seem to notice.

"Eventually. The will required us to run things together for the season and now it's almost over." She leaned in, her green eyes sparkling. "As soon as you boys lose, I'm out of here."

His pulse skyrocketed—at her closeness, her scent, all that life and spirit she projected. But mostly he suspected it was at the thought that Violet would be gone soon—and every game he won kept her here longer. *No pressure, then.*

"Did you watch the games?" he asked.

"I did. You guys should be two and oh instead of even in the series."

This was true. He'd played well in the first game, but then the doubts came creeping in. *Things are going so well. How long before you fuck it up, asshole?*

"I'm a bit preoccupied, I s'pose."

Surprise lit up her pretty features, though pretty wasn't right. Violet was a strikingly attractive woman, with strong bone structure, beautiful red lips, and almond-shaped green eyes that seemed to see right into his dark soul.

"You have a lot on your plate," she said, unmistakable caution in her voice.

He let the silence sit for a moment, ripen. With a glance toward the hallway, he checked that no one was about to crash the intimate bubble that had somehow been crafted in the last thirty seconds. His girls, in particular, did not need to hear this.

"My in-laws want custody, at least until Kendra gets her act together. And with everything going on, it's tempting to think they might be better off."

"Is that what you think? That they'd be better off?"

No. The thought of surrendering his girls to the Gordons made him sick to his stomach.

Quickly, she skirted the island, then placed a hand on his arm. "Fight for them, Bren. Your girls need to know their dad's in their corner, that he'd do anything to protect and love them." Her eyes shone at him with unnamed emotion. Her palm on his arm was light, yet weighted with consequence.

The first time they had touched. The first time they'd actually had a real conversation.

"Is that what you wished for? For Clifford to make it right?"

Another shrug. Another slip of the sweater. "At first, but then I found out what he was like. Not good father material, but you . . . you're different."

Was he? He'd not been there for them. When he was physically present, he was emotionally absent, preferring the comfort of a bottle. And then there was the night it had all come crashing down. "I haven't been such a great dad. Done things I'm right ashamed of. Even now, I have no idea what I'm doing."

She squeezed his arm. "Yes, you do. What you feel for those girls is innate. It can't be taught. Some men's only contributions are sperm and money. That's not you."

No, it wasn't. Had Violet had another man in her life to stand in for Clifford? A stepfather or someone who treated her like a princess? Whatever her circumstances, she seemed to have come out of them all right. Bren wanted more than "all right" for his girls, however.

He knew this: he would be there for them, no matter what came barreling at him.

Her hand still lay on his forearm, its gentle grip both soothing and inciting. They stood staring at each other, the significance of the moment lost on neither of them. She broke the connection first by stepping back, releasing him.

"Harper's going to take care of everything, you know. She's already got interviews for nannies and housekeepers and tutors set up. You're golden, Scot." She picked up her opened can of LaCroix. Was that a slight shake to her hand? "And your daughters? I know they're young, but girls tend to take change in their stride."

"Better than boys?"

"Aye." She drew the single syllable out like a pirate.

He laughed at her use of his own way of affirming things, and she grinned back. He wasn't prone to happy outbursts. As frustrated as he often felt around Violet, he invariably found himself smiling—then immediately doubting his right to the joy she brought him.

A sound of heels approaching put him on alert. Harper entered, her gaze dipped to a clipboard, her cheeks pale.

"Okay, groceries done, Vi?" On seeing the cleared counter and the closed fridge, she checked off a box on the list, then turned to Bren. "I found someone to come in and clean once a week, at least temporarily while we work on a housekeeper. And I know you're worried about their schooling. I'm interviewing tutors tomorrow. This agency we're using comes highly recommended."

Bren exhaled the breath he'd been holding in forever. Since Violet had stopped touching him, if truth be told.

"I can't thank you enough. I've been out of my mind—well, you probably noticed."

Harper's eyebrow scooted up. As a team owner, and the former general manager, she noticed everything, including the unmissable fact that his play in that last game in Dallas had been less than stellar.

"I still need someone to look after them when I'm not around. And I can't dump that on you indefinitely."

The doorbell rang and Harper checked her watch. "Right on time. That's a good sign."

Bren looked in the direction of the door while Harper headed toward it. "What's going on?"

Violet winked. "Let the Great Nanny Hunt begin."

FIVE

Violet coughed loudly and held up her phone. "Ready?"

"Ready!" The enthusiasm was all Isobel. Harper merely grunted, uncaged her feet from her heels, and curled her legs under her body on the sofa in the den at Chase Manor.

"Have you ever practiced kissing in a mirror?" Violet asked.

Harper groaned. "Are these questions designed for eight-year-olds?"

"We are all eight-year-olds in hot-lady bodies. Just answer the question, Harper."

Usually their awkward sister bonding nights saw more action than this, but these days, Harper got queasy if she went more than a hundred feet beyond the radius of Chase Manor or Rebels HQ. So they were having a quiet night in asking each other embarrassing questions from a list Violet had found on the Internet. Like you do.

When she'd landed on their doorstep eight months ago, Violet had expected the half sisters she barely knew to put up more resistance. Be outright bitches, to be honest. After all, she was the by-blow, Clifford's sordid secret, who'd appeared conveniently once the old man croaked and millions of dollars were put in play. At first they'd circled each other warily like feral cats, but with each week that passed, with each sisterly get-together they muddled through, the threads between them braided into strings. Violet would never say she was a true Chase, but she could no longer claim not to be, either. One foot in, one foot out.

"Harper," she prompted.

"Okay, when I was—"

"Twenty-five?"

"Ten. I was skinny and awkward and no boys were interested. But I wanted to be ready when Ben Costigan noticed me." Harper sighed. "It took two years, and then only because I puked over his shoes during gym."

Isobel gasped. "I thought you always had guys dropping at your feet!"

"Tales of my tween prowess were greatly exaggerated, probably by me. What about you, Vi? Bet you had tons of boyfriends."

"Well, the Catholic school uniform is a guaranteed boy magnet, but the retainer and my nickname kind of left me on the outer edges of the cool kids' circle."

Harper leaned in, eyes gleaming. "I have to hear this nickname."

"Assquatch." She stood and cocked her hip, pointing at her rear. "On account of my most amazing *be*-hind. I've been crafting this baby for years, ladies."

Everyone laughed their heads off at that, before Isobel blurted, "Surprised you didn't use it for your boob job!" Immediately, she covered her mouth in horror. "Oh, God, I'm so sorry. What a dreadful thing to say."

Violet held up a hand of insta-forgiveness, not minding that Isobel had put her two feet in it as usual. "No! It's fine. I could have. The doctor gave me a choice to use tissue from my stomach or ass to reconstruct, but I decided to go the other route with the implants. This booty has been drawing them in like honeybees for so long that I can't imagine getting rid of it. It was already such a huge change, you know."

Of course, she'd had a rough time of it after her double mastectomy, her mind reeling with whether the removal of those mounds of tissue that signified to the world her femininity would make her any less of a woman. Getting the implants was a huge help in traversing that hurdle, but it still took her awhile to feel whole again. Womanly. Desirable.

Tattoos were part of her strategy. They drew attention to her well-toned arms and her fabulous thighs. She'd always enjoyed men looking at her, lusting after her, and even if she wasn't open for business, it still gave her a thrill. Some people would call her a tease, but it was her body and she would celebrate it—its strength, its beauty, its not-deadness—however she liked. But it had taken time to muster the courage to place her new boobs front and center. For months after the surgery, she wore prim, high-necked blouses, baggy turtlenecks, and full-coverage tops that sent wandering eyes away. Not anymore.

She'd survived and she had a nice pair of tits to prove it.

Her sisters nodded, and after a taut moment, Harper spoke up. "Did Clifford know? About your breast cancer?"

Sitting again, Violet felt a sharp stab of pain when she took a shallow breath. "Yeah. I didn't tell him, but I guess he'd been keeping tabs on me. Offered to pay for stuff but I—I turned him down. When you came out to see me in Reno just after I was diagnosed, Harper, it was a tough time. I know I wasn't all that welcoming." She'd been downright rude, actually.

"Are you kidding?" Harper waved her hand. "There I was trying to fix years of Dad's fuck-ups with a getting-to-know-you sister lunch. It's a wonder you didn't punch me in the throat."

Isobel smiled serenely. "We've all wanted to punch you in the throat at some time or other, dearest Harper. Let's face it, you're no picnic." She turned to Violet. "Dad owed you, and you should never doubt that. Sure, we know you have plans once the season is over, but you don't have to scoot off as soon as the last game's buzzer sounds. There's always a place for you."

Violet swallowed around the lump the size of a puck in her throat. She loved how they'd gone to such efforts to include her despite the fact she knew zilch about hockey or their world. About being a Chase. Guilt pinged her. Would they be so accommodating if they knew how her mother had gone out of her way to target a rich Hall of Famer and get him wriggling on a hook?

Harper sighed at Violet. "I'm going to miss you so much."

Violet's guilt gave way to warmth at the sentiment. "I'm not going anywhere just yet."

"I was talking to the wine in your hand." With a wink to say she was half joking, Harper gazed dispiritedly at her glass of soda water with lime. "Seven months of this. Complete. Hell. But at least I have Remy, who'll be cooking for me constantly and making sure the baby's jonesing for jambalaya the minute she exits Hotel Utero. I can't imagine doing this pregnancy business and child raising alone. Bren must be freaking out." She chuckled. "You should have seen his face today. This woman was interviewing for a job looking after children but she was dressed like a Dallas Cowboys cheerleader."

"Maybe she got confused about which sport he plays," Isobel answered between a sip of her wine and dashing off what Violet assumed was a quick sext to her boyfriend, Vadim Petrov, the Rebels' front-line left-winger.

"He should have no problems once all the help is in place," Violet muttered. All the *female* help. She hadn't sat in on the interviews, but she'd witnessed the parade of candidates. Besides the scantily clad cheerleader, there was a pretty college grad with an early childhood education degree and another woman (also pretty) in a skintight Rebels T-shirt. Talk about obvious.

Her pulse picked up, remembering their intimate conversation in the kitchen this morning. Bren St. James hadn't looked at her directly since the day they'd met in the Empty Net. The day he dodged a bar fight and she found out that she owned the Rebels hockey team. That she owned him.

Since then, she'd gotten a kick out of turning his crank. He'd always acted like she was an annoying pest, but she would often catch him out of the corner of her eye, puzzling her out. Like some ghost figure, his own sneaky gaze would slide away when directly challenged.

But not today. Today in his kitchen, she'd felt the full weight of his attention, and she wondered how she had lived without it for so long. Today they had put aside the scowls and taunts, and cracked open their respective armor plates to let each other in a little. It was exhilarating. Hearing him talk about wanting to do right by his girls had both scratched and soothed a private spot inside her.

Ah, daddy issues. The best.

"Maybe banging his nanny would be good for him," Violet said casually. "He's so uptight. Obviously needs to clear the pipes."

Isobel narrowed her eyes to slits. "I thought you had the hots for him! And now you're suggesting he bone the governess?"

"Of course I have the hots for him, me and every other woman between nine and ninety. But haven't you noticed? The guy hates my guts. Also relevant, he had his shot."

Harper straightened. "Had his shot? With you?"

Wasn't Violet just a font of emotional spillage today? She took a long sip of her favorite Malbec. "I might have made a pass at him months ago, when I didn't know who he was or that I was technically his boss. And he got all high and mighty, accusing me of being a star fucker—like I care that he's a pro athlete, who I could buy and sell, literally. So he missed his chance to tap this very fine ass and now he acts like I'm some sort of disease-ridden piece of junk."

He hadn't acted like that today, but she had no doubt their dynamic would return to the prickly, sexy surface level of before. To think she would have happily let Bren St. James be her first since her surgery! Let him touch her new(ish) breasts, grab her great ass, make her scream in ecstasy. She liked to think his rejection of her was more about him than about her, but it had definitely put a crimp in her confidence. These days, she might flirt with every Rebel, but her teases were more bark than bite.

She pointed at Harper. "You saw how he responded at Rebels HQ when I dared to talk to him in front of his spawn. He's probably disinfecting his kitchen as we speak."

"Probably."

That response was a little on the speedy—and affirmative—side. "So, he *does* hate me?"

"Hate's such a strong word. He's, uh, made it clear he doesn't want you to be involved."

"Involved in what?"

"Looking after his kids."

Violet's heart sank. She'd known he didn't approve, but to hear that he'd come right out and said it to Harper gutted her. She thought they'd hurdled something today.

What was his problem with her? Were her tattoos too bright, her streaks too pink? Did she laugh too long or remind him of what it was like to enjoy himself, back when he was downing a bottle of Johnnie Walker a day? More important, why did she care so much?

Despite growing up surrounded by the love of the man-hating Three Witches, she'd always gravitated toward guys out of her league. All-American guys who would somehow validate her, like Denny, her ex-boyfriend. Denny, who did "something in finance" and drove a Jag and wore Ferragamo loafers. Denny, who on hearing about her breast cancer diagnosis immediately focused on the upside. (*Now you can get bigger tits, babe.*) Denny, who bailed at the first sign of hair loss circling the drain of his alcove-recessed marble shower.

It made no sense why she'd want a guy like that, one who made her feel like she belonged in polite, upwardly mobile society. She knew all this about herself, so wasn't she marvelously well adjusted? Perhaps not as much as she wished.

Papa, can you hear me?

Freakin' Clifford Chase.

Getting breast cancer was a wake-up call, and not just for her physical health. The Year of the V didn't have time for naysayers and haters. Now that she knew her worth, she refused to waste it on guys who weren't as knowledgeable on this score—and that included D-bag hockey bozos like Bren St. James.

"So he hates me. Meh."

Not wanting to appear affected by inquiring further, she was still annoyingly grateful that Isobel was curious.

"Did he say why he doesn't approve?"

"Something about—look, it doesn't matter."

"Harper!" Isobel and Violet yelled in unison.

Their oldest sister threw up a hand in annoyance. "He thinks you're a party girl, kind of flighty."

"Wait, did you tell him about the dicktabase?" Violet maintained a fun Tumblr in praise of the penis. Harper had freaked out when she first heard about it, terrified the press would link it to the team, and the Chase sisters would look like the sex-obsessed, athlete-loving women they were. *If the condom fits* . . .

"Of course I didn't tell him! Look, Bren's attitude is more an indictment of his ex-wife and of himself than it is of you, Vi. He wants the kids to have a stable home life—"

"And a tatted-up, vino-swilling, penis-curating, pink-haired *chica* smacks of trouble?"

You're nothing but trouble.

She'd thought he meant sexy trouble! Guys only said that when they were thinking of how good a girl was in bed, not that she might be a bad influence on his kids. That—that—that prick. *No spot in the dicktabase for you!*

"Like I said, this is more about what he thinks of

himself," Harper said, a guilty tinge to her voice. "I shouldn't have told you."

"No, it's better to know. That way I won't mistakenly offer to do his grocery shopping or breathe a word to his kids. It's good to know where we stand."

Fucking Manilow.

Bren leaned his forearms on the front bar of the shopping cart, and for the fifty-seventh time cursed the fact that he'd not made a list before he came out. Usually he lived on coffee, cereal, and Pop-Tarts. Most days, he ate lunch with the team and dinner with Remy when he wasn't with Harper.

Who knew two tiny humans and a dog could consume so much? One week since they'd all moved back into the house, and the fridge that Harper and Violet had filled with groceries was practically empty. He needed domestic help, stat.

They were two all in the Dallas series, but at least he had a couple of days until game five, a reprieve while he busted his balls on the Great Nanny Hunt. The first batch had been more interested in him than in his kids. With more interviews lined up for tomorrow, he hoped he could find someone who wasn't a hard-ass, a soft touch, or had the hots for him. This paragon of child care had to exist.

Barry Manilow continued to assault his eardrums.

He grabbed eggs because there were lots of things

he could do with eggs. Pulling aside one headphone, Caitriona gave him the eyebrow raise she'd learned from her mother.

"I'm vegan."

"Since when?"

"Since forever."

He snorted. "You're eleven and you weren't vegan when you came to visit a month ago."

"Well, I am now."

"Do you know how to cook vegan?"

"Margarita respects my culinary needs."

Margarita was Kendra's housekeeper in Atlanta and Bren's recollection was that her pancakes were as hard as pucks. He grabbed another dozen eggs and put it into the cart, enjoying his daughter's scowl immensely.

"Where's your sister?"

"Around."

Bren looked over his shoulder at the far end of the dairy cases in Mariano's. No sign of his youngest, not that he was overly worried—she had a good head on her shoulders. Despite being allergic to a shit-ton of things, she knew better than to sample anything that might kill her.

He examined the ingredients of Kraft Mac & Cheese, 99 percent sure there was no actual dairy in it. Caitriona picked up a box of angel-hair pasta and a jar of marinara sauce and placed them in the cart.

"What're you listening to?"

Somehow she heard his question, because she answered immediately with, "Harry Styles."

"Who?"

"Harry? Styles? He used to be with One Direction?" Epic levels of disbelief were rising with each question his stupidity was forcing her to ask.

"Any good?" He had to be better than Manilow, though now Steely Dan was slowly euthanizing him.

Caitriona shrugged, grabbed more pasta.

"Pasta's okay?" When she didn't roll her eyes, he ventured, "What else? Vegetables?" He'd have to talk to Remy, maybe even ask him over to cook. That shithead loved interfering with Bren's life; he could interfere constructively by making dinner.

"Go get some produce, love," he said. *And then I'll think of a way to cook it so it's not as boring as fuck.*

He wandered a little more, then turned down the soup aisle. Soup should be safe. But what was located in the soup aisle might not be.

Violet Vasquez, shaking her sweet ass.

For fuck's sake, really? Someone up there was definitely messing with him. Donna Summer's "She Works Hard for the Money" was now playing on what Bren charitably called the grocery store's "sound system," and Violet was dancing to it.

She picked up a can of minestrone. Put it back. Her hips swayed to the music, a rhythm that pulsed his blood and hardened his dick. She read the ingredients on another can and shoulder shrugged to the beat.

A guy checking out dried soups a few feet away snuck furtive glances, his intention clear. Bren pushed the cart a few feet into the aisle, ready to intercept.

Violet continued to sing. *"She works hard for the money, so hard for it, honey . . ."*

The woman could hold a tune. Her voice was sweet, and while anyone else might have looked like the crazy person you skate your cart past at the grocery store, Violet looked hella sexy and approachable.

Too approachable. Dry Soup shifted a foot closer, but Bren wasn't a pro athlete for nothing. He wheeled his cart behind her, cutting off Dry Soup's path to glory.

The guy raised an eyebrow of, *I see what you did there.*

Bren reciprocated with an eyebrow of, *Too fucking right, brother.*

When he turned to face Violet, she was staring at him. It was possible she might have known exactly what little turf war had just occurred here. Let her know. Not that there was a thing he could do in reality, but the likes of Dry Soup wasn't going to get a look in, not on his watch.

"Hello," he said to Violet.

Instead of a saucy response, he got something distinctly unvarnished: a scowl to rival the ones he usually dropped on her. Hadn't they moved past this? A week ago in his kitchen, they'd had a real conversation. *A moment.* After months of teasing, taunting, and tempting, he'd never thought he'd miss the day Violet wasn't interested in seeing him.

She looked past him down the aisle, her brow lined. "Where are the girls?"

"I set them to work, picking up stuff. One of them is

likely poisoning herself, the other just told me she's a vegan and I might have been dismissive."

"Shooting for father of the year, then?"

"I try."

Dry Soup still hovered, now in a foolhardy loiter near the chicken broth. Bren shot a glare in his direction until he moved off.

"What's that for?" Violet asked.

"Don't like how he was looking at you. Like he's hungry."

"He's in a grocery store, dummy."

"And I'm merely being chivalrous, protecting you from unsavory pickup artists in the soup aisle. You're welcome."

It was meant as one of his rare jokes, but judging from Violet's reaction, it was interpreted as anything but. "Why do I need protection? Because of how I dress? How I laugh? How I flirt?"

Where was this attitude coming from? "Meant nothing by it."

She blew out a breath that was half growl, picked up a can of Italian wedding soup, and examined the ingredient list like she was studying for a test. Why wasn't she taking this opportunity to get under his skin using those taunts that tripped off her tongue like sensual ninja knives?

"Have I offended you in some way, Violet?"

Keeping her chin dipped, she shook her head, but it was a shake of disbelief, not of disagreement with his question.

"Violet, look at me."

Glittering eyes snapped to his, in them a flash of something—a visceral response to his demand—but it was gone so quickly that even the rewind called him a liar.

"Has something happened?"

"Look, St. James, you and I have never meshed, so we don't need to pretend to get along. We just ran into each other at the store and you 'saved' me from the unseemly interest of a fellow shopper. *¡Maravilloso! ¡Gracias!* Now you can take your steel buns and your sexy scowl off in the opposite direction."

Color flagged her cheeks, making her olive skin glow. She was furious, and he still didn't know why. He was also furious, and he had a better idea of the reason.

She'd changed the social contract. They'd been moseying along with her teasing and taunting and flirting, and him acting like it was the worst thing ever to happen to him. Like Violet's attention was a fresh slice of hell, because in a way it was. She reminded him of everything he couldn't have. She reminded him of the man he used to be. His body came alive around her, and alive was dangerous. Alive was the opposite of numb, and numb was his best defense against the demons whispering in his ear.

One drink won't hurt. Thirst like yours can't be quenched with anything but whiskey.

If he allowed himself to want her, it was a slippery slope to succumbing to the demons at the door. Of course he couldn't tell her this, so instead he latched on to her words.

"Steel buns?" There was also "sexy scowl," but he figured he'd start with the ass stuff.

She rolled her eyes, then coasted those same eyes down his body, half hidden by the grocery cart. "As if you don't know."

"That I have an ass you could bounce a puck off of?" He twisted to check himself out. "S'pose I do, lass."

She burst out laughing and muttered something in Spanish.

"What's that?"

"Not for your ears, Scot."

One day she'd tell him. One day, he'd get it out of her, preferably while her body arched into his and his body drove into hers.

He shook his head at where his brain had gone. Bad, not-numb Bren always had the worst ideas. This, along with all the other cues, should have been his signal to leave, but his feet were quite comfortable where they were. He surveyed her basket, which contained enough soup and crackers to last a nuclear winter.

"Got yourself a saltine problem, I see."

"Harper, actually."

"Franky said she wasn't well the last time they stayed. Throwing up, apparently." Recognition pinged him. "Is Harper pregnant?"

She nodded. "The morning sickness is knocking her out."

And here he was only adding to her problems. "Remy must be over the moon."

"You know it. He's already talking to the peanut in French!"

Bren smiled. There was no greater joy than that of

a man learning his child was on the way. At least, not until the day he held her in his arms and vowed to protect her with every fiber of his being. On the flip side, there was no greater sorrow than the day you realized you didn't have it in you to be that man.

"So, how's the nanny hunt going?" Violet asked.

"Interviews tomorrow. Harper can't make it so I might have the kids sit in to see if they respond to anyone."

"Letting your kids make the call? Bad move."

"My kids shouldn't have any say in who gets to spend time with them?"

"Your kids will choose whoever they think they can walk all over. Especially Franky."

He bristled, immediately on the defensive. "Franky?"

"Yeah, that one can smell weakness. They both can—I mean, they're Gorgons in disguise like all girl children—but Franky's got a sixth sense about her. Tough as nails, despite the angel act."

Should he be pissed or impressed at Violet's insight? She had pretty much nailed Franky down. His youngest was a daddy's girl, but she was also practical, meaning she'd have no compunction about leaving him with a broken leg on the site of a plane crash in the Rockies. She might come back with help. Then again, she might not.

"Heard the candidates so far were sort of mixed," Violet said.

"If by mixed, you mean crazy, aye."

"All looking to get in your Union Jack boxers."

This was the Violet Bren knew and lo—*lusted* after. Feeling unusually playful, he leaned in. "Maple leaf, actually."

"What?"

"My boxers. I'm half Canadian."

She raised a dark eyebrow. "Which half?"

"The best half."

He wasn't quite sure when it had happened, but in the past few moments he'd moved close enough to cage her against the Campbell's. Her tongue darted quickly to her lips, a sensual preview of wet pink flesh that put his groin on notice. All this time, he had thought she wasn't attracted to him, that her moves were part of a game.

This hypothesis had just been soundly debunked.

Not because she'd licked her lips and made him spark to life, but because of how her eyes flared, lust stoked and wide with want. His body thrummed with awareness, with the need to plunder and take.

"Viol—"

"Hey, Pink!"

Jumping back, Bren peered down at his youngest daughter and her arms full of snacks—ice cream, Pop-Tarts, cereal bars. She dumped them into the cart.

"You've been busy, sprite. Any real food in there?" He picked up the cereal bars, scrutinizing the ingredients, which was better than scrutinizing Violet.

"I checked them all, Dad. Not a nut in sight." She grinned toothily at Violet. "I'm allergic. To lots of things."

"I heard."

"We're going to order pizza tonight. You should come over!"

Bren clamped his mouth shut, not wanting to give voice to an opinion one way or the other. He knew what his body wanted, however, which was in itself a sign that Violet sharing a gooey, cheesy thin crust was a bad idea.

"I'd love to, but I've got a date."

His neck muscles tautened painfully at how fast he snapped his head back. "You do?"

"Uh-huh," was all she said, making him feel like an idiot for asking. He shouldn't care, so why did he?

How about because when he'd thought she had a friends-with-benefits thing with his teammate Cade, Bren had wanted to punch the two-day designer stubble off his grinning Texan face every time he saw them together? Or when he just saw Cade. At practice. At a game. Every-fucking-where.

"Well, we probably should get moving." But Violet was now rummaging in his cart. He wished that was a euphemism for something sexier than Violet fingering his groceries.

She picked up a package of tortillas. "Flour, Nessie? Corn's better."

"The girls like flour. I like corn."

"And you're such a softie you give them everything they want." She frowned. "No beef or pork?"

"We use turkey," Franky said. "It's healthier."

Though now Caitriona wouldn't eat it. Was he going to have to make multiple versions of everything?

"Hmm, maybe, but beef and pork taste better. The way my *abuela* used to make it, with her special seasoning . . ." She smacked her lips. "*Sabroso*. Tasty."

Franky squinted behind her glasses. "Are you Mexican?"

"No. *Yo soy* Boricua." Violet smiled, and Bren got a touch dizzy at how her tongue shaped the Spanish words. "Puerto Rican. Well, half."

"What's the other half?"

"Know-it-all white dude." She winked at his daughter. "Pretty dangerous combination, kid. But the Puerto Rican half is the best."

Bren coughed out a laugh, reminded of his earlier comment about his Canadian half being superior.

"Okay there, Scot?" But she was smiling, remembering, too.

"Fine."

Franky was considering Violet in that way she did when she was planning something. Best to move on out.

"Do you like apple pie?" his daughter asked Violet.

"Sure do."

"We need to get cereal." Bren pushed the cart forward, intending to signal the end of the meet 'n' greet–slash–eye fuck in aisle five.

Violet picked up her soup-heavy basket and walked alongside them.

"Do you have a boyfriend?" Franky asked her.

"A few."

"You can't have more than one, but you can have a

husband and a boyfriend at the same time. That's different."

Bren exchanged a glance with Violet. His wife's infidelity through the eyes of his nine-year-old. They reached the end of the aisle, a natural place to separate.

"So, Franky," Violet said. "What did the pirate say when he turned eighty years old?"

Franky looked at Bren, then back at Violet. "I don't know."

Violet made an eye patch with her palm and inclined her head. "Aye, matey!"

It took a second, but his little girl erupted in giggles. Bren felt his smile building, because nothing made him happier than his daughters' joy.

"It was great seeing you again, Franky," Violet said. "Enjoy your pizza."

She caught his hot gaze, and there was a moment of awkwardness as they both considered how to conclude this fun little get-together. A fortunate or maybe unfortunate pause, because it gave him a moment that led to another moment, this one of madness.

"I don't suppose you'd be interested in helping me out with these interviews? It's just that with Harper unable to make it, I'm not feeling so prepared."

She blinked at him, those emerald-fired eyes wide in surprise. A few seconds ticked by in silence while she worked out how to let him down gently.

"If you're busy, forget it—"

"No, I'm not. You're probably going to need protection from some hot Swedish chick looking to score a multimillion-dollar athlete and a green card. What time's the first one?"

"Ten o'clock."

"Okay, see you then." She backed up, her gaze still on him, and he found he couldn't break the connection.

"Enjoy your date," Bren muttered, hoping he didn't sound insanely jealous. Maybe it was Erik, that date she'd bought at the Hockey for Everyone fund-raiser. Tripping the team's goalie in practice wasn't really cool, but needs must.

"I will," she said with a sexy kick to the corner of her mouth before she swiveled that ass he wanted to take a bite out of to the ten-items-or-less line. And he let himself look and be reminded of why he had busted his balls for the past eight months doing everything in his power to ignore her.

SIX

"So, what've we got?"

Bren held open the door for Violet, not that the woman needed an open door. She was already barging in.

"The first one is due in five minutes." He looked at his watch. "She has Montessori training and was a nanny to a French diplomat's kids."

"Score one! If she can handle little mon-soors and madams, she's already ahead of the game." She caught him looking her up and down. "What? Am I not dressed appropriately to interview kid wranglers?"

He shook his head, annoyed with himself for being so transparent, especially as he'd done a pretty good job of keeping everything in check around Violet these past months. She wasn't dressed appropriately to be within a hundred feet of *him*. She wore a fifties-style red skirt that puffed out, hitting just above her knees, and he knew as soon as she sat down it would ride up to reveal those lickable rose tattoos. Her low-cut shirt showcased cleavage he wanted to bury his face and stay ensconced in for the foreseeable future. Why had he thought this was a good idea again?

The doorbell rang before he was forced to comment on her outfit, not that he should. Women should be able to wear whatever the hell they liked, but everything Violet did or said or wore provoked him. It was unreasonable, he knew, but he couldn't help how he felt.

"Let's get this over with," he muttered.

Two hours later, Bren was at his wit's end, but the one bright light in all this was Violet, who had come prepared. Bren hadn't even thought to have a list of questions, preferring to go by instinct and see how the conversation went. Before the first interview, Violet had pulled out a clipboard, held up her phone, and asked sweetly if the interviewee objected to being recorded. She then pretty much took over the whole process.

Her "process" had weeded out the first three candidates as unemployable. One because she said a light rap with a wooden spoon across the knuckles did wonders for naughty children. (Asking a nanny's philosophy on disciplining his kids had never occurred to him. Violet was all over it.) Another was dismissed as unsuitable because she said the children would need to be quiet while her stories were on (*Days of Our Lives* fan). Number three answered all the questions put to her appropriately, but she smelled strongly of onions, and while Bren liked onions, he wasn't a fan of it as perfume.

Now they were left with the final interview of the day. Bren choked back a laugh when she walked in, because this woman was straight out of central casting for

Scandinavian child-care providers. He gave his cointer-viewer a look: *gonna protect me from this Swedish chick look-ing to score a green card and my millions?* Violet twitched her lips, clearly remembering that exchange.

Now they were sharing inside jokes. Christ.

Look up *hot nanny* in the dictionary and you'd see a picture of Elin Gustafsson in all her blond, blue-eyed natural beauty. She wore a white blouse with little flow-ers on it and slim black pants that cut off before her ankles. Her English was perfect, her teeth were straight. Violet asked if she could drive and she produced her license, along with CPR certification.

Violet wasn't trying to trip her up, exactly, but as the interview went on and no immediate red flags were raised, the questioning intensified.

Are you comfortable reviewing and assisting with home-work?

Are you willing to live in or do multiday overnight stays with the children to accommodate their father's playing schedule?

Have you ever had to handle an emergency?

Would you care for a sick child? Do you know how to ad-minister an EpiPen?

Elin answered everything clearly and with no hesi-tation. She loved children. She loved unharnessing their capacity for greatness. She loved how children had so much to teach us about the wonders of the world. Bren half expected the ghost of Whitney Hous-ton to enter any minute warbling about children being the future. Of course they were, but he didn't need to hear it in such touchy-feely terms. Maybe he was looking for faults where none existed, because Elin was perfect.

Then came the true test. Gretzky trotted in, sat at her feet, and proceeded to let one rip.

"You have a dog," Elin said rather obviously.

At last, her Achilles' heel. She hates dogs.

Violet was on it. "Are you okay with dogs? The kids love him even though he's a freakin' fart machine."

"I adore dogs," she said in full-on Stepford mode, gazing on Gretzky as if he had just expelled the scent of fresh-baked cookies. She bent down to pet him, and Bren watched for the dumb mutt's reaction.

He loved it, but then he loved anyone who paid him the slightest bit of attention.

"Bye-ee!" Violet shut the door on Elin and turned to Bren. So weird, it was like they were a couple seeing off a visitor.

"She's—"

"She seems—"

At talking over each other, they smiled. And whoa, when the Scot curved his lips, it was something else. Worlds exploded and re-formed with that smile.

"Good," Violet said, eager to have her opinion out there so it didn't look like she was parroting his. "She seems really competent."

"You think so?" Smile gone, he screwed up his mouth,

rubbed his chin. The sound of palm against beard was subtle and delicious.

"Oh, yeah, didn't you? And she can start quickly. That's huge. Plus the girls liked her." Bren had asked his daughters to meet her when it looked like she'd passed the not-crazy test. Elin had been a sweetheart to them; the girls hadn't run from the room screaming.

Walking toward the kitchen, Violet heard his steady tread close behind her. "You don't think she's a bit too—"

"What?"

"Swedish?"

She grabbed her messenger bag off the chair where she'd slung it three hours ago. Frankly, the interviews had worn her out.

More likely, it was having to sit on the same sofa with Bren, her body itching to slide closer and pick up where they'd left off last night in the soup aisle. He'd come really close to kissing her with beef broth as their romantic backdrop—she was sure of it. She was also sure she would have let him, which was all wrong, because she was supposed to be annoyed with him.

She should have said no to helping him out, but he'd looked so miserable and she'd wanted to help. To feel useful. Prove to everyone there was more to her than the good-time girl who had nothing to contribute to the almighty Rebels.

"What's wrong with the Swedish? Not only are they a very enlightened people and a nation of hockey fanatics, you just *know* she can put an Ikea bookcase together. They probably have contests for that in Helsinki."

"Stockholm."

"Fine, *Stockholm*. As long as you're okay with meatballs for dinner and Abba morning, noon, and night, then you're all set."

"I suppose I could call her references." He said it like this was a hellish task instead of the answer to his prayers.

"What's your problem? You've found Ms. Perfect, a chick who won't party or let you down or be a bad influence. I thought this is what you wanted."

His eyebrows slammed together. "What's that got to do with anything?"

"What?"

"Partying? Bad influence? Where's that coming from?"

Really? She didn't have time for this. "Look, I did you a favor and asked all the hard questions while you figured out if she was a C or a D cup. Barely a B, in case you need a second opinion. She passed all the tests, right?" Her voice had gone a bit pitchy there, as Simon Cowell would say to some woebegone would-be diva on *America's Got Talent*.

She slung her bag across her body. "You deflected Creepy Soup Guy and I helped you back. We're even. You don't have to talk to me again or worry I might lead your kids astray."

He was still rocking the Bren scowl of doom. After a long beat, he uttered: "Harper."

"Yeah, Harper." She wished her sister had never said a word. Better to live in ignorant bliss about what Mr. Kilt 'n' Built really thought of her.

Time to book it out of here. She was already moving toward the door when she felt a pressure around her wrist. She looked down to find a big Scottish hand halting her progress, and she kept looking because that was generally the universal sign for *lay off, buddy!*

He didn't take the hint. In fact, *he* was now looking in surprise at his hand as if he wasn't quite sure how it had gotten there. As if forces beyond his control had made him do it. It was the first time he had touched her. It was also magnificent.

She pulled away. Not a jerk, just a slide, because she wanted to hold on to his touch for a few more pathetic seconds.

He stabbed fingers through his dark hair. "Sorry, I shouldn't have done that."

No, you shouldn't, but I will count the seconds until you do it again.

She shook off that ridiculous thought. This guy had totally dissed her to Harper, then almost kissed her after scaring away what could have been the love of her life in the soup aisle. What a dick.

Silent seething was not her MO. It was time for a reckoning.

"Why did you say that? Why did you tell Harper you didn't want me near your kids?" God, was that her voice? She sounded so . . . hurt.

"Doesn't matter."

"Fine." She pivoted and took a few steps, tempting him to touch her again. Reel her into the embrace of his big, hard body—so she could stomp on his oversized feet!

"Wait," he gritted out. "Let me explain."

She faced him, her bag on a cocked hip, giving him her best *I haven't got all day* vibe.

"When Harper talked about how she'd get all the wives and girlfriends on board to help, she started listing them off. I was grateful, and then your name came up and I felt something . . . else."

He paused, so she filled the gap. "Disgust?"

"No. God, no." He scrubbed a hand through his hair again. "You know my history. Everyone knows it. Today I'm eleven months sober."

"Congratulations."

"I think if you were in this house, I might not make it to twelve."

Oh. *Ohhh.*

"Me being near your kids—or near you—would drive you to drink?"

She stepped in close, needing to test this hypothesis for herself. Could he be serious? Admittedly, she had it going on, but surely he had enough willpower to withstand the sensual onslaught of one Violet Vasquez.

"You're kind of"—he waved over her—"provocative." She watched the bulge of his Adam's apple, how his blue eyes darkened to inky midnight. "I'm not supposed to date anyone during my first year of sobriety."

"You want to date me?"

"No. I don't want to date anyone. I'm using that word as a euphemism for everything, and I mean *everything*, I want to do to you."

She wasn't sure she had the imagination to conjure the *everything* Bren meant. She wasn't sure she needed it. His honesty toppled her.

"I—I don't get it. You've done nothing but glare at me since we met like I'm something on the bottom of your shoe."

"And you've spent that entire time getting under my skin."

They were so close now, almost skin-to-skin. "You're fun to provoke."

"Right. Fun." A breath left him, warming her lips, stoking her desire. "I can't be involved with anyone right now, not when I need all my strength for my kids and the play-offs. I'm barely holding on, Violet. I want to do everything to you. I want everything *from* you. I would consume you with need. Desire. Darkness. It'd be dirty and desperate and not very pretty. And I suspect you're the kind of woman who needs more than I have to give. A hundred percent of my focus." A hundred percent of his focus dipped to her breasts, then back up to her lips.

"I never intended to set back your recovery."

"I know that. I know it's not malicious. You're this vibrant force, a woman who lights up every room she enters. You can't be expected to dim your sun."

What a lovely thing to say. "I tease, Bren, but I never

imagined that you thought of me that way. Not seriously." That she might possess such power shocked her. Thrilled her, too. Those things he'd said. All that need he'd expressed. It had been so long since any man saw her that way, as having the potential to ruin him.

Ruin them both.

"I do, Violet. I think of you all the fucking time." He was breathing hard now, hot puffs of want drawing her close. Pulling her under. "And it's—fuck, it's killing me."

Don't die, she thought, just as his mouth descended on hers, taking advantage of her gasp to curl his tongue inside. Her shock extended past a few seconds, her brain still caught on his protest mere seconds ago.

But shock gave way to surrender.

Surrender gave way to ferocity.

His mouth on hers was everything she'd never known she needed.

He pushed her back against the fridge. Something fell—magnets, perhaps?—and then his body was a wall of heat and sinew stealing every slice of common sense. She felt his erection, hard and flagrant, against her belly. He lifted her, his hands under her ass while she responded in the only way she could: she wrapped her legs around his hips like a hussy.

If this was only a fraction of his focus, she was a goner.

He ground against her, all hard deliciousness, and her overriding thought was: *it's been so long, and this is going to be embarrassingly quick*. His beard didn't just tickle, it abraded. The roughness was divine, alternating with his firm lips and wicked tongue fucking her mouth.

His hand slipped farther under her skirt, over her ass, down her cleft, a teasing brush that found her wet and ready.

"Jesus, Violet," he muttered against her mouth. "You're soaked. You fucking need this, too?"

Her legs were wrapped around his hips in a tree hug while he dry-humped her against a fridge. These were not the actions of a woman who didn't *need*.

He stopped kissing her and stared into her eyes, panting hotly against her lips. It was as if he was look-ing for some assurance. Permission. Invitation.

"Yes," she whispered.

His fingers delved deeper, employing luscious strokes of her folds. The kissing had ended and what was left behind was sheer, terrifying intimacy. A gaze that could melt stone, a scrutiny that hungered. He fondled, rubbed, and touched, while he ground against her hard and with carnal intent. Surrounded by all this pleasure, she could only hold on, feeling like she was flying full throttle into a cat-five hurricane.

Then he ripped his fingers away and dropped her to the floor like a sack of Idahos.

"Dad!" Franky's voice called out. "Gretzky needs to go outside! Can I take him?"

Shallow breath. "Take him out front, love, but don't go near the road."

A few seconds passed. The front door slammed.

Bren rubbed his beard, then he swiped a finger still

wet with her desire across his lips. His tongue darted out to taste her, and briefly he closed his eyes in what looked like absolute bliss.

Violet's legs were a jellied mess, the fridge holding her upright. "That's some hearing you have there, St. James. Positively bionic."

"Skill of the single dad." His eyes snapped open. "I shouldn't have done that."

"Well, I didn't exactly resist," she said, laughing off the knot of dread behind her breastbone that he had regrets. After all, she was *trouble*.

"So, you understand? Why this can't happen?"

"Oh yeah. The sex would probably cause a tornado. We owe it to the world not to give in to our inappropriate lust."

He didn't laugh. This guy needed a humor transplant, yet the grumpy thing really worked for her.

Still, she had to gain some measure of control here. "Anyway, you screwed up."

"Had better kisses, then?"

"Oh, not that. The kiss wasn't half bad." *The kiss seared my soul.* "No, meaning you had a chance when we first met in the Empty Net and you turned me down. Now you've had a little taste so you know what you're missing." *Gotcha, Scot.*

He squinted at her, more of the grouch. If he kept that up, she'd be climbing him like a tree in two seconds.

"Guess I should call those references."

She sighed, not sure if any progress had been made

here, though no girl despised being considered a temptress of the highest order. "Yep. Better snap up the Swede
before someone else does."

And then she left before she begged him to bone her
on the kitchen island counter.

SEVEN

Bren looked up at Remy, who was mouthing something. With a sigh, he slipped off his headphones, which until now had been doing their job of helping him tune out the locker room noise.

"What?"

"I asked how the nanny interviews are going."

Every player had their rituals before a game. Petrov put two extra knots in his laces. Burnett put his socks on before his shorts, and his shorts on before his jersey. And Bren listened to violent, crush-your-soul death metal. You didn't mess with a man's pregame ritual, and you certainly didn't mess with it to ask how the interviews for his kids' nanny were going.

But of course, that's not what the Cajun was asking at all. He had this twinkle in his eye that spoke to mischief on the horizon.

"Found one," Bren said, praying that would shut him up.

"The hot Swedish chick?" Remy was curiously well informed.

Erik Jorgenson, obviously no stranger to the charms of his countrywomen, perked up. "You're hiring a Swedish nanny?"

"Thinking about it. She comes with good references." Or he assumed she did. A day later, and he hadn't quite gotten around to calling. He told himself it was because he was focused on game five, though really it was because that kiss with Violet was taking up all his brain power. Right-hand power as well.

He'd known it would be spectacular. No, that was overstating it. He'd known it would be good. A good kiss. Put it down to the months of circling each other. All that pent-up tension between them, along with the pent-up tension in his balls, meant that Bren could have kissed Gretzky and pronounced it out of this world. He was in dire need of getting laid.

Yet she'd been so wet. *For him.*

As for her taste . . . Jesus, her sweet tang was better than whiskey. Maybe that kiss and the memory of how she'd tasted would tide him over. He could use it to jump-start his fantasy life. *Yeah, because you haven't been using your wicked fantasies about that smart-mouthed girl already.* She took a starring role, all right. He just hadn't reckoned on the reality outshining the fantasy.

"Yeah, Violet said she was a winner," Remy commented with a half grin. Fucker.

Petrov raised an imperious Russian eyebrow. "Violet has met her?"

"Sat in on the interviews, I heard." Remy again, as if Bren wasn't even here.

"Violet's helping you find a nanny?" Erik looked confused. "Perhaps you should just hire her."

Remy smirked. "Yeah, Saint, perhaps ya should."

Of all his teammates, Remy was the most attuned to the undercurrents between Bren and Violet, and he never stopped giving Bren shit about it.

Erik leaned in. "You do not approve of Violet, I think, Captain. She lives her life out loud and this bothers you."

Bren hadn't realized his weird vibe with Violet had affected anyone else on the team. "No, she can live her life any way she pleases. I'd like to hire someone who's qualified to watch children."

The Swede wasn't listening. "Ever since Cade announced he likes men, she has been sad. Heartbroken." He sounded much too hopeful.

Cade shouted from the other side of the locker room, "For the last time, Swede, she knew I was gay before any of you kickers and she is in no way heartbroken. Just go on that date with her already. Hell, she already paid for it."

Bren swung back to Erik. "You haven't gone on this date?"

"Not yet. She has been very busy."

So Violet wasn't on a date with Erik last night. Who else on the Rebels roster did he need to cut down in their prime?

"You want to date her? For real?"

"Why not? She is a beautiful woman and she likes to laugh. We would have a good time together, she and I. Very compatible."

Well, that was just fan-fucking-tastic. Seeing Cade and Violet together—and Bren was right pissed at himself for being so relieved to hear they were only fake dating—had driven Bren wild these past few months. Not that he could, or would, do a single thing about it, because Violet was all wrong for him.

He could still feel the imprint of her kiss on his lips, her taste better than wine, her body like liquid fire in his arms. It was bad enough he'd spent months using her as fantasy fodder when he thought she was with one of his teammates; knowing how she tasted, felt, and sounded up close and personal was a particular cruelty.

I think if you were in this house, I might not make it to twelve.

For alcoholics, one drink was too many and a thousand were never enough. He suspected it would be the same with drinking down Violet, an addiction he couldn't risk.

"Hey, boys, are we ready to play?"

Bren's eyes snapped to the new arrival—the woman they had just been gossiping about. Those same eyes almost popped out of his head. *Sweet Jesus.* Violet stood at the door wearing a cheerleader outfit in Rebels blue and white. A deep-plunging shirt with a large R molded to her perfect breasts above a pleated skirt that barely skimmed her pert ass. In her hands? Pompoms!

Occasionally Violet popped into the locker room before and after the games. "Morale building" she called it. Bren preferred to label it what it was: a complete and utter cock tease. But she'd never looked so blatantly provocative.

"Gimme an R!" With each letter of the cheer, she bestowed her favor on one lucky player. A kiss on Cade's cheek, a squeeze of Remy's bicep, fanning herself with a pom-pom in front of Petrov, which made the Russian laugh. Then she stood in the center and placed her fists on those shapely hips.

"Well, boys, we're in with a shot here," she said gruffly, a pretty spot-on impression of Coach Calhoun. "Home ice. The people of this city are behind us with our lovable loser status and shit."

Everyone laughed, charmed by the impression and the sentiment. The city couldn't be more excited and Violet's spirit was infectious. Coach wasn't so great at the motivational speeches, but at this point, they didn't need it. Each man on the team had his own reasons for playing lights-out hockey.

"When can I get that date, Violet?" Erik asked with a cheeky grin.

She stroked his chin and fluttered her eyelashes. "Soon, my hot Swedish lover. Soon."

Erik looked like every single one of his Christmases and birthdays had come at once. Prick.

Violet caught Bren's eye, the first time she'd looked his way since she'd come in.

"So sad, Scot. Need a special cheer?"

He stood, his body itching for battle. For her. Did she think he'd forgotten how she tasted, how her supple skin felt beneath his fingertips? Did she think he'd forgotten a single fucking thing about that kiss?

The locker room buzz was loud enough that no one would hear what he said to her. "You're playing with fire, lass."

"Just doing my part for the team." She fluffed a pom-pom under his chin. "Make me proud, handsome."

Before Bren could comment, Coach Calhoun walked in.

"Okay, boys, we're in with a shot here . . ." The rest was drowned out by the sound of everyone cracking up. With a final wave and salutation of good luck, Violet swayed that fine ass out of the locker room with every unattached guy's gaze still affixed to it.

They lined up to head into the tunnel. A few reporters milled about, but they were experienced enough not to mess with the pregame routine.

"Hey," Bren said, low enough so only Remy could hear. "Congratulations, Dad-to-be."

Remy smiled over his shoulder. "No secrets in this family, I see."

"Nope. I'm thrilled for you, brother."

Remy nodded, his emotion appearing to get the better of him for a second before he said, "So. Hot Swedish chick?"

"Fuck off," Bren muttered. He needed to purge from his brain all thoughts of Violet. In AA, you followed something called the twenty-four-hour plan. No pledges to never drink again, just an effort to get through it a day at a time. That's how he approached his drinking, and that's how he would approach Violet.

The Rebels had a game to win, and tonight, his kids were in the owners' box with Harper. He would make them proud. Then tomorrow, he would call the references of his future nanny.

EIGHT

Harper jumped up from a chair in the emergency room waiting area the minute she saw Bren pounding through the door. They'd been up 3–2 after a couple of hard-fought periods when Coach approached him in the locker room and asked him to step outside.

Never a good sign, though typically Coach wouldn't give him a heads-up that his play was piss-poor enough to bench him for the third. He just wouldn't send him in and no one would question it because he was the fucking coach. Dante had been waiting outside the locker room, and that's when Bren knew.

Something had happened to one of his girls.

Apparently, Franky had eaten something from the owners' box buffet that had given her an allergic reaction, but she'd received an EpiPen dose and was reportedly okay. He wouldn't believe it until he held her tight enough to feel her little heart beating against his chest.

"Bren, I'm so sorry," Harper said. "I should have monitored all the food in the box. It didn't even occur to me that the brownies might be a problem, and then I stepped out for a second—"

"It's okay, Harper."

Caitriona sat in a corner chair, nose to her iPad, Beats on. She hadn't even acknowledged him. "Love, what happened?"

She still didn't respond, so he hunkered down in front of her. She removed her headphones.

"Are you okay?"

"Yeah."

"How come your sister's eating stuff she shouldn't?" He couldn't be there 24/7. Sure, Caitriona was only a kid, but she was older and had to look out for her little sister.

His daughter shrugged. "I can't watch her all the time. She's supposed to ask an adult if she can eat something before she puts it in her mouth."

That was true. Franky knew better. Parenting was hard, and there was no good reason why he should expect his oldest daughter to step into that role.

He straightened. "Where's Franky now?" he asked Harper, who was still pale and shaky. He couldn't blame her. Watching someone else's kids took work, and with Harper suffering in the first trimester of her pregnancy, her mind couldn't be on his problems 100 percent.

"She's in an exam room down that hallway."

Alone? She must be terrified. Why wasn't Harper with her?

No. Step back. This isn't Harper's responsibility. These kids are your responsibility.

With a nod at Harper and one last look at Caitriona—who was back to ignoring him—he headed off to see his daughter. He rounded the corner, his heart expanding in relief at hearing Franky's laugh. Thank God. Then his chest tightened at the sound of another voice—a husky, calm, straight-to-his-balls one.

"So, which one is your favorite?"

"Rathouisiidae," Franky said cheerfully, sounding none the worse for wear after her ordeal. "They're carnivorous and they eat other slugs, but you only find them in Southeast Asia."

Holy Rathouisiidae. Violet Vasquez was discussing slugs with his daughter.

"Why do you like them so much?"

"They're survivors," his daughter said, so simply it broke his heart. "People think they're ugly pests. Nature gave them a way to make it."

"Especially when they're biting the you-know-whats off boy slugs."

His daughter giggled. "I'm never getting married."

He wasn't sure how that was relevant, but Violet didn't question it. She merely responded with, "Neither am I, kiddo."

His phone chimed with a message from Remy: *Franky okay?*

He texted back: *Just fine.*

Remy: *Good. By the way, we won, asshole. No thanks to you.*

Bren smiled, then rubbed his beard because he wasn't sure he had a right to this sliver of joy. Putting on his game face, he walked into the room. Violet was sitting on the bed, still in her cheerleader outfit, one long wave of perfect inked thigh filling his eyeballs. Franky was leaning in to examine one of the tattoos on her arm.

"Hi, sprite. Heard you've been making trouble."

"Dad!" She bit her lip and her eyes went wide, welling with the beginnings of tears. "I'm sorry. They looked like the brownies Margarita makes back home. I know I should have asked."

He hugged her hard, replenishing his life force with hers. "Yeah, you should have. But I'm glad you're okay."

Violet watched him, and Bren felt like he was being weighed and found wanting.

"Violet said she's done the Epi a million times before. She knew exactly what to do."

What? Bren snapped his full attention to that green-eyed gaze. She could have been her usual smartass self, but she played it straight.

"A million times before, huh?" was all he could say. The woman he'd said wasn't fit to be around his kids had just saved his youngest daughter's life.

"Yeah, my mom's allergic to peanuts as well," Violet said, as if it were nothing. "Never grew out of it, so it was something I was trained on early. Any chance I have to stab a needle into a thigh, I'm all over that."

She smiled at him, a dazzler that knocked him over. "I'd best be off. Harper's freaking out, which means my night playing nurse is only beginning. But first, I have a question for you, Franks."

His daughter sat up straighter. "Okay."

"What did the baby corn say to the mama corn?"

"I don't know."

"Where's popcorn?"

Pretty lame, but Bren would suffer through a million terrible jokes just to witness the smile Violet put on his daughter's face.

Franky grabbed her hand. "I could show you those other slugs tomorrow. They're not as fascinating as the Rathouisiidae, but they're still interesting. I have them in a terrarium at home."

Kendra had never been encouraging of Franky's interest in wildlife and science, preferring to direct her energies to dolls and clothes, pursuits that Franky didn't care for. Though his daughters never said it, he suspected Kendra's ambivalence to motherhood shone through, and this is why they'd wanted to live with him. His kids needed accepting adults in their lives, and he waited with bated breath for Violet's response.

Violet squeezed Franky's hand back. "Wow, you sure know how to sell it, kiddo. Let me see. I've got improv class in the afternoon, but maybe we can figure something out." She was clearly trying to take the middle ground here—not hurt his kid's feelings and still keep with Bren's ill-conceived wishes that she not spend time with them.

He was such a jerk. He'd made this big to-do out of Violet and his kids because *he* wasn't strong enough to be around this beautiful steak of temptation.

"See ya, Franky," Violet said, pulling her hand away

gently. "And remember: always ask before you chow."
She nodded at Bren as she headed out.

Bren leaned in and kissed Franky on the cheek. "I'll
be back in a sec, sprite."

He caught up with Violet a few feet away outside the
room. "Vi." *Vi?*

She turned, obviously surprised. "Oh. Hi."

"Thanks for doing that. For having the presence of
mind."

"No problem. I mean, it was pretty fucking scary, but
I knew Harper had one with her and luckily she'd left
her Kate Spade in the box when she stepped out."

"Kate Spade?"

"Purse, heathen."

He rubbed his beard to hide his budding smile.

"Don't be too hard on Caitriona," she said softly.

"Why do you say that?"

"I know she's older, so I'm guessing you expect her to
look out for Franky. But she's just a kid herself, and she's
kind of self-absorbed right now for self-preservation
reasons. I remember what that was like when—well, I
remember. These past couple of weeks have been trying
for you all."

Worst father ever right here. He couldn't think of a
single thing to say. For years, he hadn't needed to because he was: (a) married and (b) reliant on alcohol to
make him more palatable to those closest to him.

Violet didn't seem to care. She could have stepped
into the silence, but she just stood there, waiting for
him to get his personality together.

"Franky really likes you," he said.

"Well, she has excellent taste." Wink and grin. "She's pretty special herself. She's going to either rule the world or destroy it. Maybe both."

"Yeah, sometimes I think she's hovering on the edge of the dark side." Talking about his kids was easy. For the past eleven years, his marriage had survived on conversations about the girls, which was perfect for the man who lived inside his head and made rare visits to the world of normal adults. He'd made a terrible husband, and not just because he was a drunk. Now, if he ever got around to dating, what the hell would he talk about?

Violet was surprisingly easy to talk to when he wasn't trying to ram his tongue down her throat. He wished he'd tried this sooner instead of scowling at her for the past eight and a half months.

"When's the hot Swede starting?"

"I haven't called her yet."

"Oh?"

He shook his head, unable to verbalize it. Ms. Ikea would have done a fine job saving Franky tonight—of that Bren had no doubt. But she wasn't the one on the spot. This woman was.

"Could you come over tomorrow like Franky asked, for the slug show? After your improv class, if that's a real thing?"

"Oh, it's a real thing. I'm also learning flamenco. Building my résumé."

He had no idea whether to believe her. But he wanted to believe in something.

"Her mom wasn't the most encouraging of her interests." He refused to feel bad about guilting Violet into a visit, not if it pleased his daughter. "If you have time, Franky would appreciate you stopping by."

"Only Franky?"

"Not sure Caitriona appreciates anything right now."

She smirked, a smartass look of *I've got your number*. She'd meant: Would one Bren St. James appreciate a visit from one Violet Vasquez?

"I'll see what I can do, Nessie."

She sashayed off down the corridor back to the waiting room, leaving him bewildered and questioning everything he thought he knew about women.

NINE

The next day Violet still hadn't shaken off the events of the night before. Bren's little girl could have died, and Violet's dreams were filled with Franky's blue lips and desperate wheezes. What if Harper had taken her purse with her to the restroom? What if she'd forgotten to pack the EpiPen? What if Violet hadn't known what to do? So many what-ifs standing between happiness and heartbreak.

Violet turned her car onto Hazel Avenue in Highland Park, drove twenty feet, and slammed hard on the brakes. *¡Dios mío!* What was that? Eyes frantic, she scanned the sidewalk for the culprit that had just scared the living crap out of her.

Ah, just as she suspected: she had almost killed St. James's mutt. This family was going to be the death of her!

With clearly no sense of remorse at having aged Violet ten years, Gretzky sniffed at a fire hydrant outside the open gates to Bren's home. Inhaling a deep breath to calm her nerves, Violet parked her beater and got out. What the hell was he doing out on the road where unsuspecting motorists could mow him down?

"Come here, puppy."

He lifted his head and wagged his tail, then returned to sniffing the hydrant. Heady stuff, apparently.

"*Tu pequeño bastardo, ven aquí.*" *That* seemed to get his attention. Interesting. In fact, he seemed to appreciate her pissy tone as well. Having grown up on the receiving end of Spanish orders, Violet could appreciate its utility for others. Mom shouting at her to do her homework, tidy her room, or eat her dinner always sounded more threatening in the mother tongue.

Gretzky left off from his sniffing, wagged his tail, and then launched himself at Violet with such force she fell back on her ass. "Hey!"

She pulled herself upright and, still shaking slightly, pointed at the house. "*¡Entrar en la casa! ¡Ahora!*" Yes, she was the domme here. Then she headed that way herself, watching to see if her doggie-sub would follow her. He did, still wagging his tail, still joyfully clueless. Passing through the gates, which were wide open—defeating the purpose of uh, *gates*—she spotted a woman on the sidewalk in jogging gear so tight it must have cut off all circulation to her extremities. Pink all over, too: headband, tracksuit, sneakers. Probably one of the neighbors.

The woman threw a look at Violet's crappy car, Violet's current ensemble—denim skirt, teal leather jacket, and Frye booties—and Violet's coif, still pink streaked.

"Hey there!" Violet called out with a wave before

following Gretzky, who had overtaken her and then stopped to wait for her. Such a gentleman.

She walked up the drive, realizing that she probably could have parked closer to the house, but the damn dog had spooked her. The St. James house was actually one of the smaller ones on this street filled with McMansions and faux colonials. This one had *only* five bedrooms, whereas all the others had eight or more. But it had character, from the stained glass lintel over the door to the Tuscan slate tiling the kitchen floor. It was the perfect house for raising a family.

No one answered the door, which was not exactly the welcome Violet expected. She was a special guest at Chez St. James after all. Somehow, Bren had gotten ahold of her number, though the text she got this morning was definitely from Franky.

You don't want to miss out!!! Followed by a photo of a slug in a jar.

¡Mano! How could she resist?

She tried the bell again just as the door flew open. Caitriona stood there, looking like Violet was a slug. Her gaze fell to Gretzky. "He shouldn't be outside."

"Yeah, I'm guessing not. He was in the street and I almost ran him over."

The girl's eyes flew wide and she hunkered down, hugging the dog so hard Violet swore she heard him squeak. "Oh no. Dad'll kill me." She peered up. "I put him outside while we were cooking, but I must have left the side gate open."

This was the first real emotion Violet had witnessed

in the girl. She wouldn't judge, because everyone handled disruption differently, but she had to admit some small relief that Caitriona wasn't a complete robot.

Sensing an opening, Violet asked, "How about we forget it happened? Let's just say you owe me."

Caitriona nodded. "Okay." She closed the front door behind them. "Come on through."

Violet trailed after Cat and Dog, the kitchen their apparent destination, the sound of music getting louder as she approached. As she walked in, the first thought that entered her brain was: *wow, that's a lot of flour.*

And it was everywhere. The counters. The floor. Bren's hair.

Bren's beard.

That should have been the best part, but it wasn't. Not even close. Bren St. James, aka Lord of the Puck aka Hell's Highlander aka the man who might have played a very minor part in Violet's vibrator-fueled fantasies over the past eight and a half months, was wearing an apron.

A pink, frilly apron with ponies—no, even better, *unicorns*—and rainbows on it.

With fists on hips, he assessed his youngest daughter's efforts as she kneaded pastry. Even Violet could tell that stronger, less patient hands were required to get that dough into shape. Big, manly hands like those meaty paws belonging to the Scotsman.

Stop fantasizing about his hands with his children in the room.

Bren kept those patient hands patiently on his hips while he patiently watched Franky push the dough around the counter. Flour rose, plumed, and fell on every nearby horizontal surface.

"Like this, Dad?"

"Just like that, sprite."

"And Violet likes apple pie?"

"Everyone does."

What was this? Violet's pastry needs were being considered here?

Caitriona was on the other side of the island, bobbing her head and mouthing the words to a song, the one everyone knew about Hamilton not throwing away his shot.

"Who was at the door, love?" Bren asked.

"Me."

Bren and Franky looked up, both surprised.

"You're early!" Franky said.

"My class was canceled so I came right over. So, you're baking?"

Bren smiled, and yet again, she was struck at how affected she was by it. She was supposed to get a mini-orgasm at Grumpy Scot, but this . . . this was impacting her a couple of feet north of the nether regions. Guys had smiled at her before, so what the hell was this flutter in her tummy about? And since when did she use the word *tummy*?

"Yeah. The girls had their first lesson today with the new tutor, so we decided to have some fun baking. We're getting the apple pie done before we start on dinner."

"I could go if this is a really bad time."

He looked horrified. "No! Don't leave me." Now he looked doubly horrified. "That came out a little unmanly."

She rolled in her lips. Bren St. James was pretty adorable right now.

"I'm building a slug empire," Franky said, apropos of nothing, and that was pretty adorable, too.

"This one is a spotted garden slug."

Sitting on a weathered patio chair overlooking the somewhat overgrown backyard, Violet feigned interest in a mollusk with a particularly slimy trail. She used to fake orgasms, so she figured this couldn't be worse than some of the guys she'd dated.

Franky sat cross-legged on the patio while she added a few twigs to a glass terrarium, which already had a layer of soil and leaves. An empire couldn't expand in a jar, after all.

"So, Franks, what was that you were saying earlier about me liking apple pie?"

One of the slugs—out for a walk, Violet liked to think—made slow progress a few inches away from its new digs. Franky switched her focus to it, stroking it with her index finger, and watched its response to the stimulus of touch.

"It's part of the plan."

"The plan?"

"I'm not supposed to say."

Curiouser and curiouser. "So, what do these puppies eat?"

"They're mollusks, not puppies. And they eat greens. Kale, spinach, lettuce. But not iceberg lettuce. It has to be dark green and leafy . . ."

She carried on, talking about slug diets and how you shouldn't put a bowl of water in the terrarium because they might drown and something about a mister, which Violet realized after about three minutes meant a spray bottle.

"How does pasta sound, sprite?" Bren stood at the door, still floured, still aproned, still adorable.

"Okay," Franky said absently.

"Hey, Franks, what do you call a fake noodle?" Violet asked, and when Franky looked curious, she went in for the kill. "An impasta!"

"That's silly." But she grinned all the same.

"Yeah, I know, but it's okay to be silly once in a while."

"You staying for dinner?" her father asked Violet gruffly.

"Sure! When you ask so nicely, how can I refuse?"

He shook his head and returned to the house.

Ten minutes later, Violet was in heaven because Bren St. James made a mean bowl of ziti à la pomodoro. There was garlic bread, too (store-bought, but you couldn't have everything). About halfway through dinner, he turned to Violet and said, "Sorry I don't have any wine. I haven't had guests in a while."

"Dad emptied all the bottles in the sink last week," Franky said. "They smelled terrible!"

A look of such discomfort crossed Bren's face that Violet wanted to hug away his pain. These girls, too. She'd noticed a bottle here and there in the cupboards when she put away the groceries.

"Water's fine."

The apple pie sat on the counter, cooling. Gretzky sat in front of it, drooling.

"You're not worried he'll try to grab it?"

"I like to torture him," Bren said, matter-of-factly. "He likes it, too."

"Speaking of what we like, I'm all in with the apple pie."

Bren raised his chin. There was still a spot of flour in his beard—several spots of flour—which gave his facial hair a gray-speckled, distinguished quality. Violet longed to stroke her fingers through it, feel that springy growth against her skin.

He slid a glance at Franky, who muttered guiltily, "I didn't say anything."

"She won't agree to it," Caitriona said, probably the first thing she'd said since they started eating.

Father and daughters exchanged glances, like they were planning a caper and Violet was the target. Or maybe she was the accomplice who needed to be brought into the fold for one last score. She preferred that last interpretation.

"Girls, how about you take Gretzky outside into the garden?" Bren asked. "He's not getting any younger watching that pie."

The girls knew a ruse when they heard one, but dutifully did as they were told, leaving Violet alone with Bren.

"Done?" he said, standing and nodding at her empty plate, then taking it when she didn't answer.

She picked up her glass of water, stood, and leaned against the counter.

"You don't want me looking after your kids, St. James, last night notwithstanding. That was a fluke, really. Next time, who knows."

"They like you."

"Even Caitriona?"

"She doesn't like anyone right now."

True, and Violet knew better than to take offense. "What about Ms. Volvo? She's perfect."

"I know. And her name is Ms. Ikea." He sighed. "She didn't even screw up her nose when the dog farted."

"That's a good sign."

"Is it?"

She wouldn't argue with him. This was not a reason to choose, or not choose, a qualified nanny.

"I called the agency about her references and . . ." He rubbed his mouth.

"And what?"

"She took another job. I waited too long and now I have to start over."

For fuck's sake. "St. James . . ."

"Look, I understand that you have a busy life. You seem to have a lot going on with your improv classes and your flamenco lessons."

Now he was making her sound like a dilettante. "And don't forget all I do to support the team. Advising Moretti on acquisitions as long as the players are hotties. Boosting team morale with my pregame pep talks." She touched her shoulder to his big, beefy bicep. "And how could you ever trust me not to dye their hair and pierce their ears?"

"Maybe you should try some pie."

"What's that about, anyway? Franky seems a bit obsessed. In fact, you all do, weird St. James family."

Bren stroked his beard. "When I wasn't . . . such a mess, I'd return from away games, and after catching some shut-eye, make an apple pie with the girls. It was this coming home ritual, a way of grounding myself and reconnecting with my sprites. They loved to help me. And then when I was drinking more, I stopped because I had more important things to be doing."

Like sleeping off a hangover and getting trashed all over again, she supposed. The bitter tinge in his voice said it all: he'd not yet forgiven himself. And was he *trying* to break her heart with the apple pie story?

Those blue eyes implored her. "I'd need your help for just a few days."

"Tsk. You're assuming you're not going to get past the first round? Nice attitude."

"Just a realist. What I do know is I'll play better knowing they're with someone I trust."

He trusted her? She walked over to the window and took in the domestic empire she could rule for a brief moment. Caitriona was throwing a probably germ-ridden tennis ball to the end of the yard, but Gretzky couldn't find it because Caitriona still had it in her hand. This subterfuge apparently didn't square with Franky's sense of fair play, as she struggled mightily to pry it from her older sister's claws.

Violet had always wanted sisters. Don't get her wrong—she hadn't grown up lonely, not with her mom and two aunts. There was a lot of love in that cramped apartment in Reno, but she would have enjoyed playing with someone closer to her age.

She wished she'd known Harper and Violet sooner. All that wasted time.

"If only they were cuter," she muttered.

Bren snort-laughed behind her. Turning would only give him the satisfaction of knowing she'd enjoyed his reaction, so she didn't move an inch. Her heart beat wildly in her chest. She felt hugely vulnerable about this trust he was placing in her.

"And what about us?"

He was close to her now, his breath a whisper of warmth against her cheek. "Us?"

"You said that me near your kids—near you—would interfere with your sobriety."

"I realized that the welfare and happiness of my daughters is more important than anything."

Even his attraction to her, which he didn't deny. This wasn't a decision made lightly. Creating a stable environment for his daughters was the prime directive, and whatever existed between him and Violet was barely a blip compared to the well-deep love he had for those girls.

This was good. Today, Bren St. James with his adorable apron and floury beard had struck her as a little too human, a little too *viable*, no longer just a piece of ass she could tease and taunt. This wasn't the kind of man she could easily put in her rearview when she took her cut of the franchise and ran. The barrier between them would exist for good reasons all around.

Because she hadn't answered, he continued making his case. "You can use my SUV while I'm gone, and it doesn't have to be live-in. We won't have to spend time together, just the handoff. When I'm here, you don't have to be."

But what if I want to be? If she valued her mental health, then she'd best nix that notion. It sounded like the ideal setup, except she would now be responsible for the nearest and dearest people to this man's heart. This was madness, but apparently she'd gone a little mad herself.

Most important, it felt significant, something to give her purpose.

"Until the end of the play-offs, whichever round that is," she said.

His broad shoulders relaxed. "Thank you. Now let's have some pie."

TEN

Violet: *Hey, Nessie.*

Bren: *Are the girls okay?*

Violet: *Yes. Do you think I'd text you while you're at an away game with "Hey, Nessie" if they weren't?*

Bren: *Okay. Can I help you?*

Violet: *Oh, the answers I could give. LOL.*

Bren: *. . .*

Violet: *;P (that was me sticking out my tongue, spoilsport). So I'm checking in to see how late is too late for them to drink soda.*

Bren: *What are they telling you?*

Violet: *That they usually drink it with dinner and then again with their cookie snack at 8 p.m.*

Bren: *Lies. All of it. No soda or cookies after 6 p.m. Not unless you want to be up all night with them.*

Violet: *Nessie has spoken!*

Fifteen seconds later . . .

Violet: *Oh, they don't like that. But you're the bad guy, so I'm in the clear.*

———

Violet: *Hey, Nessie.*

Bren: *Is everything okay?*

Violet: *Uh, we've covered this. Yes.*

Bren: *. . .*

Bren: *?*

Violet: *Sorry, Gretzky was getting a little familiar with the chica parts there. Anyways, we have a problem. The girls have never seen* The Princess Bride.

Bren: *Of course they have. Everyone has.*

Violet: *Nope. I was quoting all the best lines and they were clueless. Mawage. Inconceivable. ROUS. Nothing!*

Bren: *Way to make me feel like a failure as a parent.*

Violet: *Right, because it's all about you. Okay for them to watch?*

Bren: *As you wish.*

Violet: *Nice. Have fun storming the ice field!*

Bren: *Rink.*

Violet: *Whatevs.*

—～——

Violet: *Hey, Nessie.*

Bren: *Hey.*

Violet: *So why do bagpipe players walk while they play?*

Bren: *. . .*

Violet: *To get away from the noise!*

Bren: *Ha-ha.*

Violet: *I know. Classic, right? Sorry about the game last night.*

Bren: *Thanks. We still have one more shot. How was the movie?*

Violet: *Didn't watch it. Figured you might want to see it with them the first time. We watched* The Lego Movie *instead, and through the power of product placement, you're now on the hook for all sorts of useless plastic shit.*

Bren: *Uh, thanks?*

Violet: *No problem! BTW, Cat's no longer vegan . . . you're welcome! Night, Nessie!*

"Mami, what's the best way to get blood out of clothing?"

Violet held the phone between her cheek and her shoulder, wishing she'd put it on speaker. Too late now, as she was already scrubbing a T-shirt with dish soap in the kitchen sink at Bren's house.

"You haven't called in weeks and this is what you

open with? Have you finally done away with one of those rich white girls?"

Violet sighed. Since her mom had moved back to Puerto Rico eighteen months ago, she'd been a touch snide whenever Violet called, partly because Violet didn't move with her. San Juan had never been her home, and it sure as hell wouldn't start being so now.

But mostly her mom's attitude stemmed from the fact Violet had moved to Chicago to get to know her sisters. Louisa Vasquez thought Clifford Chase was the devil and his spawn not much better—present company excluded, of course.

"I talked to you three days ago, so quit exaggerating. And we always talk about the same things. The weather, your lumbago, the weather, how it affects your lumbago—"

"Okay, okay, point taken. And now you want to talk about covering up some crime involving blood-spattered clothing."

No wonder Clifford Chase had run a mile. Of course, he'd recognized a gold digger when he saw one and he was smart enough to ensure that his latest baby mama wouldn't get a dime for herself. Violet's Catholic school tuition fees at St. Ita's were paid directly by Clifford's lawyer. Anything else had to be itemized and justified as necessary to Violet's upkeep. Louisa's scam hadn't left her any better off, just on the hook for an unwanted child.

Violet had found that part out later. Before the age of thirteen, she'd never doubted her mom's love for her, that Violet was wanted. She knew Louisa loved her in her own way, but unfortunately it was tangled up in something ugly and sordid.

Biting her lip at her uncharitable thoughts, she tried a reboot of the conversation.

"*Hola*, Mami, how are you? How's the weather? Is your lumbago acting up? Any tips for getting blood out of a shirt?"

"What kind of material?"

"Cotton. A T-shirt belonging to one of the girls. Franky, Bren's youngest, had a nosebleed."

Violet had already filled her mom in on her new position. Expecting pride that Violet was doing something more productive than answering phones in a tattoo parlor or slinging hard liquor in a biker bar was probably too much. That she was looking after rich *gringitas* was an extra dose of salt in her self-inflicted wound.

For most of Violet's childhood, Louisa had worked two jobs—one as a hotel maid, the other as a diner waitress—and now that Violet was a wealthy woman, all her mother could see was the hoops Violet had to jump through to get what was rightfully hers as Clifford Chase's daughter. Picking up after rich white people was just another mark against Clifford and the tentacles he seemed to extend from the grave.

"I did not raise you to be a maid to some rich man's children."

"I'm a nanny, and it's temporary."

"I don't understand why you are there at all. Why have you not sold your share? That's your money. It's what you are owed."

It was what Louisa was owed. The fruits of the score she'd set in motion all those years ago.

"I'm waiting until the end of the season, Mami. I told you. The franchise will be more valuable if the Rebels are champions. They'll have to give me more."

That knot between her lungs pulsed at her mercenary thoughts, but she had never lied to Harper and Isobel about her plans. They knew this life wasn't for her.

"Just remember," her mom said. "Those girls are not your real family. Don't get soft and let them off the hook."

"Bloodstains?" She was beginning to wish she'd just Googled it, but she'd assumed her mother might enjoy feeling useful. The woman enjoyed something, all right.

"Put baking soda in water to make a paste. Spread it on the stain, let sit for thirty minutes or overnight. You could also use lemon juice or hydrogen peroxide."

"Thanks. Now that wasn't so hard, was it?"

Her mother sniffed derisively. "This man you are working for, the alcoholic?"

"Done some research, then?"

"Have *you*? What if he goes on a binge? Takes it out on you? If he hits you, call the police. Or better yet, get a gun."

"Mami—"

"Your aunt didn't call the police and she got into trouble later."

Aunt Cecy hit her good-for-nothing husband with a baseball bat instead of calling the cops. He deserved it, but the police didn't look kindly on the introduction of weapons into the situation. All her mom's and aunts' experiences with men were skewed, so much so that Violet wondered how she'd made it out of their man-hating cocoon free of their bitterness.

Maybe she hadn't. She wasn't exactly interested in anything long term.

"Bren's not like that. He's a new man." She didn't know what he was like before, but she saw no evidence that he was in imminent danger of falling back into his old habits. His daughters meant too much to him. "And I can handle myself. You know I can." She'd broken up plenty of bar fights and knew how to throw a punch. Not that it would ever be necessary with the Scot. The guy wasn't dangerous.

At least not in the way her mother thought.

She was having a lot of fun texting him about silly things, as if she didn't know sugary sodas after 6 p.m. were the work of the devil. Maybe she liked the idea of them making child-care decisions together. *Totally whacked, Vasquez.*

Her mother's answer was another disapproving sniff. "Don't make the mistake of thinking you can rely on this man. Not after the last time."

Violet bit down on her lip, annoyed to be reminded of "the last time" and the man who had let her down when she'd found out about the big C. The minute things got tough, Denny Carter got slithering.

Babe, I can't. It reminds me of my grandma's last days.

He'd reached out when her father died, a call that,

funnily enough, coincided with her inheriting a professional sports franchise. Subtlety had never been one of Denny's strong points. She wasn't fool enough to fall for him again. She was all out of second chances.

Because her mother was paying rent inside her head, her next words weren't all that surprising. "They're not like us, Violet. That bastard screwed with their minds, and now they are warped by too much money and not enough love. Don't forget who was there for you through the bad times."

Violet knew better than to rely on anyone but those closest to her—the women who had raised her. As soon as the play-offs were done, she'd move on.

"I won't forget, Mami."

"Good. And don't leave it so long to call your mother next time." She clicked off.

ELEVEN

Gretzky attacked as soon as he walked in the door.

"Down, fella," Bren shout-whispered as he reset the alarm. Kendra's birthday. Probably should change that.

Five in the morning, so his girls would be asleep. Violet, too. With the weight of his daughters' care off his shoulders, he'd played a blinder in game seven, scoring a goal and racking up three assists.

They'd made it to round two.

Winning also meant that Violet would have to stick around for another few weeks. He smiled to himself, strangely pleased with that notion. He'd barely seen her before he left for Dallas, as Harper had brought her up to speed with to-do lists and emergency numbers and Franky's medications.

He dumped his bag at the bottom of the stairs, knowing he'd have to do laundry later. Maybe the girls' laundry as well. Harper had hired someone who could come in once a week on Thursdays—who knew housekeepers were so hard to find?—and she wasn't due in until . . . what day was it again? Friday morning. So she would have stopped by yesterday.

He couldn't think about this now, not when his bed was calling him softly.

He stopped outside Franky's room and pushed the door open. She had fallen asleep with her glasses on—a typical occurrence—and her Kindle was resting on her chest. She was rereading *Harry Potter* for the fifth time. He stepped in, pulled gently on her glasses, and laid them on her nightstand along with the e-reader. She stirred a little, but didn't wake.

A feeling of such overwhelming love enveloped him that his knees almost buckled. *Don't fuck up, Bren. Do not fuck up.*

He put his head around Caitriona's door. The sleep of the dead for that one, which made him smile. He hoped she'd start talking to him soon. His smile faded, remembering how he'd hurt her. Hurt them both.

Halfway to his room, ready to drop like a log, he decided he probably should make sure Violet had actually stayed the night like she was supposed to. Not that he doubted she would, but it was his duty as an employer to—

Ah, shut yer hole, St. James. You just want to see her.

The door to the guest room she'd taken was open, close enough to the girls if one of them called out. Of course, she wouldn't be sleeping here while he was, except for these brief few hours when their time in the house overlapped.

Over the past three days, he'd spoken to her a couple of times, just to check in. Texted more, which worked better for him. That way, he could think about what to say, though it wasn't exactly producing polished gemstones of wit.

He looked in, needing to verify she was here. Safe.

If he wasn't already sure that someone up there hated him, the sight before him would have confirmed it. She lay sprawled on her front, the edge of her white panties riding up to showcase the curve of her perfect ass. The comforter was pulled back, one of her legs twisted in it. Buttery stripes of light through the blinds splashed the back of her thigh, illuminating those inked vines that stretched around her legs. He knew the front of her thighs were tattooed with roses and other red, pink, and orange blooms.

Would they unfurl if he touched them? Would she?

Some asshole tattoo artist had sat beside her, hunched over her luscious skin while he applied the tools of his trade. Bren wondered if it had hurt her, then decided that she was a tough woman. She had to be, given how Clifford had treated her.

During his musing about her body ink, his eyes had adjusted better. The panties had writing on them, a couple of words in a tiny script emblazoned across her ass, too small for him to read from this distance.

He moved closer. N-O-S . . . A smile cracked his face, enough of a surprise that his facial muscles protested slightly. In tiny text, the message on Violet's ass spelled out:

NOSEY

FUCKER

Jesus, this woman was going to be the end of him.

She turned over. He stepped back, but it was too late.

"Hey," she whispered, swiping a hand over her eyes. The watery dawn light spotlighted the curve of her breasts in a way he should not be noticing. She wasn't overly ample, but there looked to be the right amount to fill his hands.

"Sorry, I didn't mean to wake you. Just checking on my girls."

"Your girls?"

He heard the smile in her voice at what she might consider a slipup, and perhaps it was. *Violet, his girl.*

He cleared his throat. "How were things?"

"Good. They have a lot of energy."

On the subject of energy, and more specifically on how to temper it, he shoved his hands into his jean pockets and backed up a few steps to lean against the doorjamb. Talking about his daughters with their nanny was perfectly appropriate. Just a standard debrief. *De. Brief.*

Christ, the comforter sat at midthigh, providing no coverage whatsoever. From this angle, there was no missing that dark shadow of hair behind the white fabric of her panties. Through his pocket, he knuckled his hardening cock, willing it to behave.

He should leave, but something—someone—was cementing his feet to the floor. No traces of self-consciousness showed on her face. In fact, she cat-stretched her arm above her head, the pull of the fabric over her breasts downright delicious.

"Need me to make coffee?" she asked, her voice a lazy tease.

He hauled himself back from the brink. "No, I should get to bed. Didn't sleep on the plane."

She nodded. "You played well, St. James. The girls are very proud."

He backed out, slowly, so as not to fall on his ass. As he turned away, he heard her say in a soft voice, "So am I."

———

He awoke to the sound of laughter, and for the briefest moment, he thought Kendra was here with the girls. He shook himself awake. Not Kendra.

Her.

He'd know his girls' laughter anywhere, but why did it sound even better with the addition of Violet's husky chuckle? Then Gretzky's bark joined the heart-affirming chorus. They must be in the garden.

Swinging his legs out of the bed, he stood and ambled over to the window of his bedroom, rubbing the sleep from his eyes. Christ, he ached something fierce. He'd had the requisite rubdowns and check-ins with the physio after last night's game, but the stiffness often hit him in the morning. He was turning into Old Man DuPre, who was always complaining about his broken-down body. Remy said he was retiring because he was skating on fumes, but Bren knew the guy had a few more years in him. His friend was stepping down because he saw a life after hockey and it had finally come into focus when he met Harper. The guy who needed the Cup to complete his career was content to let it slip through his fingers if this season didn't pan out. This year or never. Must be nice to have it all worked out.

Bren had never felt so out of his depth in his entire life.

Not strictly true. Fifteen months ago, he'd hit rock bottom. The memory of his girls' eyes still haunted him, the terror he'd inspired in them a crushing weight on his chest.

Kendra must not have told her parents what he'd done, because they sure as hell would have brought it up if she had. She'd held it over him for more money, sole custody, a brand-new house in Atlanta so she could be with Drew. Bren could have fought, but he would have lost.

He'd put his daughters' lives at risk—and his wife had used it as leverage.

Kendra had never wanted kids. She'd wanted the life of a pro hockey WAG, and a child was her most direct means to that end. An accidental pregnancy a few weeks after he signed his first pro contract—it didn't take a genius to figure out that one.

He'd liked her well enough. He'd fancied the hell out of her. And she was having his child. He was on top of the world, and when Kendra suggested they get married, he hadn't even questioned it. A child of divorced parents, Bren only got to see his dad during the summers in Canada. Bringing his daughter up in a two-parent home was a no-brainer. Hadn't he already bought the house? And now he had the hot wife, the gorgeous baby, the lucrative contract. Now he had the life he'd always craved.

Within a year, he and Kendra were at loggerheads. She wanted a bigger house. She wanted to live downtown, where there was nightlife and better restaurants. Decaying in the suburbs was not what she'd signed up for.

She threatened to leave him—or maybe he threatened to leave her?

Then she found out she was pregnant with Franky, and there was no more talk of divorce. They had kids— two beautiful, bright-as-buttons girls—and Bren let Kendra have her way. Her own apartment in the city, which she'd descend on as soon as he came back from an away game.

I've been holed up here for days. Now it's your turn.

She went through money like water. When he had to go away for a game, she'd return as if on sufferance. As if spending time with her girls was a chore.

A flick of the cord opened the blinds and let in the midday sun. But the ball in the sky had nothing on the brightness shining in the garden. Two little sprites, a demon on four legs, and a—what should he call Violet?

A siren. A temptress. A pain in his ass.

More like your balls, St. James.

She was at it again with the short denim skirt, revealing all that ink he wanted to run his tongue over.

Would inked skin taste different from uninked? He owed it to himself to find out.

Violet held a tennis ball high in the air and pointed at Gretzky with her other hand. Trying to teach him to sit up and beg, perhaps. A losing proposition.

The big black mutt just stood there on all four legs, tail wagging in adoration, waiting for her to throw the ball. Franky was giggling, and even Caitriona looked amused. He hoped he'd made the right decision and that it wasn't his dick talking. He could resist her.

If he could resist a drink, he could certainly resist the charms of Violet Vasquez.

Siren. Temptress. His daughters' primary caregiver.

TWELVE

"Yoo-hoo!"

Violet turned to the grating voice behind her. It belonged to the jogger from a week ago, who was now dressed in tight yoga pants and a hot pink tank top, showcasing a great rack. Violet would know, as she was a bit of an expert on breasts that had a good surgeon at their root. This doctor had done a very nice job.

"Hey there!" She power-walked up the drive, arms bent, fists as pistons fueling her stride. Blond hair scraped back in a ponytail. Makeup perfect. "I live next door and we just got back yesterday from St. Barts. My kids, Jeremy and Lance, used to play with the girls."

Violet assumed, no, *prayed*, that "the girls" referred to Franky and Cat, not the puppies packing the tank top.

Jogger in Pink yammered on. "They're at school right now, but I know they'd love to come over to hang out. Supervised, of course." She wrinkled her nose, taking in Violet's denim skirt, sloppy tee, and cowboy boots. Violet as supervisor did not pass muster. "I could bring them by later and—oh, I'm sorry. I haven't introduced myself. I'm Skylar Nichols."

Violet shook the proffered hand. "I'm—"

"Violet Vasquez," Skylar finished. "You own the Rebels with your sisters. And now you're looking after Bren's kids."

She made it sound like this was the oddest set of circumstances imaginable, and perhaps from the outside it was.

"Everyone's pitching in."

"Consider me part of the team!" Skylar beamed, not unlike a crazy person. "If you need a break from the little monsters, let me know. Or I can always bring wine!"

Hey, Skylar, you're all right. "So, Tarquin and Persephone?"

"Jeremy and Lance," Skylar said with good humor. "I'm guessing the girls are being homeschooled because it was too late to get them in anywhere? They might like a little company their own age."

"Sure, I'll run it by them."

After a few more pleasantries, Skylar jogged off with plenty of jiggle. Once inside, Violet smiled to herself. She'd ask her charges if Jeremy and Lance were worthy of a visit. Girls matured a lot earlier than boys, and they might have already outgrown them.

She checked the time on her phone. Seven fifteen. The girls would be up soon, scavenging for breakfast, not that she really needed to be present to give it to them. They tended to make a lot of noise as they clanked around the kitchen. Tonight was game one of round two against the Detroit Motors, and their dad needed his rest.

Violet ran a finger along the mahogany bannister as she walked by. After six days of playing nanny, she'd decided she loved this house, though really she loved the "home." How it came alive with Bren and his girls in it.

What had happened between the man and his wife?

Sure, she knew the broad brushstrokes. Alcoholism was to blame for the demise of many marriages, but they'd had eleven years. Eleven years of togetherness, raising their two girls, in this house. His adoration for his daughters was unquestionable, and Violet suspected he'd once looked at his wife that way.

Perhaps still looked at her that way.

Not that she cared.

She walked into the kitchen and was confronted with a sight that every woman should have access to early in the morning.

Bren stood at the counter with his back to her, and what a back it was. Pure muscle, carved out of . . . more muscle. At the top of that perfect triangle, broad shoulders tapered to a trim waist and narrow hips, barely covered by gray sweats (the best color sweats!). Slung dangerously low, too. If he turned—

He turned.

Her knees lost all their power as her mouth lost all its moisture. Hooray for low-slung, because those were some mighty fine hip-to-groin indents being framed perfectly by those sweats. She assumed that if she looked up, she'd find more of the same perfection. So she did her hormones a favor and zipped past the goodie trail, abs, nipples, pecs, and went straight for the eye contact.

It's for your own damn good, she asserted to every screaming body part that insisted she'd somehow failed in her womanly duty to report all the facts.

"Morning," he said. "Wasn't expecting you."

"I thought I'd come in and make the girls breakfast. Try to keep them quiet while you rest."

He smiled, and her knees melted again. *Come on, knees, you're better than this!*

"I couldn't sleep. Never can on game days." He held an egg in his hand, next to a bowl of more along with other ingredients. Bread. Milk. Cinnamon.

"*You're* making breakfast?"

"Aye. Used to do this for the girls when they'd come visit. French toast casserole."

First the apple pie, now the most important meal of the day. Pretty swoon-worthy. "I hear that in Scotland they fry everything five times to make sure it's dead."

Slight uptick at the corner of his mouth. "My cooking prowess comes from the Canadian side."

"I'll get out of your way, then."

He passed over that. "Thanks for taking care of the laundry. You could have left it to Mrs. Higgins." That was the woman who came in once a week.

"What else am I going to do while they have their lessons?"

"Take it easy? Put your feet up?" He returned the egg to the bowl and folded thick arms across his thick chest. "You're not here to do housework."

"I've been doing housework all my life. I prefer to feel useful."

"Then get to making the coffee." He turned his back, her acquiescence assumed.

She smiled at his gruff but affectionate tone. For the next ten minutes, they worked side by side, not speaking, the comfort level surprising, because usually around him, she felt tense. Needy. Horny.

Oh, don't get her wrong. Needy and horny were still predominant, but not so tense. More . . . loose.

She opened a cupboard, and as she reached for the sugar bowl because she didn't like Splenda, her gaze fell yet again on that bottle of Johnnie Walker Double Black. No change in the level, still three quarters full. She'd seen it there when she put the groceries away. Noticed it every time she reached for the sugar. Wondered why he hadn't dumped it like he had all the others.

Suddenly he was behind her, grabbing the bowl for her. Like something out of a rom-com, his hand covered hers, his chest leaned into her back. If she moved back an inch, what else would she find leaning in?

"I've got this," she said.

He didn't remove his hand. "You sure? You're kind of short."

On tiptoe, she cupped the bowl with a shaky hand and twisted to face him. She was now caged with that broody Scot looking down at her intently. His broad chest gleamed and she tightened her hold on the bowl, so she wouldn't be tempted to reach out and touch. As if it could protect her from an incredibly sexy, yet undoubtedly poor, decision.

"Why do you keep that bottle in there?" Damn, it was none of her business. "Sorry, I shouldn't ask."

Silence ruled for a long beat, then: "No, you should. I need to be held accountable, and with you taking care of my girls, it's only right that you question anything that might put them in danger. I need you to always question that."

"But they're not in danger from you. You'd never hurt them." If there was one thing she was absolutely certain of, it was Bren St. James's absolute devotion to his daughters.

"No." His brow crimped. "At least, not now. I keep that bottle to remind myself that I'm one drink away from disaster. When I got out of rehab, I used to order shots in bars and not drink them, or I'd sit off in a corner and brood while my teammates had their fun. But I don't go to bars much anymore now that the girls are here."

When Violet had first arrived in Chicago, she'd spent a lot of time with the team at their usual watering hole, flirting and laughing, but Bren was always on the outside, watching and waiting. "Was that my fault? Did you stop hanging with your teammates at the Empty Net because I was there?"

Wry smile. "No. I needed to be alone for a while after rehab but still close enough to know I was part of the crew. The distance was necessary while I worked on . . . forgiving myself, I suppose. They were there with open arms, but I'd let them down, and I wasn't ready for them to embrace me back into the fold." He raised his gaze above her head. "The bottle is here to remind me to never again take a single thing for granted. And speaking of taking things for granted . . . I don't think I've thanked you enough, Violet."

"Thank me with cash." She shrugged, oh so nonchalant. "Not that I especially need it, but I'm not working for free."

Putting this on a boss/employee footing seemed best. Except she was his boss on the team and he was her boss in the . . . Not the bedroom. No. He had employed her to look after his kids. But she hadn't forgotten his mouth on hers, his fingers' rough stroke between her legs, his eyes dark with want. Like now.

"I wouldn't dream of taking advantage," he murmured.

Please do. "You know I washed a few T-shirts with the last load."

"I did thank you."

"Meaning you should wear them. Cover this"—she gestured at the gloriousness that was *this*—"up."

The slightest smirk teased his mouth. "This?"

"Mrs. Higgins is going through menopause and it's not helping her hot flashes. Then there's the kids' tutor. Very young and impressionable—"

"She's middle-aged, happily married, and completely incorruptible."

She sighed, affecting boredom. "Okay, it's kind of distracting to me."

He looked a little surprised by her honesty. Then a little smug. "Could say the same thing about your teeny-tiny shorts."

"I'm wearing a skirt today." *For your improved access, sir.*

His gaze dipped over her denim skirt, lingering on her inked thighs. "Like that's better." Gaze back up, sensual fire in those blue-on-blue eyes.

Had she mentioned that all this time he was still looming over her, those thick arms boxing her in? No? Well, he was, and it was delicious.

"So, neither of us are fans of the other's wardrobe choices," she said.

"Guess not."

Something shifted between them—it had been shifting since the moment they met, ebbing and flowing—but this was a strange charge that could be labeled only as one thing: honesty. A recognition that they were both incredibly attracted to each other and had decided to be open about it. And with it came a certain sadness. They couldn't act on it for a zillion reasons.

She fell back on her usual defense strategy: humor.

"Kind of a cliché, isn't it? The single dad with a thing for the nanny."

That dampened the flames, all right. He drew back and she hated every inch he and her smart mouth put between them.

"That's me, one giant cliché."

The oven timer dinged, and they went back to their lives before that conversation had rocked them both.

Bren stared at the swirls he'd generated from stirring his coffee with his spoon. He liked coffee in porcelain mugs, the kind of mugs you got in diners, the kind of diners like this one in downtown Riverbrook. Call him old-fashioned, but coffee was meant to be drunk out of something real, not polystyrene or paper or whatever you got in Starbucks.

The door to the Bottomless Cup opened, but it wasn't who he was waiting for. This gave him more time to think on that moment with Violet in the kitchen this morning.

He hadn't expected her, and he was oddly touched that she'd shown up early so he could get more sleep. Seeing her walking into his kitchen, breezy and free-spirited, had sent a pang of longing through him the likes of which he'd never experienced, not even after long periods playing away during his marriage. Sure, he felt a version of it around his daughters, but never with a woman, not even his ex-wife.

Of course, Violet made a habit out of upending all his expectations.

That little cha-cha they'd performed in the kitchen, the one that ended with them all but admitting they wanted each other, had taken him by surprise. Acknowledging this ongoing attraction should have freed up his brain, but knowing she felt the same way, that it wasn't just a passing flirtation, had crashed through him like a fireball.

Just your weak body talking. If his coffee date would only show up, then he could maybe get his head on straight. He needed to be at the practice facility in an hour.

The door opened again and Bren's head raised instinctively. About fucking time.

Kevin McCordle lumbered in, looking like he'd barely survived a rough night on the tiles. Bren wasn't overly concerned. Kevin had ingested so many illegal substances in his life that he could easily wrest from Keith Richards the title of "who smoked and shot up everything." No amount of clean living could turn back that clock.

He shuffled over and sat opposite Bren in the booth. "Christ, you look like shit, St. James."

Sure thing, pot. The man's sponsorship style was tough love laced with insults. Bren wouldn't have it any other way.

The server stopped by and took Kevin's order for coffee. When she stepped away, Kevin cracked his knuckles and cocked his head.

"You haven't been at meetings. Thought you'd dropped off the face of the earth."

"Been busy getting my kids settled, and oh yeah, taking my team to the play-offs for the first time in fifteen years. AA meetings take a backseat to that."

Kevin looked unimpressed. One, his wife had divorced him ten years ago and they didn't have kids. Two, he was a baseball fan with no interest in hockey. It was one of the reasons Bren had been drawn to him as a sponsor. There'd be no time wasted on hero worship and angling for game tickets. Kevin hadn't even known who Bren was when they first met.

Like Violet that first day in the Empty Net. Christ on a Zamboni, had Bren really turned her down? To think that the first woman he could have buried his body to the hilt inside since coming out of rehab could have been the one who had haunted every erotic dream since.

She was right. He *had* blown it.

Kev's coffee arrived and he made a big deal out of adding his sugar and cream.

"I've hired a nanny," Bren said, and it came out in a barely contained burst, as if it was desperate to find air.

Kevin squinted. "Swedish?"

"Latina. Young, sexy, and my boss." Bren explained the curious setup and strange dynamic as best he could.

"Let me get this straight. You hired this woman during one of the most testing periods of your life," Kevin said over the lip of his mug. "She's off-limits for a number of reasons, yet you've decided to place her front and center."

"It's not as bad as that. When I'm home, she's not there." Except for this morning. And a couple of days ago when he stood at her bedroom door like a creeper. He squirmed in the booth. "I trust her—with my kids and with me. In fact, she's better at resisting my charms than I am hers." That shouldn't have bothered him.

Whereas before she was Ms. Flirtation whenever he walked into a room, now she was all business. That was good, wasn't it?

"You want full custody, don't you?"

"Of course I do."

"Then don't give your ex any fodder. Pounding the nanny is just the kind of thing her asshole lawyer will use to prove your unsuitability."

"Like I said, that's not going to happen." Bren hadn't thought of Violet as being a threat to anything more than his sanity, but Kevin's comment gave him pause. He needed to live a life a hundred times more blameless than Kendra, because his alcoholism would always trump her infidelity—and he recognized that was as it should be. He'd made mistakes. Put his kids in harm's way. If he wanted them back in his life for good, drawing—and continuing to draw—that boundary between himself and Violet was even more important.

Kevin sniffed, sipped his coffee. "So you're under a lot of pressure right now. The play-offs, your kids, your ex." He waved over the rest, meaning Violet. "That's a lot to deal with. Any lapses?"

"No." This was one of the things that Bren had resolved to be honest about. If he fell off the wagon, he would tell Kevin, who never judged and would ask how he could help. The guy had been a firefighter in his previous life and had seen a shit-ton of drama, including the worst humanity had to offer. "There are times when I'd like nothing better than to stuff it down with brown, but then I look at my girls. Being given this chance to be with them more, to make it up to them, makes me want to be a better man."

"What about when their mother is back on the scene? Because you know that's going to happen."

Oh, he knew. As sure as the sun set in the west, Kendra would show her tight little tush when it was most convenient for her. He was still trying to work out her endgame. He didn't believe she'd had an attack that warranted a long rest in some jumped-up spa. Almost two weeks, and she hadn't even attempted to contact her daughters. What Bren knew of Kendra, it was that she had a plan, and the closer he got to a finals run, the more likely that plan would manifest itself. More money, more notoriety, maybe even a shot at one of those *Real Housewives* shows.

When she came back, Bren would be ready for her.

THIRTEEN

"So, how's the Italian Stallion doing? Still putting it to you good?"

Violet peered over her sunglasses at her best bud, Cade "Alamo" Burnett, leading defenseman for the Chicago Rebels. A Texan cliché, he wore a Stetson pulled down low over his forehead to block the unseasonably warm mid-May sun. Close to eighty degrees and Chicagoland had gone berserk. People walking around in shorts, sidewalk cafes busting open, and gorgeous gay guys lounging shirtless in Adirondack chairs in the burbs.

Her own gorgeous gay BFF didn't even look at her as he answered. "My hot boyfriend is just fine, and why yes, Vasquez, the sex is awesome." He whispered that last part so impressionable ears wouldn't hear. Which reminded her: time to check in with her charges.

"How's it going, girls? Any questions?"

"No, we've got it," Franky called back.

Violet had set them a Saturday morning task to weed the flower beds in the backyard. Children needed sunshine and fresh air—she'd read that somewhere—and putting them to work had a triple benefit: keep 'em busy, keep 'em healthy, and get the garden ready for planting. They'd embraced it with a lot more enthusiasm than she'd expected.

Bren had left as soon as she returned from Home Depot with supplies. He hadn't said where he was going, just that he'd be out for a couple of hours. She wondered where he was, then wondered why she cared.

The past two weeks had gone so well. The Rebels made it through round two of the play-offs, beating the Detroit Motors 4–1 in the series. The semifinals started on Wednesday in LA.

Eyes closed against the warm sun, she asked Cade, "Have you and Moretti done anything public yet?"

"Why, because all gay guys are into exhibitionism?"

She turned to him. "That's not what I meant. You came out at a press conference a month ago, and yet no one knows that you and the team's general manager are a soap opera supercouple."

Cade rolled his beautiful hazel eyes. "It's tricky for him. Hell, you've seen some of the shade people are throwing at me online. And him."

The tweets and social media comments were vile, most of it aimed at this sweet, brave man who had come out in the face of an inevitable hurricane of hate. Some assholes were also blaming the hiring of Dante as GM and how he must be pushing "the homosexual agenda." Why else would a healthy, red-blooded Texan specimen like Cade "turn" gay?

Cade sighed. "Dante's had to deal with a lot of negativity getting to the top of the hockey management food chain, and he doesn't want to look like he's taking advantage of me. We're waiting until after the play-offs to debut Cadante, so for now, we're getting to know each other better."

"Burnetti has more of a ring to it." She heard the smile in his voice, his acceptance that Moretti, his boss as well as his lover, had to do this his way. But she didn't agree. If you loved someone, then shout it out. Violet was the kind of person who went all in, to hell with the consequences.

If Clifford Chase had given her even a smidge of encouragement, she would have shown him how lucky he was to know her and have her as a daughter . . . She shook off that thought. *If wishes were horses.*

"Have to say I'm surprised you took this on," Cade said.

"What?"

"Nannydom."

"That makes two of us." She could feel his eyes on her, so she continued, her voice low. "We already kissed. Got it out of the way."

Cade pushed his Stetson up with an index finger. "You didn't think to share this tasty nugget?"

"Nothing to report. It was just okay."

"Just okay?"

She shrugged. "Yep. Nice but nothing to text my BFF about. And knowing that there aren't any real sparks between us meant I could happily take on this job without that hanging over us." Did she sound like she was overdoing the protest? She *felt* like she was.

Cade remained quiet, so she filled the silence.

"I can see he's objectively hot. The beard, the bod, the burr. But when all's said and done, he's a mess and I don't have time for all that drama. The Year of the V is all about *me*, not some guy with issues. He needs to focus on those two and his career."

She chanced a peek at her friend, who considered her thoughtfully.

"You've changed your tune. For the past nine months, you've been taunting him with your Latin booty, driving the man nuts, and now you're pulling the rug out from under him?"

"Believe me, this is better." For him, but mostly for her. Bren St. James was the kind of guy Violet could fall for. She never would have thought it before, given that she usually liked flashier guys. But having talked to him more in the past month than she had all year, having seen how he was with his daughters, she knew this proximity was dangerous.

"Not sure he's as much of a mess as you're making out," Cade said. "Now, I know it's kind of hard to distinguish between happy Bren and miserable Bren—"

"Beard rubs," she said. "Beard rubs increase when he's in a good mood."

Cade shook his head in pity, a knowing grin playing on his lips. "If you say so. It's clear to me that he's in a much better place now than when he was drinking. Drunk Highlander got into fights, on and off the ice.

Missed practices and games. Hell, we had to leave him once in Toronto because he'd gone on an all-night bender and stolen a horse from the mounted police!"

"Seriously?"

"Yep." He cast a quick glance to the girls and lowered his voice. "Now he's focused, present, rock solid. I've no doubt it's still a struggle for him, but the guy's in a better place. The least you could do is throw a blow job his way."

"Cade!"

"Oh, like it's never crossed your mind." His phone vibrated and he picked it up, already smiling. A quick read of the text, and Cade took a sharp breath. That was an *imma get some* inhale if ever she heard one. "It's been swell being your muscled eye candy, but I'm out of here. Bye, Cat! Bye, Francesca!" He left the yard with a haste that might be considered indecent.

With Cade out of her hair, she decided to check in on the seasonal workers.

"How's it looking, ladies?"

Franky peered up through her glasses. "I found two more citizens for Slugville." She pointed at two slugs on a patch of grass, nudging each other in a manner that Violet assumed was slug flirting.

"What about you, Cat?" Caitriona had already started planting, so points for initiative. Violet knelt down beside her and dug a petunia out of the plastic tray. "We'll want to place these at least four inches apart."

"I know," Caitriona muttered. "It says it on the tag."

"Awesome! Sounds like you've got it." She sat back on her haunches. "So, do you guys know the boys next door? Godfrey and Sebastian?"

Caitriona blushed. Interesting. "Their names are Jeremy and Lance."

"Their names are Dumb and Dumber," Franky said.

She looked to her sister for confirmation, who merely said, "They're boys." Confirmation enough.

"Well, I ran into their mom a while ago and she said that they'd like to come over to see you guys sometime. I figured I'd ask before we set something up." It would be good for the girls to have someone else to hang with. This homeschooling business wasn't exactly conducive to the development of social skills.

Franky checked in with Caitriona again. Something passed between them, and Franky—who Violet was figuring out was the leader despite being younger—pronounced the sisters' decision. "Maybe on Monday after lessons."

They spent the next hour planting the beds with colorful petunias and pansies. Just as they were finishing up, Violet brought out the hose and its spray nozzle attachment.

"Stand back, ladies." She watered the newly planted beds, and then Gretzky jumped into the stream because he was a total drama hog. "Dog!"

The girls laughed, so she turned the hose on them. Ha! After a few yelps, they managed to work together to wrestle it from her—okay, she might have let them—and turned it on each other, then Violet herself.

She didn't mind. She was wearing a bikini, cut generously so there were no visible scars. Still made her boobs look *awe*some, and awesome boobs needed an audience, right?

"Dad!" Franky screamed.

Well, what do we have here . . .

Violet had no choice but to pivot—would've been weird if she didn't greet the man of the house—and face him in all her slick and wet bikinied glory. There was no missing the flare of surprise in his eyes. Maybe, more. And the *more* lasted a lot longer than was decent considering his spawn was nearby.

Seeming to realize the inappropriateness of it all, he dragged his thermonuclear gaze away. "What's going on here, then?"

"We're planting," Franky said. "Violet says it's healthy for us."

"Does she now?" Bren's gaze found Violet's again, this time dipping over the thin fabric clinging—just—to her breasts. She didn't usually let them all hang out, but she'd be lying if she said she didn't want him to look at her. To see her as a woman. And oh, how she enjoyed the way Bren St. James assessed her, like she was the only thing worth having on the menu. He ate her up with a heady regard that made her dizzy.

So she did the one thing guaranteed to cool everyone down: she grabbed the hose from Franky and turned it on the boss.

His grin lit up her world while the way his wet tee clung fondly to his pecs and six-pack lit up places that hadn't experienced these kinds of heat levels in a long, long time.

Not such a great plan after all.

"I'm hardly wet," said his soaked-through nine-year-old.

"Into the shower, Franky."

"I'll have dry clothes ready for you," Violet called out as Franky plodded into the bathroom. She was still at the age where baths were a chore. It might have been unseasonably warm, but he didn't want his girls catching a chill. Hot showers were the solution.

As for himself, a cold shower might be best, because Violet Vasquez now stood in his youngest daughter's bedroom looking like something out of a wet T-shirt contest. It wasn't the most revealing bikini he'd ever seen, but combined with the Daisy Dukes, it was doing a fair-to-decent job of making him lose his mind.

Today's AA meeting was supposed to help him to refocus on what was important. His team was through to the semifinals. His girls were settling back into life in Chicago. He had almost convinced himself that the attraction between himself and Violet was all in his imagination.

And then he'd come home to find his daughters' nanny holding a dripping hose like she might hold his cock. His thick, leaking, hard-for-Violet cock. A savage kick of lust had almost paralyzed him.

He wanted her to stroke him roughly, squeeze his fat head, milk every drop, and run her tongue around the rim. He wanted to see that flash of pink tongue as she teased him with whether he deserved a blow job or if she'd allow him the privilege of entering her body— slowly, until he was seated deep and all he could feel was Violet, Violet, Violet.

Until now, he'd mostly focused on her ass, because had you seen her ass? Beautifully rounded, high enough to park a mug of coffee, close to perfect in every way. As wowed as he'd been by her rear, he'd not spent nearly as much—or enough—time on her breasts. All this time, he'd been missing out, because these beauties were teardrop-shaped, firm and high, ready for his mouth . . .

"We should hit the shower as well," he muttered, and immediately felt his cheeks heating at that verbal slipup.

Her grin was slow and knowing. "We?"

"You're wet."

"I am." Another grin.

"You'll catch a cold."

"Or maybe I'll catch a fever."

Her skin gleamed, those tattoos running down her arms drawing his greedy gaze. Better he focus there than on her tits. But inevitably, his brain returned to those beautiful swells like a magnet, hauling very willing eyes with it.

She inhaled deep, thrusting her breasts forward in invitation. Not deliberate, he was sure. Breasts had a habit of filling the space in front of them, usually through no fault of their own. His cock stiffened, trying to RSVP with a resounding yes!

"Can I borrow a T-shirt?" she asked, low and husky.

"Must you?"

She smiled. "I thought you preferred when I cover up. Less distracting."

"Never said I preferred it."

He kept his eyes on her face, and then without his knowing quite how it happened, his hand found the curve of her jaw. She trembled under his touch, as affected by receiving it as he was by giving it.

"You're so fucking beautiful," he whispered.

Her breath hitched in her chest. "Bren—"

"I'll get you something to wear." He cut off whatever she was about to say, telling himself he was in control, when they both knew each day was another chip in the wall of his resistance.

She slipped by him, her scent sweet and floral. Scent of a woman, which was catnip for a man who'd gone so long without. But that made it sound as if any woman would do.

Only this woman would, and that was not a good conclusion to reach.

"Stay for lunch," he said, pleased to hear his voice was steady. "The girls would like it."

A slight pause, then a small "Okay."

He headed into his room, adjusted his painful erection in his jeans, and changed into a dry tee. For Violet, he lay a pair of drawstringed sweatpants and a Rebels

T-shirt out on the bed, then headed downstairs to make lunch. This was good. He'd passed a test. *The* test. He could view a teasing, taunting, sexy-as-hell Violet and not paw at her. Much. *Congratulations, St. James!*

Five minutes later, a sound behind him made him turn, expecting to see one of his daughters. Instead it was Violet, but something wasn't quite right. Like his job of assessment on the rink, he weighed all the details. The T-shirt swam on her; the sweats weren't much better, and had one leg rolled up. Her hair was wet, straggly, and uncombed. Was that shampoo dripping from the ends?

Most disturbing, those green eyes were wide and dazed with something he'd never have expected to see: fear.

"You okay?"

"I can't—I can't stay. I need to leave."

"What's happened?" Because something had to have occurred in the past five minutes. He moved forward, closing the gap between them quickly. "Are your sisters okay?" That was the only thing he could think of that would make her act this way.

She backed up toward the front door, shaking her head as if she was afraid his touch would send her into some sort of downward spiral.

"Th-they're fine. Just tell the girls I had to leave."

"Viol—" But she was already gone.

FOURTEEN

Sheridan Road had never looked more verdant, its grand houses standing sentinel over her journey home. Or what she called home these days, like she was playing house with borrowed dolls and Monopoly money. She shouldn't be driving, not when the tears blurred her vision like rain on the windshield. She needed wipers for her eyes.

Oh, God, this couldn't be real. Not again.

First, you can't believe it's happening to you. That might sound stupid, because cancer doesn't discriminate, but you start off in a cloud of disbelief. You have time bombs for breasts, and this body you've always trusted was now turning on you. Cancer instills bone-deep fear, yet the idea of parting with these weaponized masses of tissue is almost as bad as knowing how they'll harm you if you let them stay.

When she was initially diagnosed over two years ago, her mind could barely process it. *I'm too young. I shouldn't have to go through this, not when I have so much I haven't done yet. So much I want to see and do and feel. I don't want to suffer.* And then, vainly: *I don't want to lose my breasts, my hair, my dignity.*

She'd done it, though. She'd gone through the radiation and chemo, traveled that road to hell and back. A double mastectomy was supposed to prevent recurrence. Of course, no surgery was 100 percent, but this one—this excision of what made her a woman—was supposed to be as good as. Her monthly breast self-exam wasn't due for another week, but something had made her check. A slight ache in her shoulder, and there it was.

A pea-sized lump in her armpit.

It might be nothing, but she'd said that before and it wasn't. *It. Wasn't.*

She swiped at the tears and slammed a hand on the steering wheel. Fuck. This wasn't fair. She'd come through and was finally getting her life back on track. Getting to know her sisters, making friends, feeling like she had a purpose—first with the team and then with Bren's little girls.

Well, universe, looks like you've got me!

Make an appointment. That's what she needed to do. Since arriving in Chicago, she'd seen a physician recommended by Harper twice for a check-in. A-okay. But not anymore.

The bastard was back.

An SUV cut her off, the driver shaking his fist like some *Scooby-Doo* villain because she'd veered into his lane. She really should not be driving.

Pulling over to the side of the road outside a glorious colonial in glorious Lake Forest, she stabbed at the dash for the hazards. If only there were a button that could rewind back to a time when she didn't know about this lump. Or fast-forward to a time when it was over.

The in-between was the worst.

Were her hazards on? Her noisy thoughts allowed nothing else to penetrate, so she pressed several buttons. The radio burst into life and with it the voice of her icon.

"You touched my hand, I played it cool . . ."

"Seven Wonders"—not one of Fleetwood Mac's most popular songs, but like all of their tunes, Violet loved this one. Composed during one of the band's crazy interludes when they weren't talking to each other because so-and-so was still bitter about who slept with whom, it was particularly memorable for Stevie Nicks's crazy mullet-perm in the video.

Violet sang along, tearfully letting herself fall into the words, assigning stupidly deep meanings like people do when they need something to latch on to. What would Stevie do in this situation? Probably a line of coke and one of the guys in the band. *Zing!*

"If I live to see the Seven Wonders . . ."

Time dragged, sped up. She had no idea. Minutes. Hours.

The passenger door opened; the car's weight shifted. She turned, shocked at the sight of Bren. Or shocked at how relieved she was to see him.

"Nice parking job," he muttered, and she was so

grateful that he didn't immediately launch into *what's wrong?* that all she could do was stare. His nose was a little crooked. She hadn't noticed that before, but then she was usually trying not to get all caught up in his Celtic glimmer.

An electric moment passed—a Bren and Violet moment—as they held each other in thrall. He was waiting with the patience of a man who was used to enduring.

"I think it's back," she finally rasped.

"What is?"

She couldn't say it. The C-word. "I had them removed." She pointed at her tits—at her beautiful, perfect, reconstructed tits. "These are fake. I had them cut out and now I think it's back."

No shock from the unshockable Bren St. James. Instead he leaned in and cupped her face. "Tell me why you think that."

She pulled at his free hand and pushed it under the T-shirt he'd given her to wear.

This was not how she'd imagined the first time he would properly feel her up.

"Here." She guided him to her armpit, absorbing how his fingers brushed the side of her breast. No bra, because she'd been wearing a bikini before the shower. Smugly tempting the man who claimed he would lose his mind if he let her in.

What the hell was wrong with her?

She felt that brush of his fingers as one would feel knuckles grazing an arm. Not sexual, just an awareness of a human touch to her skin. Placing his fingertips over the armpit, she pressed them down. "Right there. A small lump. Feel it?"

He nodded gravely. Did that word come from *grave*, as in the hole you dug to bury someone?

"When did this happen before?"

"Two years ago. It runs in my family, and while it was only in one, there was enough about my genetics to encourage me to have the double mastectomy. It's not supposed to come back, Bren. It's not—"

His thumb stroked her lip, as much comfort in it as a hug. "It might not have. We'll get you in to see a doctor tomorrow. Today. We'll get it taken care of. You can handle this. You did before."

With her mom and aunts around. She didn't think she could go through this again, not with these people. Shared DNA, yet strangers to her. But she would, because the only way out was through.

He followed her home to the cottage at Chase Manor. Only when he got out of the car did she think to ask, "Who's with the girls?"

"I took them next door to visit the neighbor kids, the Nicholses."

"Oh, okay. Tristan and Balthazar. You should get back to them."

"They'll be fine for a while." He followed her into the cottage and closed the door.

In her small kitchen, the one she had decorated with

thrift store bits and bobs, he looked solid and present and surprisingly at home. "Thanks for seeing me back."

"We should call Harper."

"No! She'll call a million people, drag some doc out of his golf game."

"And that's a bad thing?"

She opened a cupboard to get a glass for water. Her mouth was dry, words hard to form. "I don't want her or Iz to know. Not yet. There's so much happening with the play-offs that this is just a distraction."

"A distraction." He leaned against the counter. "That's what you do best, though, isn't it, Violet? Distract?"

She stared at him, trying to reckon with his meaning.

"You're the queen of distraction." He raised a hand away from his body. "Telling people to look here because you're doing something over here." A gesture with his other hand in the opposite direction. "With Cade. With other players."

"That's not why I was with Cade. He needed a cover and he's my friend."

"Aye, but it suited you, too. Kept you safe when you knew I'd be gunning for you if I thought for a second you were free."

How the hell did they get onto this topic? She had bigger problems than whether Bren St. James thought she was a tease.

"Like I said, you had your shot."

"And you've spent the past nine months reminding

me of how I fucked up that day in the bar." He shook his head, shook off his frustration with her. "But that's a conversation for another day. For now, we're going to focus on the current problem, and when that's resolved, you and I will have that reckoning."

She was a fake-boobed, possibly cancer-riddled mess and he still wanted her. Or wanted her enough to get some sort of revenge for the torture she'd put him through these past few months. Her entire body warmed at the prospect of being . . . used.

"Why wait?"

"Why wait for what?"

"This reckoning." She moved forward and placed both hands on his chest. His breath caught, his pecs rose beneath her fingertips. "Maybe you should just take that revenge now."

"Revenge? That's not it. A little punishment, per-haps." His fingers dug into her hip, a subtle display of dominance. "But you'll not use me to blank out your problems, Violet. I know all too well the dangers of using. Sex. The bottle. When I fuck you, there'll be nothing clouding your judgment."

"So sure it's going to happen, Scot?"

"It's inevitable, lass. We can fight it or accept it. First, we'll take care of you, then we'll take care of each other."

She had started to shake, and the only way she could think to stop was to sink into him, all that strength. His arms encircled her and pulled her flush. She knew she must look a fright with her half-rinsed hair and his

oversized sweats, but none of that mattered while Bren
held her. Head tucked beneath his chin, she closed her
eyes, inhaled his scent. Soap and a hint of coffee. She
knew he wouldn't break first. It would be a point of
pride with him.

In the arms of this warm, breathing monolith of a
man, she felt safer than she had in years.

"I should take another shower," she murmured
against his hard, wonderful chest. "Rinse out the shampoo."

He drew back. "Do you have an oncologist in Chicago?"

She shook her head.

"Go take care of yourself and I'll make a few calls."

"Not Harper."

"Not Harper. But this isn't how we're doing this
going forward, Violet."

"Doing what?"

"You need help, you ask for it."

"I don't—" He stopped her midsentence with that
famous St. James scowl. "I got through this before."

"On your own?"

"No, my mom. My aunts." Her mom was back in San
Juan and no way was Violet calling her or Tía Cecy—
next in line to the mom throne—with news of a possible
recurrence. This is how she'd handled it back then.
Didn't spill until absolutely necessary. It was weird
sharing this with Bren, and while it should have felt
like a relief, it didn't. It felt like another weight in their
already taut relationship.

She was too tired to argue. "I'm going to take that shower now."

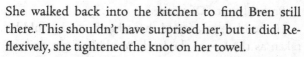

She walked back into the kitchen to find Bren still there. This shouldn't have surprised her, but it did. Reflexively, she tightened the knot on her towel.

He looked up, and she assessed his gaze for changes. Would he view her differently now that he knew she wasn't the same person as he'd suspected? Would he think she was a fraud because she had provoked and teased, sold him a fake bill of goods?

She felt different because of what she'd found under her arm and the knowledge he now had about her. This last part should have made no odds, but it did.

"I thought you would have left."

"What gave you that idea?" He gave her an up-down look filled with what could only be called carnal interest. Maybe he did it to make her feel better. *It's okay, Vi. I'm no longer attracted to you, but I'll play along to make you feel better.*

"The girls need you," she said.

"They do," he said simply, and there it was again. That unshakeable feeling that every time he mentioned his girls, she was included.

"I made a few calls," he went on, "to get the names of the best oncologists in the city. Everyone I talked to said you'll need to see your regular GP first. You have one? Nearby?"

That's what she'd figured. "Yes, she's at the River-brook Medical Building. I'll call her on Monday morning." Today was Saturday, so she'd have to wait.

He nodded. "And you'll take one of your sisters with you. Or Cade."

Probably not. "Of course."

He nodded, so assured that what he said would be taken as the law of the land. "You'd best get dressed and dry your hair. You're coming back to our place for lunch."

She swallowed. "No. I mean, thanks, but I'm not good company."

"I'm not letting you stay here to brood. One of us with that attitude is bad enough."

Said as if they were a couple who needed to balance each other out. *Shut up, Vi, that's your underarm lump talking.*

"I'd really prefer to be alone." It was a lie, and he knew it. She always did better around people. She could go stretches without them, but she needed the energy of others to refuel her. She looked around at her kitchen, this place she felt ownership over. This place she was prepared to leave in a heartbeat as soon as the dumb hockey season was over and she had that big, fat check in her hand.

He waited. As before, when he held her in his solid embrace, she got the impression he could wait her out forever.

She didn't want to be alone here. She wanted to be surrounded by love, even if it wasn't for her. "I'm going to get dressed."

Not a word from the Scot, but then he'd known she just needed time to get used to the idea.

"You'll be here when I come out?" She tossed off the question as if his stubborn streak was annoyingly inconvenient, but her breath held in anticipation all the same.

"Aye, lass. I'll be here."

FIFTEEN

Bren put his head around the door of Franky's room. She was parked in front of Slugville, taking notes.

"All right there, sprite?"

"Yep, Dad," she said without looking up, but as he left, she called out to him.

"What, love?"

"Is Violet okay?"

He stepped back inside. "Why do you ask?"

"She seemed less . . . Violet yesterday."

Yesterday being the day she'd found out her cancer might have recurred. He'd brought her back to their place for lunch, and she'd tried valiantly to be her usually cheery self. They'd eaten pizza, then settled in and watched movies, including *The Princess Bride* and *Ferris Bueller's Day Off*, a favorite of Caitriona's.

The shock at Violet's news had lingered overnight, and he'd awoken this morning with his mind chock-full of thoughts of his children's nanny—except this time, it wasn't the usual overheated sexual fantasies. This time, he was thinking of how he wanted to hold her forever like he had in her kitchen. Tell her it would be okay. *He would make it okay.*

"She wasn't feeling so good," he said, soothing his worried daughter. "A headache. But today's her day off, so she's probably resting after we wore her out."

Franky wrinkled her nose, a signal that she was plotting something. "Should I call her and ask her if she needs anything? She might want to come over and see the slugs. Or make an apple pie."

"You could text her, I suppose. Just to check in." *He could text her, but he didn't want to crowd her. Instead he'd rather use his youngest child to do his dirty work. Classy, St. James.*

"I'll text her," Franky agreed.

Rather than wait around like an idiot, he went in search of his other daughter. When he'd only had one weekend a month with them, he'd filled the time with trips to the zoo, cupcake runs, and movies. They'd loved it. Now that he had them constantly, they didn't seem as interested in his efforts to entertain them. This was more like his life when he was still married to Kendra, who went to great lengths to shove them off on neighbors and slumber parties when he wasn't playing. She'd never enjoyed doing things that involved all of them. Said he'd be bored.

His daughters could never bore him. He loved spending time with them, loved especially watching their faces light up when they came across something new to them. They were still young enough to perceive wonder, and it made him feel young to see that wonder filtered through their eyes.

He found Caitriona curled up on the sofa in what Kendra used to call the music room because it contained the piano. The instrument that Caitriona hadn't played once since she'd come to live with him a month ago.

As he entered, Caitriona looked up guiltily from her iPad and turned it off.

"Texting with one of your friends?"

Her eyes flew wide. "Yeah. Sophie from my old school."

He wondered. His recollection was that one of the Nichols boys had been sweet on her when they all lived here together last year. Maybe Bren had jump-started that again when he dropped them off with Skylar yesterday.

"I know you must miss your friends back—" He almost said *home*. "Back in Atlanta."

"It's okay here. It's quieter."

"Oh yeah?"

"Mom and Drew fought a lot. Kind of like you and Mom, which makes me think Mom might be a bit of a drama llama."

"Neither of us are saints." He refused to criticize Kendra in front of the girls. God only knew he was a tough man to live with.

Taking advantage of the unusually pleasant father-daughter vibe, he ran a finger along the piano. "Do you want to start up lessons again?"

"Not really."

"Thought you liked playing." She loved music, had

every soundtrack of every Broadway musical memo-
rized.

She shrugged. "It's kind of lame."

He sat beside her on the sofa. "Lame? You've been
playing for five years. When did it become lame?"

"Mom likes it. She thinks it's elegant." Air quotes
around *elegant*. "But . . ."

"But what?"

No response. Caitriona had always had a hard time
expressing her feelings. She was so like him in that respect.

"I know you miss your mom, love. Have your grandparents mentioned her?"

"They said she wishes she could be here, but she has
to take care of herself."

That sounded like Kendra, looking out for number
one. He couldn't believe that she'd made no effort
to get in touch with her children. To be honest, Bren
hadn't pushed the issue with her or her parents, because Kendra's bad behavior would be to his advantage
during any future custody hearing. He hated that his
daughters were suffering because their mom was so
selfish, but if it meant he was one step closer to getting
them back permanently, he was prepared to put up
with it.

"Well, she needs a long rest. But you'll see her again
soon and she might like it if you could play her a tune
on the piano."

Franky wandered in. "I texted Violet. She said she's
fine and she'll see us tomorrow."

Two minutes later, he headed into the kitchen and shot off a text to his children's nanny.

> *Sorry about Franky bothering you on your day off.*
> *She was worried.*

A full minute passed before she responded.

> *She's sweet.*
> . . .
> *Like her dad.*

He didn't feel sweet toward Violet. He felt positively savage.

What the hell was wrong with him? The woman was sick with worry and he wanted what, exactly?

To drive deep between her thighs until she was shaking with the force of the orgasms he'd given her. That's what.

He texted back: *I'm not sweet. I'd just prefer not to look for another nanny.*

Shit, that came out all wrong. He was going for a joke but it sounded like he thought she might not be around. As in, *permanently* not around. He started typing again, then stopped because he had no idea what to say. He hit the call button.

She answered immediately. "Nessie."

"I'm sorry. That was in poor taste."

"Forget about it. I know your big thick Scottish fingers and puck-concussed brain are virtually incapable of stringing a sentence together."

When had it become so easy with her? The strains of "Gold Dust Woman" filtered in from Violet's end, and he was reminded of how she'd been playing another Fleetwood Mac song in the car yesterday. And "The Chain" that day he came across her filling his fridge.

"Do you have some sort of Fleetwood Mac kink?"

"Kink? No. I'm a fan, like any right-thinking human."

"Okay, weirdo."

"Name three songs of theirs you don't like."

"'Don't Stop' is pretty overplayed," he said, warming to the subject. "'Tusk' is sort of strange, but also crazy compelling. And . . . that's about it. Touché."

She laughed. "See? The Mac are near perfect, and Stevie Nicks is the greatest rock 'n' roll frontwoman of all time."

"Vasquez, I already acknowledged that they have a decent catalog, but this Stevie Nicks business is a bridge too far."

"Name another," she challenged.

"I'll name five others. Joan Jett. Grace Slick. Ann Wilson. Tina. Aretha."

Violet scoffed. "They're all power. None of them have the ability to do vulnerable and raw sensuality. None of them have that smoky-sweet quality like Stevie. *And* she's a fashion icon as well as having led a life of great drama. It all combines to make her a true artisan."

"You've given this an oddly specific level of thought."

"I have!" She chuckled softly. "And nothing you can say will change my mind."

He laughed, feeling unexpectedly joyful. It surprised them both enough to create a taut silence in its aftermath. There was a moment's pause while they both figured out how to navigate it.

"Caitriona used to play the piano." So it might've sounded like a non sequitur, but they *were* talking about music.

"And she doesn't anymore?"

"Says she's not interested. I feel like she's punishing me. She knows her misery makes me miserable."

Violet snorted. "Right, she's *that* evil, every thought and action centered on how to ruin your life."

"I knew you'd understand."

"She's eleven and she misses her mom. It's hard on all of you."

Bren sighed, wondering if he should share more of why Caitriona wasn't happy with him and how he had betrayed his daughters.

One hand on the wheel, another turning the ignition. Headlights illuminating the drive to the street, but not enough to overcome his blurry vision.

Sharing might be initially cathartic, but ultimately would result in Violet looking at him differently. He found himself desperately wanting her good opinion, this warm glow of basking in her good favor.

"Have you talked to your sisters?"

She hesitated. "Not yet. I was going to head up to Chase Manor later and fill them in."

"If you need a ride to the doctor, you just have to ask." He assumed she'd be on it tomorrow, Monday. He'd cut practice if necessary.

In the distance, he heard something crash, then the sound of raised voices. One of his daughters called the other one stupid. Ah, the poetry of parenthood.

"The girls are fighting. Want to come over?"

Her husky chuckle went straight to his balls. "Adios, St. James. And thanks for—well, just thanks." She clicked off, and he went to break up World War III.

SIXTEEN

The waiting was the worst.

Doctors' offices. Preop prep. Postop recovery. Test results. For a girl who wasn't patient, it made her the worst patient in the world. (*Ha, see what she did there?*)

Pretty pleased with her mental pun, she smiled at the receptionist in Dr. Lowell's beige-on-beige waiting area, but got nothing in response. Nice bedside manner, lady.

Luckily the girls had a field trip to a museum with their tutor this morning to see the *Jurassic Park* exhibit, so Violet was able to get away and "run an errand" without anyone asking questions. That the doc could see her so soon was a minor miracle.

Her thoughts wandered back to the day before yesterday. After she'd dried her hair, Bren had driven her back to the house on the lake and made lunch. His reasoning was sound: she needed to be around other people and it was easy to lose herself in the girls and Gretzky and even Bren as he laughed at something one of his girls did or said. And then they'd watched movies as though it were perfectly normal.

Like a family.

But they weren't her family. They were spoken for; especially him, if not by his ex-wife then by the addiction that had him in its grip. This ghost in the corner of her eye, a shadow looming over everything. Like she didn't have enough shadows to deal with.

The door opened and the nurse smiled at her. "Violet? We're ready for you."

He slammed the door of the SUV so hard it was a wonder the windshield didn't crack. The force was necessary to announce his presence. His fury.

The girls' tutor had called to say she was bringing them to the Field Museum, but when he asked if Violet was there, he was told she'd slipped out on an errand. A doctor's appointment. There was no reason why this should have bothered him except for three salient facts:

One: Cade was still at the rink, working with Isobel on his skating motion.

Two: Bren had spotted Harper in the stands chatting with Dante during morning skate.

Which meant that three: unless Violet had someone else in her life whom Bren didn't know about, she had gone to that appointment alone.

He didn't know the location of her doctor's office, but he did know that he wouldn't be civil if he called her. So here he was, slamming the SUV's door outside her cottage so Violet would know how furious he was. Her piece-of-shit car was here, so she would be as well.

If it was good news, surely she would have called him. But then she didn't owe him a thing, did she?

The door to the cottage opened and she was there, alive and bright and *withholding*.

"Bren, what—"

"The *hell* are you doing at the doctor's by yourself?"

She looked taken aback. Oh, he'd take her aback. He'd take her over his knee for a spanking.

She started to speak. "I—"

"This is not how you do this, Violet. You should have brought your sisters to that appointment. Or Cade."

Or me. You should have brought me.

Irritation pleated her brow. "I had it handled."

"You had it handled. You had it *handled*?" Was she trying to fuck with him?

That must be it. She was back with the MO of the past nine months, messing with his balls and his mind. Now she was barely breathing, staring at him like he was a madman, and in that moment, he knew. This was not a woman with a death sentence.

Still, the words tore from his throat in an anguished yell. "*Are you okay?*"

"Yes!" she screamed back before covering her mouth like she couldn't believe she'd stooped to his rage-driven, let's-shout-about-our-feelings level.

"Good!"

"Then why are you still shouting at me?!"

"I don't know!"

But he did. In the process of learning she would be okay, he had learned something about himself.

He cared about this woman, and Christ Almighty, self-discovery sucked.

She tilted her head to the sun, and if it had been raining or cloudy he would have moved heaven and earth to make that sun appear. When she faced him again, her eyes glittered with unshed tears.

"Apparently my armpits need to go on a diet."

He blinked in confusion. "Uh. Okay."

"That's what the lump is, a fatty deposit called a lipoma. Usually they'd leave it because it's not typically health threatening, but because of my history, we're going to take it out. It's a simple outpatient surgery."

The tight ball of stress he'd been living with for the past two days unfurled and flooded his chest. "They know for sure it's not something else?"

"They'll check when it comes out, but right now, the doc said it feels soft and it moves around. That's what sealed it for her. It's mobile under my skin." She smiled, a star-bright curve of her lips that felled him. "I was worried about nothing."

"Not nothing."

"No, not nothing."

"I'm sorry I shouted," he muttered, feeling foolish for overreacting and revealing so much. "You shouldn't have been alone. I would have come with you." He would have done anything to ensure that she didn't endure that solo.

"You had practice. In fact, I'm pretty sure you *have* practice."

"When you have as many problems as I do, people tend not to question when you leave a practice early."

"St. James . . ."

"Vasquez . . ." He added an eyebrow raise to let her know he would brook no disagreement here.

A tear escaped the corner of her eye, a strange sight from this woman who always projected such toughness. Before he could stop himself, he had caught it with his thumb. He longed to taste it, but he preferred to remain connected to her, skin to skin, so he let his thumb remain over her cheekbone.

"I thought it was back, Bren. I thought I was going to have to go through it again, and I wasn't sure I was strong enough."

"You would be. You are. But luckily you don't need to test that strength."

She exhaled, her breath soft against his chin. He released her and stood back.

"Well, it's good that you're okay." It came out sounding formal.

Not a word from her. She stood, staring at him, as he backed up. Backed away.

She was fine now. She didn't need him to hold her hand at the doctor's. She didn't need him at all, and God only knew his needs were unimportant. But he'd like her to know he had the capacity to be there for her.

He closed the gap between them and placed his

hands on her upper arms, then inclined his head to kiss her . . . forehead.

She made a small sound of disbelief. His dick agreed wholeheartedly.

He peered down at her. "What?"

"Must I do everything, St. James?"

His frown must have conveyed his confusion, because all it earned him was an eye roll.

"I won't seduce you, Scot."

"What if you already have?" Seduction could be as much mental as physical, and he had been thoroughly mind fucked by Violet Vasquez. He moved his lips from her forehead down her nose. Her breath hitched, a sweet invitation, so he slipped his mouth to her jaw, testing. Then her earlobe, tasting. Then a sensitive spot at the juncture of neck and shoulder.

Tormenting. Them both.

"Bren," she rasped, turning her head just in time for her mouth to crash against his.

This wasn't a textbook or fairy-tale kiss. This wasn't smooth or gentle. It was hard and needy and unrepentant.

It was Violet.

It was Bren.

It was everything.

Bren St. James was kissing her . . . voluntarily.

Not that their previous makeout session had required all that much coaxing, but there had been a smidge of reluctance to it. Like Violet had somehow trapped him into doing it.

Not this time. This kiss was Bren going all in, and it was glorious.

He pushed her back toward the cottage, over the threshold, into the kitchen.

"Tell me to stop," he whispered against her lips.

"Are you crazy?"

Brow crumple. Super sexy. "I don't want to take advantage while you're feeling at sixes and sevens."

She coasted a hand down the front of his sweats, where it met considerable resistance. "I could say I don't want to take advantage of your unbelievably hard boner"—she gave it an earthy rub—"but that would be a lie as big and fat as this fabulous erection."

He groaned. "You can take advantage of me anytime."

"And what about your sobriety?"

He didn't even flinch. They'd reached the point where they could talk easily about this.

"Just replacing one drug with another."

"Bren—"

"That came out wrong. I never seem to be able to say what I mean to you. What I'm trying to say is that getting lost in you would be good for me. Good for you, too, I think."

He was right. He was what she needed, and she would gladly give him this while taking a slice of heaven for herself.

"Take me to bed, Scot."

He hitched her up around his hips while she explored his mouth with hers.

"Need direction," he murmured.

"Been that long?"

"Hilarious. I mean, where is this bed you speak of?"

"It's a cottage, not a penthouse." At his growl, she cut him some slack. "Behind me, first door."

She returned to her explicit exploration. Usually, guys with facial hair did little for her, but Bren St. James did pretty much everything for her. *Delicioso.* She licked the corner of his mouth and felt his lips quiver, his entire body harden.

Inside her bedroom, he placed her down on the bed gently.

"Don't treat me with kid gloves," she warned.

"How about you let me decide how this goes, Violet?"

The Scot was going to be bossy in bed. Yes!

Being a bit of a smart mouth, she often found that most guys mistook her attitude for tough-girl aggression. Not so at all. She just liked a guy who could match her verbally, and then she liked a guy who took charge sexually. Relinquishing control was a good way for her to forget about her problems. Thinking too much during sex was not.

The bossier the guy, the better.

He was still wearing sweats and then he wasn't and she approved of the not-sweats situation immensely. The Scot had a body that required all her attention. Tat-free, no need to paint those beautiful muscles.

Better to see them—and him—in all their blocked and ridged glory. She'd been with guys who had a lot of ink, even piercings in interesting places. They all seemed like poseurs compared to the guy before her. Bren St. James didn't need to gussy up that body or accessorize his dick.

She swallowed. *Yes, that's one mighty fine piece of equipment you have there.* She had some experience here—not that she had a long list of past lovers—but the dicktabase gave her a good frame of reference. She'd seen it all and she knew what she liked.

Bren St. James's cock was perfect.

"You're staring," he said, and was that shyness she heard in his voice? So cute.

"You're beautiful." And she meant it, her voice almost breaking with her appreciation.

He stroked his erection, almost in warning, and her mouth watered at that extra squeeze to the plump head—and the bead of delicious moisture it produced.

"Need to see you, Violet, love. Don't think I can wait much longer."

He needed to see her. *Oh.* She hadn't really thought this through. Of course he did, but that meant she had to strip. Which shouldn't have been a problem, but she hadn't done that since before her surgery. A two-year dry spell.

He continued to pump. Up and down. Hard and rough. "I need to see the ass that's been driving me wild for months, the breasts I've dreamed of sucking, the pussy I've imagined gripping me hard."

Okay, so not only did the Scot *look* perfect, he had all the words.

Pulling her upright, he tugged at the zipper of her denim skirt and slid it down. Then he gripped the hem of her T-shirt.

She nodded, raising her arms to help as he pulled it up over her head.

His eyelids fell to half-mast, his gaze moving over her body and the straight-out-of-a-catalog breasts that filled her teal bra perfectly. His knuckles skimmed the side of her breast, yielding a whisper of sensation. He seemed to be trying to see everything at once as he coasted both of his big beautiful hands down to her hips then clamped them over her ass and drew her flush. Her breasts smashed against his chest.

"Is there anything I shouldn't do? Anything that won't work for you?"

His fingers were already seeking pleasure between the backs of her thighs, beneath her thong, stroking in to the point she had to close her eyes to stay upright.

He didn't need to know that her nipples lacked the nerve endings to feel sensation. Nor that her breasts, while beautiful, would never truly contribute to her sexual satisfaction. If they gave him pleasure, then that would be enough.

She suspected Bren had plenty of ways to make up for their lack.

"Treat me like any other woman, Bren."

"Not like any other, Vi." His mouth stamped on hers, an oral claiming that made her believe. She wasn't any other woman to him. She was Violet, his girl, and she had never felt more desired.

He pushed her onto the bed, no longer gentle. This element of roughness thrilled through her.

"Turn over and show me that sweet ass."

Oh. My. "God."

She twisted onto her stomach, and maybe she wasn't fast enough, because he lifted her onto her knees, so her ass took a starring role in the proceedings. Her thong bisected her ass cheeks in a way she suspected drove him a little crazy.

"You have any idea what this ass has been doing to me since the moment I met you?" He looped a finger in the waistband and pulled. Or perhaps twisted with his finger? She couldn't see. But she felt the tug against her wet flesh all the way to every extremity.

She tried a wiggle. Got a throaty groan in return.

"Tell me, Scot. Tell me what this ass has been doing."

"Making it so my cock is raw from jerking off. Contributing to every wank session in the shower, every sleepless night in my bed. This ass has been the bane of my fucking existence and I plan to use it hard. I plan to use this luscious body hard. You got a problem with that?"

He jerked the fabric of her thong, pulling it through her slippery folds, making her mindless with need.

"Dios, please."

"Yeah, you'd better pray to your god, 'cause I'm going to take you to the edge and pull you back. I'm going to show you the meaning of torture, woman."

Well, the joke was on him, because she was close. That's what happened when you were primed from months of using your fantasies of a bad-tempered Scot to get off. She had her own stories to tell.

Another saw of the fabric through her sensitive flesh. Another flicker of warmth stoking the fire. Another—ack!

He pulled her thong down, and she mourned the loss of friction. Two large hands grasped her ass and then she felt something soft and at the same time firm—not his cock, but his lips. A teasing graze over her spine, down the cleft of her ass, but always stopping short of where she needed him to be.

"*¡Malparido!*"

He chuckled, the sound a mix of smoke and sin, the vibration against her slick flesh unbearable.

"Bastard!" She shoved her body back in obvious invitation. *Take it. It's yours.*

His tongue licked one long, filthy-gorgeous stroke through. It made her buck, hurled her to the edge. She clenched her muscles, desperate to push herself off that cliff to climax. Must she do everything?

He turned her onto her back, gently forced her legs apart, and stared at what he had created.

Wet, pulsing, wanton, and begging.

"Look at you. So ready for me." He licked his lips.

She had both hands free and could have used them. One quick stroke and she'd be there. But watching Bren savor her like this was the biggest turn-on. His cock jutted proudly from his body, its broad head slick. They were both so close, yet holding this moment seemed hugely important.

"Inside me." When she came the first time with Bren, that's how she wanted it.

He appeared to shake off his trance. "I don't have protection. I didn't plan this."

She leaned over and opened her side table drawer, then handed him a three-pack of condoms.

"I'm expecting great things, Scot."

Smirking, he tore open the packet and secured the protection, then he slotted between her legs, still careful not to touch her. It was as if they both knew the second it happened, the world might explode.

"Take off your bra. Need to see those gorgeous tits."

It should have ripped her out of the moment, placed her back in her head, but it felt right to be showing him everything. She loved how he gave her ownership of this. Even better, she loved the crude words he used. These breasts deserved no special handling. Today their purpose was pleasure.

Leaning up, she unhooked the bra and drew it away from her body, letting it slide from her fingers to the floor.

With the backs of his knuckles, he glanced his hand first over her left breast, then over her right. He cupped one, testing its weight and feel, shaping it with his palm. She felt his touch as one would a light brush over skin, but true sexual sensation didn't magically return because Bren St. James had touched her. Yet something inside melted while somewhere below heated.

He rubbed his sheathed length against her ready flesh, his eyes wild as they wavered between her face and her breasts. She arched into him, eager to take him inside her.

"Please."

Gripping her ass, he pulled it toward him at the same time as he sank in slowly.

Oh.

Oh.

Yes.

His eyes fluttered closed briefly, then on an exhale, he drove deeper.

"Christ," he muttered. "If I'd known . . ."

She usually liked it fast, needing the friction to get her there. But with Bren, the languor and his awestruck wonder was its own form of spine-melting pleasure.

The feeling of fullness was exquisite. She had missed sex. Missed the weight of a man, the grunts, the moans. This physical connection had always made her feel alive, and while she walked in the wilderness, she'd wondered if she would ever feel this way again.

With Bren, those sensations came barreling back, bringing with them novel twists to a familiar tale. Old and new joining.

Bren moved inside her, withdrew a few inches—and the man had inches to spare—and plunged again. That hold on her ass was perfect, keeping her rigid while he found a rhythm and used her as he'd promised. His eyes glued to hers, looking for a response—*oh, there!* He changed the angle of his thrust so it brushed right over her clit.

"Yes," she whispered. "Just like that."

The tempo increased, took over, as he slid in and out. Thrusting and testing, seeking and finding. Her loud cry as she shattered released a wild man. He dug his hand into her ass, to the point of bruising her, and pounded hard. No mercy, his eyes burned into her, his thrusts savage and almost cruel.

"Yes, yes. Take what you need."

He did, giving her more in return. The buildup of tension surprised her as did the fall, another orgasm that triggered his and a groan, long and low.

She was out of breath, completely sated, perfectly boneless. Eyes fluttering closed, she let the stress of the past few days and the pressure release of the past few moments overtake her and send her to sleep.

SEVENTEEN

She looked calm, an angel while she slept.

Had he taken advantage? He suspected he had. He also suspected he didn't care.

If he'd given her one small moment of peace during this turbulent time for her, then he refused to regret a moment. Violet was a passionate woman both in and out of bed, a woman whose emotions needed to be fed.

Slipping inside her, he'd found her hot, tight, as new as the first time he'd been with a woman. He wanted to touch her again, trace his fingers over every tattoo, explore her more thoroughly. He wanted to learn all her secrets. For now he let his eyes run point, not wishing to wake her. He'd have to get back to the house soon to take over for the tutor.

His phone buzzed in the pocket of his sweats, now pooled on the floor. Leaning over the side of the bed, he removed it and grimaced at a text from Remy: *You okay?*

Shit, he'd charged out of the locker room two hours ago without a word to his teammates.

Yeah, just had to be somewhere.

A pause while Remy typed. *Anything you need to tell me?* How about, *I'm not drinking but I've found a new addiction?* The last thing he needed was Remy getting in his business, but the man was born to interfere. He didn't want to alarm him and say there was a problem with the girls—or break Violet's confidence, because he was guessing she hadn't told her sisters.

A friend needed my help.

Let me know if there's anything I can do. We're gonna need you at 100% this week.

Bren smiled grimly at the phone. Since coming across Violet in her car and learning what was troubling her, he'd been unable to focus on his game and it had shown in practice. Quick dispossessions, sloppy passes.

He put the phone back into his pocket and let his gaze wander around her bedroom. Like Violet, it was a mishmash of styles that somehow managed to come together in a way that worked. A half-finished abstract mural took up the west wall, photos of what looked like her mom and maybe her aunts took up the east. Violet had certainly put her stamp on this place, which was strange, considering she was supposed to be leaving soon.

He turned north and found a pair of startling green eyes smiling at him.

"Uh-oh," she said.

"What?"

"I know that look."

"What look is that?"

"The look that says you might be regretting what just happened here."

"Not regretting. Never regretting." He'd stopped beating himself up over crappy decisions months ago. "I just worry I might have taken advantage."

"Pretty sure I took advantage of you, Nessie." She turned over to face him, and he couldn't help but notice how her breasts moved.

They'd felt different in his hands. Not in a bad way, but in an undiscovered country kind of way. He knew she was self-conscious about them, but when everything about her was perfect to him, she needn't be.

"You had just heard some emotional news."

"So had you."

True. Knowing she was going to be okay had stripped his insides.

"So, really, I took advantage of your relief the nanny wasn't about to buy the farm. God knows you don't want to lose your child-care solution in the middle of the play-offs. Kind of sneaky of me, don't you think?"

"Very." He'd let her have this if it made her feel better. They both knew the truth.

Coming together like this was as necessary as breathing.

"When are you going to tell your sisters?"

She motioned between them. "About me joining Club Chase-Bangs-a-Rebel?"

"About your health scare."

Her mouth thinned and it took her a moment to reply. "Why worry them? I'm okay."

"Yes, but not telling them, Vi . . . That's not right."

"I don't want to put this on them. It's not . . ." She shrugged one beautiful shoulder.

"It's not what?"

"My role."

He leaned up on his elbow. "Your role?"

"In the family. *This* family. You know how everyone's got a part to play? Harper's uptight Ms. Judgment, the one who tells you where you're going wrong—all with the best of intentions, of course. And Isobel, she's the peacemaker, the one who wants everyone to get along."

"And what's your role?"

"I'm the mixer. The troublemaker. Bringer of fun. I get into the middle of this fucked-up Chase family dynamic and question the status quo. When I arrived, everything with these girls was hockey, hockey, hockey— and don't get me wrong, it still is. But now they're less guarded with each other and with Remy and Vadim. I like to think I've helped them see their lives from another angle."

"Violet, love, you make it sound like you're a cross between Mary Poppins and that angel in *It's a Wonderful Life*—"

"Clarence."

"Yeah, Clarence. Fixing problems, setting people straight, and then *poof!* you're out of here to go make someone else's problems go away." The thought of

Violet leaving, for that's what she'd eventually do, made him queasy and angry. Quangry.

"Poof?"

"That's what I said."

"I like collecting wings."

"But what about you? Who fixes your problems?"

"I do, Bren. I fix them. I'm one of those self-rescuing princesses you may have heard about."

"And then you're out."

"It's no secret I'm not sticking around."

This was not news, and there was no good reason why this should have made him furious, but it did. He stared at her, willing her to understand what he couldn't verbalize properly. Framing it as a family problem instead of a Bren problem seemed best.

"Your sisters want to be there for you just as you've been there for them, Violet. Don't leave without giving them that chance. I've known this family for a long time. I know how Clifford ran it. He left scars." On this woman, too, even if she refused to admit it. "Sure, you're the catalyst, Violet, possibly the best thing to happen to them." *Possibly the best thing to happen to me.* "But it's a two-way street. You have to be willing to accept the love back."

"I—I'll think about it."

He nodded. That would do for now.

She leaned over the side of the bed, giving him the perfect vista of her truly exceptional ass, and popped back up with her bra. Turning slightly away from him, she started to put it on.

He cupped her arm. "Do you have to?"

Her mouth went slack a little. "I thought that maybe we—"

"Were done?"

Gently, he removed the bra from her fingers and threw it so it landed on a dresser. A girlish titter came out of her mouth, so odd because Violet had never come across as nervous before.

"Were you thinking I'd bang and bolt? Or is that what you'd like me to do?"

"I don't want you to think you have to stay." The vulnerability in her voice snapped a clamp around his heart. Whether she knew it or not, she'd crossed a forearm over her breasts. "You said before that you couldn't give me 100 percent, and that's fine. I don't need that. Five percent. Maybe ten if you're feeling generous."

He cursed his previous declaration, which had made Violet doubt that she deserved everything that was in his power to give. But she was right about one thing: his life was being pulled in a million different directions at the moment, and he didn't have the bandwidth for a relationship. Neither did he want to give his ex any ammunition for when she came at him next.

Yet giving this up wasn't an option.

He curled a finger over her wrist and pulled gently. "I don't want to confuse the kids and I don't want people in my business."

"Meaning Remy and all those gossipmongers on the team."

"Aye, they're the worst."

She grinned. "Harper and Iz are the last people I would tell about this. Neither am I looking for hearts and flowers. I'm not planning to stay long enough to let you in, Bren St. James, but for the time I'm here, this body belongs to you."

No strings, the perfect offer, especially for a man who couldn't commit to more than one day at a time. Especially for a man who didn't deserve a woman as good as the vision before him.

Hungrily, he scanned the gift she was giving him.

"If this body belongs to me"—he coasted a palm over her generous hip, moving higher to stroke the side of her breast—"then I'll need to know everything. What turns you on, what makes you hum, what gives you pleasure." With the backs of his knuckles, he stroked the tops of her breasts. "Can you feel when I touch you here?"

"Touching them is more about comfort than discernible pleasure. The nipple is purely cosmetic. Tattooed to add color." She traced an erotic circle around it, then moved his hand around the side. "I feel more here, and if you were to taste them, my brain would make connections from the visual. More because I'd assume you're enjoying it rather than the fact of pleasure itself. A feedback loop."

He loved her honesty. Had he ever met a woman more in tune with herself and her body?

Thin scars edged along the underside of her breasts, reminding him of her bravery, of what she had endured. His fingers mapped the side, where she'd directed him, then he inclined his head and slicked his tongue over the nipple on her right breast. It felt weird to do this, knowing it did little for her.

He peered up to see her reaction. Her eyes were heavy lidded. "More," she whispered.

He sucked on the faux bud. It looked like a real nipple. It felt like one on his tongue.

She made a low sound in her throat and his dick responded, pushing against her thigh. She shifted her body slightly, raked her fingers through his hair, and all the while she stared at him with those eyes he wanted to sink into.

Out of the corner of his eye, he saw her hand move, her fingers slipping between her beautiful thighs. She stroked gently, then harder, and it drew his moan, a vibration along her breast. Locked together they continued—him sucking on the breast she couldn't feel, her touching herself with long, slick strokes. She was finding a way to make it work. To craft her own pleasure, and his with it, because her pleasure was his.

He slipped two fingers inside her and their hands worked together to get her to that peak. It didn't take long, her body a responsive instrument beneath his touch, its clench around his fingers the ultimate reward. And then he watched her lazy smile in the aftermath while she watched him grip his cock and stroke hard.

He knelt over her, using rough and mean pumps to draw out his pleasure, but really it was her eyes that got him there. In them he saw a surrender of trust that broke him open.

At the last moment, she whispered, "Mark me."

He came all over her perfect breasts, a ropy spurt that lashed across her body, and branded her as his. With her he felt renewed. Changed. Worthy.

With her he felt like the man he was meant to be.

EIGHTEEN

Semifinals, Game One
Chicago Rebels at LA Quake

Violet added the last tortilla to the warmer on the kitchen counter and called out, "Come and get it!" A herd of footsteps, some clacking, others softer, echoed and grew louder.

Somehow, Addison Williams-Callaghan, wife of right-winger Ford, beat everyone to the punch. Normally this wouldn't have been surprising, because as a former lingerie runway model, she clearly knew how to strut her way to success. But she also happened to be eight and a half months pregnant. Glowing with it, too.

"Vi, this spread looks amazing!"

Violet grinned, pleased at the praise. She'd made her favorite Puerto Rican dish, *mofongo*—fried plantains with pork cracklings and chicken broth. Also offered were *rellenos de papa*, stuffed potato dumplings fried to golden perfection. No harm in bringing a little PR flavor to suburban Chicago, even if there was a certain weirdness to playing host at Bren's house without the man himself present. But it had the best TV room setup, and this way, the girls would be more comfortable in their own place while they watched the game.

Violet might not be a hockey fan, but there was no denying how much the sport meant to Harper and Isobel. For them, it was the family business, and getting this far in the season meant everything. A win tonight would be one step further than the team had gone in years.

A win tonight would keep Violet in a job and in Bren's life.

So tonight she was a Rebels fan.

Isobel started spooning steak and onions onto a tortilla. Usually she would have traveled with the team, but she'd stayed behind to hang with Harper, for whom the rougher-than-average initial weeks of pregnancy had prevented the trip to LA for the first game of the semifinals. "How come you never cook like this for our awkward sister bonding nights?"

"Because those nights are for cookies, ice cream, and wine," Harper said. "Except now, no wine."

"Uh, get over it," Addison said, rubbing her very swollen stomach.

"You're at the end of it!" Harper exclaimed. "I have six months of wine-free hell to go."

Violet called out to the living room. "Cat! Franks! Food's up."

Addison looked over her shoulder, and seeing that the girls had yet to arrive, she asked, "So how's it going?"

"Good. They're amazingly well behaved, which makes this job easy-peasy."

"I meant with the hot Sco—"

"Hey, guys!" Violet cut Addison off on the arrival of Franky and Caitriona.

"Mexican food!" Franky said, and Violet didn't correct her, but Caitriona spoke up.

"It's Puerto Rican. It's different." Cat shot a glance at Violet, then averted her eyes quickly. "Like Lin-Manuel Miranda. He wrote *Hamilton*."

"Yes, it is different," Violet said, surprised at Cat's interest. She was still pretty reserved around Violet. "Very different."

Everyone loaded up their plates, and Addison and the girls headed back to the TV room to get settled in.

Violet couldn't help noticing that her sisters had remained behind. Isobel took a bite of her fajita, then around her chewing said, "So, you and the hot Scot."

"Excuse me?"

Middle Child wiped her mouth with a napkin. "Addy seems to think there's something going on."

"Well, Addy can think all she wants."

Isobel shrugged. "I think you'd be good for him. Bren could do with a bit of sunshine in his life. He's always so serious."

"Nah-ah," Harper said. "That's a terrible idea."

The *oh really* stares of Violet and Isobel affirmed that this was particularly rich, coming from the woman who was now carrying the child of the man she'd once declared to be off-limits.

Harper waved at them in annoyance. "Yeah, yeah, I know. But there's a lot of baggage there, Violet. A guy with a tricky ex situation, two kids, and a drinking problem."

"Good thing nothing's going on," Violet lied.

Annoyingly, Harper refused to let go. "As hard as I know he's trying for those girls, he's still got issues. In fact, he cut practice early a couple of days ago with no explanation. There was a lot of that unreliable behavior back in his boozing days, so I'm hoping it's not going to be a problem."

Damn. He'd cut practice for her. No way could she live with herself if Bren was taking the fall for her crap. She recalled his advice, how she needed to be up front with her sisters. Change the course of how things were done in the Chase family.

You're the catalyst, Violet.

"Bren did that for me. He cut practice to come see me." The enormity of it washed over her again.

Harper's mouth pursed. "For you?"

"I need you both to promise you won't freak out."

Isobel frowned. "That's *so* not a good way to start whatever it is you're about to tell us."

"First of all, understand that I'm fine. I went to the doctor and it was a false alarm, but a few days ago, I found a lump under my arm and I thought the worst. Bren witnessed my freak-out, and then a couple of days ago, he found out that I'd gone to the doctor alone. That's why he left practice early. To ream me out."

Isobel's frown had vanished, now replaced with a hard, angry glitter in the green eyes they all shared. "You went to the doctor by yourself? You had this for days—"

"Four days. I felt it four days ago."

"And you didn't tell us."

"Iz, I'm sorry. I'm not used to this. The last time this happened, I had my mom and aunts." She gestured between them. "We're all still in this weird getting-to-know-you space."

"It's been months," Isobel shot back. "And I seem to recall you being pissed as all get out at me holding on to secrets a few weeks ago."

True. Violet had gone batshit crazy on Isobel when she heard Middle Child was prepared to risk her life trying out for the Olympics after she'd been told by doctors that playing hockey again might kill her. "So I don't know how to practice what I preach. I'm a failure at life."

"None of us have the sharing gene," Harper said. "And God knows I haven't exactly been the most open person. But it's probably something we need to nourish." She threw an arm around Violet's shoulder. "So it was a false alarm?"

Relieved that the reaction drama was over, Violet described her lumpy armpit, which they both found amusing now that the life-threatening element had been removed.

"I'm going to schedule the outpatient surgery when Bren's back in town so the girls' care won't be interrupted."

Isobel held her gaze intently. "We'll be there."

It was on the tip of Violet's tongue to say they didn't have to be, but she merely nodded instead. Apparently, they needed this more than her.

"Remy's giving a pregame interview," Addy called out from the living room.

Harper shrieked. "Pause it! I miss that face."

Once she was out of earshot, Isobel leaned her elbows on the counter, cupped her face coquettishly, and delivered an all-knowing grin.

"You've already paid a visit to the Scottish lowlands, haven't you?"

Fobbing off Isobel had always been harder—they were just two years apart and had connected more easily when Violet first moved to Chicago. She was also dying to share it with someone.

"Yes!" She grabbed her sister's shoulders dramatically. "And it was so fucking good."

Isobel chuckled, then said in a singsong, "The single dad and the nanny. Sounds like a nineties sitcom."

"I know, I know. Clichés abound. But it's been building for a while and now the balloon has been—"

"Pricked?"

"Yeah. Pricked big time."

"And what comes next?"

The billion-dollar question, but only if she assigned it more importance than she should. "Neither of us is looking for anything. He was just there at the right time."

"Aw, hell no," Isobel said. "You mean, you heard you weren't dying and you banged him first thing? Do I need to kick some hot Scot ass? Because it sounds to me like he took advantage of your frazzled state."

"No one took advantage. Jeez, it was"—*crazy emo-*

tional, hot as fuck, the best sex I've ever had—"just a roll in the sheets. A relief bang. A 'yay, I'm still here, let's finally do this' screw. That's it."

Isobel didn't look as gleeful as when she'd first guessed the big news. "And now you guys go back to before like nothing happened?"

"Why not?"

Iz shook her head. "Not how it works, Vi. The relief bang has a habit of becoming a 'one more won't hurt' bang followed by a 'let's get a quick one in while the kids are at violin practice' bang."

"The kids don't play violin. Stop overcomplicating it."

"You work for him. He works for you. There's nothing uncomplicated about this."

"I'm fully capable of keeping my job separate from my sex life," Violet insisted.

Isobel smirked. "If there's one thing I know from the experience of these past nine months, it's that no one in this family is capable of making *that* distinction."

Vadim Petrov opened the door to his hotel suite, shirtless. Bloody typical. The richer-than-God Russian never made do with a regular hotel room, either; it was always a hot-shit upgrade, and for away games, this was usually where the party was at.

"Captain, you are late."

"I had to check in with my girls."

The Russian widened the door and gestured for Bren

to enter. "How are your angels? Have they driven Violet over the edge yet?"

"If they have, she's not saying."

The usual suspects had gathered on the off-night between the LA games. Other team members had gone out to a trendy hotspot, but the guys Bren was closest to preferred to hang in Petrov's suite, play video games, and shoot the shit.

Bren had an inkling they did it for him. He was fine with hanging in bars—saw it as a test, to be honest—but he had to admit, the older he got, the more he preferred a quiet night in with his girls or his boys.

Or with Violet.

Since that afternoon in her cottage three days ago, he'd been entertaining strange thoughts. Notions, if you will. He'd texted her more than usual to check in, needing to read her sharp wit, relive that look on her face when he shot all over her golden body.

He'd set boundaries. She'd accepted them without argument, making it clear that Chicago was just a way station on her journey. That he was just one of the stops.

Was that what was eating at him—her ready willingness to understand he had nothing to offer her? If it was merely sex, he would have called her after the win last night, but it was late and . . . he wasn't sure where he stood. Or if he had a right to check in, plainly looking to get his rocks off.

He was living the dream. Why couldn't he just enjoy the ride?

Petrov's suite was exactly that: a humongous set
of rooms that included a kitchen. That's where Bren
headed now, drawn by the scent of cooking, and it's
where he found Remy, leaning close to a stockpot. The
smell of something amazing wafted from it.

They could have ordered room service, but Remy
needed cooking to make him feel useful. Now that
Harper couldn't travel because her pregnancy was a
little rough on her, keeping his mind occupied was key.
It had the added benefit of making them all feel like
they were kicking back at Remy's place in Riverbrook,
their usual haunt at least once a week.

"What's on the menu?"

"Étouffée."

Bren took a closer look at the fragrant stew with
crawfish. Petrov opened the fridge and handed him a
bottle of water.

"How's Violet?" Remy asked.

Two mentions of Violet in less than a minute. "Fine,
as far as I know."

"She told Harper and Iz about her health scare,"
Remy added.

The Cajun let that hang, but Vadim wouldn't know
subtlety if it pucked him in the head. "And I hear that
you were the first person she shared the news with. That
is interesting."

"Just happened to be on the spot. Purely geography."

"Is that what you're callin' it?"

Bren turned to find Cade, not looking like his usual
friendly Texan self.

"I caught her at the right—or wrong—time. Any set of ears would have done."

"Don't know about that. She had opportunities to call me or her sisters with her concerns, to ask us to go to that doc appointment with her, and she didn't. You knew about it, though." Cade considered himself Violet's best friend, and it sounded like he was pissed at being left out of the loop.

"After the fact. And like I said, if I hadn't been there when she initially found out, then she wouldn't have told me at all."

Everyone weighed this for a second.

Cade finally spoke. "Let's call it how we see it, Bren. You and Violet have been dancing around each other like porcupines in heat for months now. I see how you were in a bind with your kids and all, but I'm not really seeing how placing Violet in your home was done with any intention other than to have her close at hand for things unrelated to nannying."

Bren sucked back a few chugs of water, hoping the delay might douse the flames of fury. "Are you saying I hired her to take advantage of her? Have you met Violet, by the way? The woman is incapable of being bullied or messed with."

"Yeah, she acts like a man-eater, but it's all for show, just like she pretends that Clifford not stepping up doesn't hurt, but I know it does. And now she's in a particularly vulnerable position, thinking her cancer might have returned, and there *you* are pulling the knight-in-hockey-pads act. Probably walking around shirtless in your kitchen and being all cute with your kids. She's only fucking human."

"You sound jealous, Alamo," Vadim said. "Only, I can't decide if you're jealous of Bren or of Violet."

Cade eyed the Russian and rubbed his beard. "Hell, Russki, you might be onto somethin' there. Broody Italian does it more for me than Broody Scot, but I can't say it hasn't crossed my mind."

"Jesus," Bren said. Far too much information.

Vadim placed his hands on his hips and addressed Cade. "What about *me*? I'm the one on billboards and in magazines. Surely *I* have figured in your fantasies."

Cade raised his beer in the Russian's direction. "Keep your tats on, Petrov, you're right up there. A close second to Chrises Hemsworth and Pine."

Everyone laughed, even Bren, glad that they were on easier terms again. He'd not enjoyed the jealousy that wracked his body when he thought his teammate had something going on with Violet. The guy was a good friend, after all.

"Seriously, though, Bren," Cade said, his tone less belligerent. "Did you hire Violet so you could seduce her?"

"Seduce her? Are we in the 19-fucking-40s here?"

Both Remy and Vadim were quiet, hanging on every word.

Bren sighed. "I hired her because she's amazing with my kids and their welfare is number one with me. I'm not denying I'm attracted to her, but these days I'm a dad first. Violet and I are on the same page in this." So maybe he was a few chapters ahead, creating a story for them in his head, one where he and Violet gave this a shot. Only he suspected that if he fell, he would be falling alone.

"But you'd like something more?" Remy asked, sly with it, too, as if he knew something had already happened and Bren was itching to take it to the next level.

"I can't let my mind go there. She's made it clear she's not here for the long haul. She doesn't want to stick around, and I can't get my kids' hopes up." He couldn't get *his* hopes up.

Only, he was afraid they were already sky high.

NINETEEN

His mouth sought hers and she gladly let him find it. Their moves were frantic, every touch magnifying their desperation. A solid kick of his sneaker slapped the door to the cottage shut, then he lifted and deposited her on the farmhouse table in her kitchen.

She tore her mouth away, her breaths labored. "Did you park down the street?"

"Aye."

"And you were careful about anyone seeing you?"

He held her face with both hands, his intensity cutting through her worry. "No one knows I'm here. But when I make you scream, they might."

"Cocky."

"Yup."

They'd been meeting most mornings he was in town, postpractice, while the girls were with their tutor. Though *meeting* was too tame. More like crashing and hurtling into each other, every coupling filled with urgency and hunger.

He shoved down his sweatpants, his erection already

huge and heavy. How did he walk several blocks with that thing? The thought sent her into giggles.

"You didn't just laugh at my dick."

"Sort of. Just wondering how you get through the day with that beast getting in the way of everything. It's so . . ." She wrapped two hands around it and stroked up to the dark, plump head.

He shut his eyes, drawing a shallow breath. "It's so . . ."

"Monstrous. All this time I've been nicknaming you Nessie, when really this is the true creature of the deep. It'd be very popular in the dicktabase."

Lust-glazed eyes snapped open. "The what, now?"

"Just a little hobby of mine. A Tumblr where I catalog and celebrate the beauty of the male form."

He looked a little shocked, if Bren St. James was capable of reaching such range of emotion. "You collect porn?"

"Women like porn as well. Don't worry, I'm discreet."

Bren's eyelids grew more heavy lidded with each stroke. "If your porn addiction gives you ideas, then I'm all for that. Right now, though, I've got a few ideas of my own."

He inched the hem of her skirt to the tops of her thighs. Strong, roughened fingers delved and found her wet and wanting.

"No panties."

"No barriers."

Looking into his eyes, she felt the truth of her words

applying to so much more than a lack of underwear. Whereas before he was guarded, since they'd finally given in to the need clawing at them, he now displayed nothing but naked hunger whenever he looked at her. Both in and out of bed.

It was electrifying to be the subject of Bren's attention.

With each deepening stroke through her, she felt drawn to him in a way that terrified her. Sex had never been like this with anyone else. Freeing and honest and scary.

Out of control.

And she needed to haul it back.

"Want to taste you," she whispered before pushing him away from her body and slipping off the table.

"Violet," he gasped as she knelt before him. This way she could focus on his pleasure without risking a complete loss of herself in the moment.

But . . . "You're too tall. Sit."

He did as he was told, kicking off his sweats at the same time.

"Take off your shirt," she ordered, enjoying the rare assumption of a bossy role.

He peeled the shirt off and threw it onto the floor of her kitchen. She took his sweats and folded them up, placed them under her knees. Leaning forward, he ran his thumb along her bottom lip.

"I dream of this mouth, Violet. I dream of it wrapped around my cock, sucking me to the back of your throat, getting wet and slick as I fuck it. But first, I need to see those gorgeous breasts and that perfect ass. *Your* shirt. Off. Now."

Command given, he released her, leaving her a quivering mess on the floor. The strength had left her arms, all sensation snaking through her descending to that aching spot between her legs.

How had she thought this might give her control? That she had any hope of retaining a splinter of it when in this man's presence?

"Violet." Her name on his lips was a demand.

Get a grip. She obeyed. Her oversized tee slipped over her head, revealing her breasts encased in red satin. Instead of removing her bra and skirt, she hiked the skirt up over her hips. His nostrils flared, and she knew he enjoyed the sleaziness she'd brought out to play, a half-dressed, disheveled, dissolute woman.

"Now, suck my cock, *mi reina.*"

My queen. The endearment—and in Spanish, too—was so unexpected she almost fell over. To cover her surprise, she averted her gaze from his and held the thick weight of him in her hands.

It felt like she was holding power, life, this man's future. She'd started out thinking a blow job would put her in charge. Three minutes in and she'd never felt more rattled.

It's just sex. It's just smokin' hot sex with a Scottish man-god. It's just a beard of awesome and a cock of wonder. It's just—she took him inside her mouth, and their joint groan affirmed that *just* was the most inadequate word ever invented.

His hand came around to tunnel through her hair, hold her in place. But he didn't push. He didn't need to.

She was all in and all his.

If she didn't look at him, she could get through this with some semblance of self intact. So she kept her gaze dipped, her eyelids at half-mast as she worked him with a messy tongue bath and jerky strokes of her hands. She used to be better at this, surely. Apparently, overthinking and fuzzy emotion had negated her once-admirable BJ skills.

That strong hand at the nape of her neck applied a slight pressure—not to make her go faster or harder, but to angle her head for further demands.

"Look at me, Violet."

She was powerless to disobey him. Something about his voice toggled a switch inside her. Giving over control now seemed like the easiest way to retain some measure of it, but staring right at him was like looking at an eclipse.

She'd always enjoyed living dangerously.

"That's my girl," he whispered as their gazes sealed together like powerful magnets. There was no escaping his draw. "Take it all. Take it all down."

He jerked. She took everything he had to give her, craving his taste, loving the surrender. And within seconds, she found herself straddling his lap, his fingers fondling her in a leisurely motion that in no way matched the urgency of her need.

"Please," she begged.

Still, he kept his stroke slow, each pass making her

mindless and driving her closer to the edge. She shook her head, no longer able to verbalize how much she wanted to come. How much she wanted this to be over but also never to end. How much she wanted.

Those magic digits sought more begging, sensitive flesh, finally reaching her burning clit. The first touch was so gentle she wanted to scream. The second an outright tease. The third accompanied by a kiss, his tongue moving in time with his fingers. She was grinding on his hand, muttering curses in English and Spanish, crazy for her climax.

With one hard swipe, her vision went dark at the edges as pinpricks of light exploded behind her eyelids. Her body shuddered with sensation, her thighs shook with the force of her release. She slumped against him, her head on his shoulder.

The next thing she knew she was waking in her bed with Bren wrapped around her.

He wasn't asleep. His body was relaxed against hers, but not completely.

"How long was I out?"

"Just an hour. You needed it. I worked you good."

She snorted. "So full of yourself, Scot."

"Aye." His breath was soft against her ear and he snuggled a little tighter. That slight shift felt more intimate than anything they'd done so far. "Could stay like this all day."

"But you won't. You have responsibilities, young man."

He felt the curve of his lips over her neck. He enjoyed

that observation. He enjoyed responsibility. It had been tough for him at the start of the season when Remy was traded in, a situation that challenged Bren to step up and lead.

"Do you like being the captain?"

"Wouldn't do it if I didn't. But yes, I like it. I used to be better at it, so I'm trying to relearn some of those behaviors." He paused. "Not just with my captaincy."

She turned over, needing to see his face.

Oh, how she liked this face. It looked older than thirty-one, which may have been the beard, but was more likely all that experience. Both good and bad.

"You mean, being a dad?"

"That, and being a man. Though I wonder if I ever really got it. You think the dad thing is innate, but in truth, I winged it for so many years. I tried not to drink around my daughters, keeping it for when I was at away games, but it inevitably crept in. I scared them. I—" Color tagged his cheekbones, and in his eyes, she detected shame. Her heart crashed in her chest, anxious to escape and soothe him. "I did something I regret. Lots of things I regret, but this one thing . . . I have to live with it, how I almost went to a place of no return."

Guilt hung over him, heavy and dark. She wanted to ask more, but figured it was hard for him to express even this much.

"So this might seem like a dumb question. I know alcoholism is a disease, but is there more to it than that? Is there a reason why you couldn't stop after one?"

He pushed a lock of hair behind her ear. A few moments passed while he gathered his thoughts.

"For me, it's mostly a lack of confidence. My dad and my Canadian cousins were all hard drinkers—it was ice time followed by brews and then more ice. Once I moved to Winnipeg to live with him, it was a way to fit in, keep up, please him. I see it now, that he was a raging alcoholic, but I always thought that wasn't me."

"Is he still around?"

"Died ten years back, cirrhosis of the liver. But he got to see me play in the NHL and he held Cat once." His smile faded with a different memory. "I've always lived inside my head, and drinking made me feel like I could be someone else. More interesting. More brave. You ever heard of Jake LaMotta?"

"The boxer? *Raging Bull*?"

"Yeah. He once said alcohol gives you false courage, but it's really masking true fear. Alcoholics don't like themselves much and they tend to diminish their talents. Here I was, with a skill someone's willing to pay me millions of dollars for, and I couldn't appreciate it. Sober me is serious and hard to know. Drunk me doesn't have to make the effort. Sober me was—is—not all that likeable. Drunk me is the life and soul, your best friend."

She rubbed his jaw, enjoying the roughness of his beard. She couldn't believe a man as strong and vital as Bren could ever lack confidence.

"Sober you is focused, intense, all in. Sober you is a great dad. Sober you is awesome in the sack. Multiple-orgasms-in-minutes me approves wholeheartedly of sober you."

He chuckled. "Been a while since you had some. You're easily satisfied, woman."

"I am," she admitted, only to have him roll his big body on top of her. She loved the weight of him, the feel of his hairy body against her smooth skin.

"You close?"

"Jesus, St. James. You haven't done any work yet!"

"But looking at me"—he ground his already considerable hardness against her—"is enough, right? You just cream at the sight of me, dontcha?"

"This from the guy who says he's lacked confidence."

His brow darkened, and she immediately regretted bringing it up. She shouldn't joke about something he'd felt drove him to seek comfort in an addiction.

"It's not just that. It's—" He took a moment to find the right words. "I've always felt like I don't deserve my good fortune. That all of my blessings were accidental. My career. My children. My wealth."

That he didn't mention his wife did not go unnoticed.

"For most of my adult life, I've imagined the rug of success could be ripped from under me at any second. I didn't deserve it, so I'd inevitably be found out. As an imposter, a fraud. Know what I mean?"

"We all feel like that sometimes. For me, it's living in two worlds. Not Latina enough for some people, too Latina for others. Not officially Chase, but the daughter of an NHL great." Though her sisters had never let her feel anything less than welcome, she still operated in this world as "other." "So I know a little bit about feeling like you don't fit in, but I made a decision after getting breast cancer that I wasn't going to listen to haters, doubters, naysayers. I was going to be fearless. Try new things, meet new people, as Isobel says, 'grasp life by the reconstructed tits.' Or as I say, the Year of the V."

"The Year of the V? I like that." He coasted a giant paw over her hips, then her rear. "Voluptuous Violet and her very versatile—" He screwed up his mouth in query.

"Vibrator?"

His eyes brightened. "Voluptuous Violet and her very versatile vibrator ventured forth seeking variety, virility . . ." He rubbed evidence of his virility against her. "And . . ."

"Victory!" She should add vindication and validation to that mix. To feel valued.

"So you threw yourself into the world of pro hockey and crazy sisterhood and boosting team morale."

She laughed. "*Visiting*—see what I did there?—the locker room to avail of the perks of team ownership is my favorite thing in the world, Nessie! Of course, I was always hoping to catch a certain Scotsman with his globes of perfection on full display, but alas, the broody bastard never obliged."

"He has a sixth sense about imminent objectification. So what does victorious and valiant Violet want?"

"Other than a versatile vibrator?" Shyness at sharing too much made her mentally squirm, but Bren just watched her intently, nothing but encouragement in his eyes. Ah, screw it. "I'd like to go to college, maybe be . . . a teacher? I've always worked at jobs with few prospects, always assumed striving for more wasn't really in my wheelhouse. And then I got sick and I realized we've only got this one life. I'm still not sure what I want to do with mine, but I know I don't want to waste a single minute."

He smiled, a heartbreaking curve of his lips. "Knowing that is half the battle. You'll figure it out. Find your talent."

She stroked his jaw, letting her fingers tangle in his beard, shape the curve of his sensual mouth. "Just like you did. You've worked hard for everything you have, Bren. No one falls into fortune like yours by accident."

Not like her with her inheritance, "earned" by her mother's gamble in hitting on a famous pro athlete. There was only one imposter in this room and it wasn't the Scot.

"I'm trying to think more like that," Bren said. "I'm trying to count my blessings and recognize that everything given to me is a gift. Like you."

Her heart seized. "Bren, that's . . . uh . . ."

He grinned, evidently sensing her discomfort. "Now, don't freak out, Vasquez. I'm not trying to change the rules. People enter our lives, and sometimes it takes a while to understand their purpose. Harper is one such person. Without her, I'd be out on my ass, probably separated from my kids and drunk in a gutter somewhere. Remy's another. He arrived when I couldn't be the leader my team needed. He carried the baton until I was ready to assume it again." He rubbed his nose against hers. "And then there's Violet Vasquez. Vibrant, vital, va-va-voom Violet. Your appearance in my life and in the lives of my daughters is a true gift. You're special, I appreciate you, and I need you to know that, okay?"

She barely managed to choke out a rusty, "Okay."

He licked the seam of her lips and tugged her mouth into a kiss, so sweet she could feel tears stinging her eyelids.

"Now, speaking of gifts . . ." He rubbed his erection along her tingling flesh.

Appreciation that he'd moved on from the serious conversation flooded her chest, yet the words he'd used to describe her lingered. Vibrant. Vital. *A gift.*

She was in the right place at the right time, that's all. A set of special circumstances had thrown them together, but it was nothing more than a confluence of weather patterns.

Nothing more.

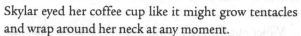

Skylar eyed her coffee cup like it might grow tentacles and wrap around her neck at any moment.

"Nothing stronger, then?"

Violet pulled clean plates out of the dishwasher and stacked them on the counter. "It's 11 a.m. and I'm on the clock. What if I had to rush one of the kids to the ER?"

Skylar's expression said it all: in the event of misadventure, *her* kids would need to make their own travel arrangements. "Probably best not to have any booze in the house anyway," she said, lowering her voice conspiratorially, even though the kids were in the yard and couldn't possibly hear her. "Remove all temptation."

Well, not all temptation, Skylar.

Skylar, along with Jeremy and Lance (formerly Tarquin and Tristan), had become semiregular visitors these past few weeks. Apparently they were a year apart, but Violet couldn't tell which was which. Both were curly-haired freckle magnets who made a lot of noise and smelled funky. No wonder their mother was fond of day drinking.

"Any idea what's going on with Kendra?" Skylar asked, fishing.

"No." Bren never talked about her. She never came up with the girls, either, though she supposed their grandparents might be keeping them in the loop. "I expect she needs some time."

Skylar snorted. "Yeah, right. That woman never appreciated what she had. But then he wasn't exactly the easiest to man to love." She shook her head. "Those poor kids."

Violet put the plates away in the cupboard. The kids seemed fine with Bren, now that they were no longer in a toxic environment. This man was incapable of hurting them. Violet would go so far as to say he was very easy to love.

By his girls, she added.

"You know she got knocked up on purpose to catch him."

Pulse rate booming, Violet turned back to Skylar. "That's a pretty serious allegation to make."

"Well, she told me. He'd just been drafted to the NHL, big contract, barely nineteen, and the future looked bright. She didn't want to risk him slipping from her grasp, so she made sure he'd be put in a position to do the right thing. The kids were like trophies for her."

She supposed it shouldn't have been that surprising. People did shitty things to other people all the time. Exhibit A: her own mother's behavior in trying to trap Clifford into a big payday. And here was Violet with her hand out waiting for the ultimate prize.

Oblivious to Violet's discomfort, Skylar nattered on. "I've never met anyone less cut out for motherhood. Half the time, she was always sending them to friends' houses. Rehab, my ass! I'll bet that whatever Kendra's doing, she's not thinking of her daughters."

A noise at the kitchen door made Violet turn. Caitriona had just stepped inside, and the look on her face said it all. But how much had she heard? Without another word, she walked through the kitchen and out of the room.

Skylar made a grimace. "Sorry."

Thanks, Skylar. "Could you keep an eye on the others while I take care of this?"

Violet headed after Caitriona and found her in her room. On first seeing it several weeks ago, Violet had thought it a little on the pink side. Even now, the Disney princess wallpaper threw her, because Cat wasn't really princess material. Seemed a bit old for it, to be honest. Perhaps her mom liked her girls to act a certain way.

She was sitting on the bed, her Beats on, her iPad in her hand but not having moved beyond the home screen. She made no acknowledgment of Violet.

Violet sat down. "Hey, kitty cat."

Nothing.

"Fair enough. I'll just poke through your stuff and be generally annoying." She headed to a dresser littered with Post-its with tightly cramped text that she recognized as Cat's. One said: *The heart fixes what the mind can't.* Another: *You can't hurt me, only I can.* Deep stuff.

"Writing poetry?"

Caitriona jumped up and snatched the notes from Violet's hands. "That's private."

"You left it lying around."

"In my room. Which you shouldn't be in." She sat back on the bed. "Mrs. Nichols doesn't know anything. Mom didn't like her. Said she was fat and had fake boobs."

"That's a mean thing to say."

Caitriona shrugged, picked up her headphones, then put them down again. Violet waited, sensing that the girl needed time to think through what she wanted to say.

"Mom always said the truth was more important, even if it hurts people's feelings."

"That's one opinion. Another one is that kindness is the most important thing of all. There's always a way to make something sound better."

"You mean lie?"

"I mean be diplomatic."

Cat thought on that for a second. "Mrs. Nichols told the truth down there in the kitchen. Mom was always trying to get rid of us, and it's true—she hasn't called us."

"Mrs. Nichols doesn't know what's going through your mom's mind. No one does but your mom, and when she's ready, she'll reach out." Violet sat on the bed. "That's my truth."

"Lies to not hurt my feelings?" The words might have sounded tween-jaded, but Caitriona's mouth wobbled, the answer to this hugely important to her.

"A different way of putting it. What I do know is that your parents love you. I see how nuts your dad is about you. I wish my dad had loved me so much."

"I thought you had the same dad as Harper and Isobel."

"I did, but he wasn't around. He wasn't in my life in any meaningful way."

Caitriona's brow crimped—so like Bren. "My dad won't always be here. He might leave like last time, go into rehab again. And then we'll have no one."

These girls had put up with a lot of uncertainty in their short lives. They had to be terrified of what might come next.

"He made some mistakes, but he's trying his best to

be better. Sometimes people hurt us, and the only way forward is to forgive them."

Cat's eyes, as blue as Bren's, blinked at her. "Did you forgive your dad?"

Violet had never thought about that. She'd arrived in Chicago filled with curiosity, a need to figure out her place—not just in the Chase family, but in the world. It had never occurred to her that Clifford might be deserving of forgiveness. He certainly hadn't asked for it.

Instead he'd dropped her into this foreign country, one where she had to forge new connections and her own path. His mind games might have sent her here, yet they also ushered in the most fulfilling period of her life. Still her heart rebelled at having to thank him for it.

"I've forgiven him," Violet said, surprised to find she meant it. "As for your dad, he's hurt you both and he knows it, but now you and Franky are his number-one priority. Nothing else matters to him, not hockey or the Cup or even pepperoni pizza."

Caitriona made a sound, like she was trying not to laugh. "He likes pepperoni pizza!"

"No, he *loves* pepperoni pizza, but he loves you and your sister more. So much more. And that's saying a lot, isn't it? You're better than pizza, Cat!" Violet shook the girl's shoulders until those bubbling giggles in her throat broke free.

"I suppose!" Serious again, she said, "I don't want him to get back with Mom. They don't make each other happy."

"I don't think that's going to happen." The thought of Bren with this woman made Violet sick to her stomach. She told herself it was just a reaction to the idea of him in an unhappy situation that she wouldn't wish on anyone. But eventually, he would meet someone. Bren was too hot a commodity to stay off the market for very long.

And now the thought of Bren with *anyone* else made her not just ill, but . . . angry.

Shaking the negativity to the room's pink corners, she refocused on Caitriona with a motion to the Post-its. "So, tell me about these. Are they quotes from something?"

"No, they're song lyrics." A blush suffused her cheeks and she added in a whisper, "That I wrote."

"Wow! You're writing songs? That's awesome. Do you write music, too?"

"Just in my head. I know a little about notes from piano lessons, but I don't want to play it on that. It's too . . ." She waved a hand, looking for the word.

"Formal?"

"Yeah. Mom wanted me to play, but I wanted to do something else. Guitar, maybe. Mom said I'd end up being a drug addict."

That was quite the leap. "Not exactly seeing the connection. You know who plays the guitar and *isn't* a drug addict? Remy. In fact, his dad is a Grammy Award–winning musician. Also not a drug addict."

Caitriona's face lit up. "That's so cool."

"Yep, it is. Maybe he could show you a few chords. Is

that what they call them? See if it's something you want to follow through with."

"Maybe." The word was casual, but there was hope in those two syllables that made Violet's heart burst with the joy of making a connection. Caitriona was a tough nut to crack. Also not unlike her dad.

"In the meantime, you could try one of those song-writing apps. Something that helps you get your ideas down so you don't lose them on little bits of paper and have Mrs. Higgins cleaning them up or the nosy nanny asking all sorts of dumb questions."

"They're not dumb. Well, not totally." She hit the app store on her iPad and ran a quick search. "There's a lot of them on here."

"Then we'd better do some research."

TWENTY

"Looks like you have visitors, *mon capitaine*," Remy said.

Bren looked over the Cajun's shoulder to the tunnel in the Rebels' practice facility. His heart leaped at the sight of Violet with Caitriona and Franky, all of them waving.

He waved back and a couple of the guys went, "Aw!"

"Shut it," he muttered as he skated over.

As his daughters hugged him, he raised his gaze to Violet. "What's all this about?"

"The girls wanted to take you to lunch." She had that mischievous sparkle in her eye he loved, so something was definitely up.

"Oh yeah?"

Franky peered up. "You don't have to go out of town for the next game until tomorrow, so we have you for the rest of the day."

"Aye, I guess you do. Sounds like you have more on the menu than lunch, sprite."

She slid a glance at Violet. "Maybe."

"I have to change, so I'll meet you outside."

"In the parking lot," Violet said, to which Franky vehemently nodded her head.

Bren walked outside to the players' parking lot to find Cade and Violet standing beside Dante's midnight blue Bentley. His girls were nowhere to be seen.

He spotted the car Violet would've driven in, an SUV he lent her because her own car was unreliable. No girls. No sign of them in his car, either.

Definitely shenanigans afoot. "Where are they?"

Violet thumbed toward the backseat of the Bentley. His daughters waved, then broke into inexplicable giggles, which set Cade and Violet off.

"What's goin' on?"

"Just lunch," Violet said before she leaned up on her toes to kiss Cade on the cheek.

Cade winked. "Have fun, Highlander."

Violet opened the passenger door of the Bentley. "In you get."

Dante loved this car, and damn, was it a beauty. No way on God's green earth would he lend it to Violet. Cade, however . . . Bren could attest to how people tended to make poor decisions when cocks were involved. So when two dicks were in play . . .

"Why are we driving Dante's car?"

The girls started giggling again. "Get in, Dad," Franky yelled. "We have to go on our adventure!"

"Quit that smoldering until we're alone," Violet murmured. "You know my knickers can't handle it." Then louder: "You heard the girls. We have an adventure ahead of us."

Bren had no idea what was going on, but he did know this: if anyone was driving this Bentley, it was him.

"Give me the keys, woman."

Violet's phone buzzed and she snuck a furtive look. Crap! Cade must have caved like a cheap suitcase when Dante asked about his car.

Dante: *I'm Italian, which means I know people, Vasquez. You harm that car and it won't be pretty.*

Men, so ridiculously territorial about their penises—oops, motor vehicles.

Bren slid her a look. "Want to tell me where I'm going?"

"To Chicago!" This was Franky.

"Fun in the city, eh?"

Caitriona leaned over, touching the back of Bren's neck, her fingers playing with his hair. Violet caught Bren's secret smile. She knew it had been tough for these two to get back to whatever they had before, and that gesture seemed like a small step forward.

"Can we go down Lakeshore Drive, Dad?"

It would take longer to go all the way east, but Bren didn't even question it.

"Sure we can, sprite."

Twenty minutes later, with Fleetwood Mac's "You Can Go Your Own Way" blaring, they were zipping down one of the most spectacular curves of highway ever created. The lake had never sparkled more brightly, and the gleaming city in the distance invited them to glamour and adventure.

"Wow, that's pretty," Violet said.

"No better view," Bren murmured. "Where to first?"

"I've got a SpotHero space lined up." She gave directions, and soon they were parked and out walking along Michigan Avenue, their heads tilted back, eyes to the sky like they were country rubes who'd never seen tall buildings before.

Bren squinted as they arrived at the Drake Hotel's lavish entrance. "This is lunch?"

"No, St. James," Violet said. "This is afternoon tea."

Within minutes, Violet knew she was in serious trouble of ruining her own chances of having children because, damn, who needed freakin' ovaries anyway? Big, bad, could-crush-a-yeti-with-a-look Bren St. James was being instructed on how to eat a scone by his daughters.

"First you do the jam, then the lemon curd," Caitriona said. "The clotted cream is last."

Bren tried his best to make his big, beefy paws do the necessary to a tiny scone. Ack, the cuteness!

The tea presented a new set of problems. "Let it steep longer. Two minutes isn't enough," Franky chided after he'd made the whopping huge mistake of pouring too soon. "And you have to use the strainer."

"I know all about tea. It was only invented in Scotland, after all."

"It was invented in China, Dad," Caitriona said.

"You sure? Pretty certain it was invented by my Granny MacGillacuddy, twice removed, on my mother's side."

His daughters giggled. "MacGillacuddly," Franky said.

"Do you think we could visit Scotland sometime, Dad?" Caitriona asked around her scone chewing.

"Why not? We can go this summer, if you like."

The girls' faces exploded in joy. "Really?"

"Aye, time you saw where you come from. I have t'warn ye, it's not a fancy castle or anythin'." Thickening Scots accent? Violet squirmed in pleasure. "In fact, where my great-granddaddy lives, it's underwater."

Caitriona screwed up her nose. "Underwater? Like a cave?"

Bren caught Violet's eye and rubbed at his beard, his tell when he was trying to hide something, usually his amusement or the truth. "No, underwater in a lake. Or as we say in Scotland, a loch. And my great-granddaddy isn't the best host. He hardly every comes out to see people, but when he does, everyone screams their heads off."

"Dad . . ." Caitriona said, catching on.

"But he'll make an exception for relatives, especially pretty little American girls. He'll probably let you hop on his slimy humped back"—he leaned in close to both of them—"before he eats you all up!"

Franky screeched with laughter. "Dad, you're not related to the Loch Ness monster! It doesn't even exist."

Bren popped a chicken salad sandwich the size of a quarter into his mouth and swallowed it without even chewing. "Are you sure about that? Plenty of people have seen him. He's just shy, like me."

Everyone giggled at the idea, none more so than Violet, who was a little too charmed by the charming

Mr. St. James. Damn, what she wouldn't give to see the man in a kilt . . .

After a few more minutes of Bren regaling them with stories of his great-granddaddy, the original Nessie, Violet noticed that Franky had gone quiet. She also seemed to be fidgeting under the table.

"Everything okay, Franks?"

"Hmm, yeah." The fidgeting continued.

"What's going on?" Violet drew back the tablecloth and found Franky getting up close and personal with one of Slugville's citizens. In a soil-bottomed jar, but still, a slug.

At afternoon tea.

Franky had taken a sliver of lettuce from one of the sandwiches and was trying to maneuver it into a slot in the jar's lid.

Caitriona leaned over. "Eww, that's gross!" Said loud enough to draw the attention of everyone in a three-table radius.

"Excuse me, miss," an oily voice whispered in Violet's ear.

Oh dear.

"So, your 'friend' has to stay in your backpack, Franky, okay?" Bren impressed upon his daughter for the fourth or fifth time. It wasn't every day a party was almost thrown out of afternoon tea at the Drake. It would have been embarrassing if it wasn't so funny.

"I know, Dad," Franky said, pushing her glasses up over her nose. She looked over her shoulder to verify that the backpack's zip was open, allowing enough oxygen to penetrate. "I only did it because they deserved to have a day off as well." Quickly, she covered her mouth and shot a guilty look at Violet, who shook her head quickly.

What was going on here? He rewound what his youngest had said, examining it for clues. But it was hard to focus on that when he was in a steel box shooting upward more than a hundred stories. His daughters wanted to come here, so he would suck it up.

"Afraid of heights, St. James?" Violet asked with a grin.

"Not particularly."

"Dad hates them," Caitriona said cheerfully. "He doesn't even like flying. That's why he wears his headphones the entire time."

"Well, he doesn't have to go to the edge," Violet said.

The elevator stopped at the Willis Tower Skydeck and vomited the entire group out—and that description wasn't too far from how Bren felt right now. The glass windows were a ways off, but Bren could see that they were up far too high. As Cat and Violet rushed to the edge, he wandered over to the video screen panels, suitably placed at the center of the floor. Here you could see what it was like to (virtually) stand 103 floors above other iconic sights like Wrigley Field and "The Bean," the nickname for the sculpture *Cloud Gate*. Much safer.

Small, precious fingers squeezed his. "I'll hold your hand so you're not scared."

He looked down at his youngest daughter, this perfect union of him and Kendra, and wondered from where she'd inherited her intellectual curiosity, smarts, and bravery. Certainly not her parents.

"Okay, sprite, lead the way."

Violet and Caitriona were already on the glass-bottomed ledge, which canted out and away from the building. Surely the height factor was enough. Did they really need to add an extra element of terror to it? There were no iron girders that Bren could see—it had been designed with some sort of invisible support system. Or a nonexistent support system.

Franky placed her forehead against the glass to study the people and cars moving around like bugs below. It was scientific for her. She still held his hand, but because he didn't want to step out so far, she was eventually forced to release him so she could get closer.

"Ah, symbolism, right?" Violet murmured beside him.

Caitriona now stood beside her sister, the two of them pressing against the window, displaying no fear whatsoever.

"I'm not quite ready to let them go just yet," he said to Violet. Their hands brushed accidentally, or maybe it was deliberate. Either way, they found each other and clasped tight.

"Having fun?"

He turned to her, drinking in her saucy smile and sparkling eyes.

"I'm miserable," he lied, but he squeezed her hand

tighter, kept his eyes on his amazing daughters, and counted every single one of his blessings.

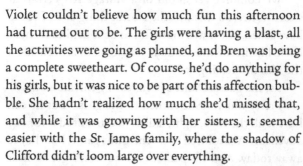

Violet couldn't believe how much fun this afternoon had turned out to be. The girls were having a blast, all the activities were going as planned, and Bren was being a complete sweetheart. Of course, he'd do anything for his girls, but it was nice to be part of this affection bubble. She hadn't realized how much she'd missed that, and while it was growing with her sisters, it seemed easier with the St. James family, where the shadow of Clifford didn't loom large over everything.

Someone else's family, a voice in her head warned. She had no illusions that this could go any further, but she'd enjoy the view for a while.

About halfway through dinner at Harry Caray's, Bren finally voiced his suspicions.

"Are we"—he looked at Violet, his daughters, then back to Violet—"reenacting *Ferris Bueller's Day Off*?"

The girls burst out laughing. "We won! We won!" Caitriona held out her hand to Violet. "Pay up."

Grumbling, Violet fished in the pocket of her jean skirt. She handed over a twenty to each of his daughters.

"We bet you couldn't go the entire day without figuring it out," Cat said, holding the bill up to the light like an expert.

"And you bet against me?" he asked Violet.

"You're not that bright. Hockey pucks to the head."

She shrugged. "How the heck would I expect you to figure it out? It's a chick flick disguised as a guy's flick."

"I like that movie." He thought for a moment. "Did we 'borrow' Dante's car like Ferris 'borrows' Cameron's?"

"We couldn't get ahold of a vintage red Ferrari at short notice, so this was the closest thing to it. I could have asked, but it was more fun to do it behind Dante's back, like in the movie. Cade was so on board. He liked the idea of 'stealing' it."

"Let me guess. Dante's been texting threats all day?"

"Pretty much." She turned to the girls. "But he can have it all the time, right, ladies? We just need it for our adventure. We wanted to do the Cubs game, but they're away today. And no parades, so we won't get to hear your dad do 'Danke Schoen.'"

"Dad's a really bad singer anyway."

"Yeah, terrible."

Bren did an impression of being insulted. "I'm not that bad. I'm better at that than Violet is at telling jokes."

"What?" Violet's mouth fell open. "I am a superior joke teller. Here's a good one: What did the ocean say to the shore?"

Bren and the girls parroted the question back at her.

"Nothing, it just waved." Groans all around, but Violet merely crossed her arms. "I don't care. It's another VV classic."

"I've got one!" Franky grinned at Violet, waiting for her nod. "Don't run with bagpipes. You could put an *aye* out." At Bren's chuckle, his youngest daughter went on. "Or get yourself kilt!"

Violet had taught the joke to Franky yesterday, and the entire table laughed much harder than it deserved. Bren's arm stretched behind his daughters' heads in the booth and stroked Violet's neck. Such a simple gesture, so comforting. She raised her eyes to find him staring with intent and mouthing *thank you*.

She tried a shoulder shrug to minimize her contribution, anything to avoid acknowledging how deeply entrenched she'd become with this beautiful family. With this beautiful man.

Once dessert was ordered—the hot fudge brownie sundae skillet—Bren left to use the restroom. The girls were looking at photos on their phones, comparing the funny-slash-terrified faces Bren had made earlier at Willis Tower. Violet checked her own phone to find a couple of new warnings from the Rebels' GM. She responded to one particularly vitriolic text with: *Is the insurance information in the glove compartment? Not finding it.*

Two seconds later, the phone rang.

"Auto body shop for Middle-Aged Phallic Compensators, how can I help you?"

Dante growled. "Tell me I have nothing to worry about."

"You have nothing to worry about."

"Why does this not make me feel better?"

"Because you tend to see the worst in people?"

"Violet . . ." He sounded so forlorn, and she realized how much she actually liked Dante Moretti.

She laughed. "Your precious is fine. Bren's been

doing the driving and he's handling the car like it's his newborn child."

"Okay, but please don't pull that stunt again." Slight pause. "How's it going?"

In that three-word query she heard a million things. She suspected Dante knew exactly what he was asking as well, so it was a surprise that her answer was so honest.

"Great. Terrible." She lowered her voice. "I don't know what I'm doing here."

Of all the people to confide in, why did she choose hard-assed Dante? Possibly because if anyone knew the perils of falling for the wrong person, it was him. She'd judged him harshly when he screwed up with Cade, but she understood now what he must have been going through. Fighting against the irresistible forces of love took an awful lot of effort.

"You're good for him," Dante said. "A stabilizing influence."

"Me? That's the last thing I'd ever be called."

"Don't underestimate yourself, Vasquez. But also, don't expect too much."

"I never do."

Dante sighed. "I don't mean because of you. Bren needs to untangle some of the knots in his life before he can be truly present. You can make him feel better, but you can't fix all his problems. You need to take care of yourself as well."

She swallowed. That was a pretty astute thing to say, and not unlike what Bren had once said about his own focus. How it would never be 100 percent on her while his life was in such turmoil. But that was okay. She refused to raise her expectations.

Just another adventure in the Year of the V. What had Ferris said? *Life moves pretty fast. If you don't stop and look around once in a while, you could miss it.*

"Oh, God," Caitriona muttered, color rising in her cheeks. Her eyes had widened to the width of the brownie sundae skillet that had just arrived, but her reaction was not dessert-related.

That's when Violet saw it. And *it* was appropriate, because several things hit her at once:

1. The Beatles singing "Twist and Shout."
2. Bren St. James strutting toward their table with—breadsticks in his hand?
3. The Scot picking up the second verse and launching into a lip-synch to end all lip-synchs.

Like Ferris in the movie.

Franky had covered her mouth with both hands, but released them to let out a squeal of delight. She didn't know where to look—at her dad, at her sister, at Violet, or at everyone in the entire dining room, who had stopped stuffing their faces and were now watching slack-jawed as one of the most famous athletes in pro sports sang to his daughters.

"Gotta go," Violet said, and hung up on Dante.

Caitriona had reddened to the roots of her hair. She shrank into her seat, trying to slip farther under the table, but her dad didn't care.

No. Her dad did what every dad has done from the dawn of time: he continued with the unrelenting embarrassment of his daughter.

Did Violet say that Bren was lip-synching? That wasn't entirely accurate. Lip-synching wasn't quite enough to get his point across; Bren was actually shout-singing over the song. And as Franky had called it earlier, he was terrible.

But he was also awesome.

Franky jumped up and started dancing, just like those German fräuleins in the movie boogying around Ferris on the parade float.

Violet turned to Caitriona, who was still blushing, but was also obviously amused. She was shaking her head, but no longer dipping it in Dad-shame. People had started clapping along, a few of them even adding their own voices to the mix.

"Come on, Cat!" Violet screamed above the hubbub, and she stood, holding out her hand. A moment's hesitation seized Violet's heart, but then the most lovely feeling overcame her. Cat placed her hand in Violet's and stood, joining just in time for the big finale.

Caitriona was the only one of them with any real talent.

But it didn't matter. Bren St. James had made his daughters' day out perfect. And if Violet wasn't already half in love with him, there was little doubt now of just how much trouble she was actually in.

TWENTY-ONE

Someone was tickling his feet. He hoped to God it wasn't Gretzky.

He cracked open one eyelid, and the sight before him melted his heart. Each of his sprites had taken charge of a foot and were doing what little girls like to do to torture their dads: painting his toenails.

This morning, he'd arrived home from LA, checked that his girls were safe, and spent close to a stalker minute outside Violet's room, his cock hard and achy, his need firing every one of his cells in want. Sleeping on the same level—and not in her bed—was impossible, so he came down to the sofa in the den. The wall clock now said 8:30 a.m., so he'd gotten just a couple of hours of shut-eye.

He blinked and raised a testing hand to his mouth. A swipe revealed no lipstick. He supposed he should be glad he hadn't woken up in full makeup.

"That's not my color," he said, though his right foot—currently being tended to by Caitriona—was being painted a very fetching blue. Something peachy was happening to his left.

Franky giggled. "We thought you were dead."

"No we didn't," Cat said. "He was snoring."

"I don't snore."

"Yes you do. Doesn't he, Violet?"

"Like a foghorn."

She stood at the door, wearing a skirt that looked like a puffy black sponge, silver kneesocks, and red Chuck Taylors. It had been three days since the St. James Clan's Day Off, since Violet had made his kids feel like the treasures he knew them to be. He didn't think he'd ever forget the sight of her dancing and singing in Harry Caray's. All that free-spirited exuberance made his heart glow.

"Did you guys congratulate your dad on how well he played?"

"He knows," Cat said, her focus on painting his little toe.

"He'd still appreciate hearing it."

Cat rolled her eyes. "Good job, Dad."

"Thanks, Caitriona."

"Finished!" Franky said. "Next customer." She looked up at Violet, determination in the set of her pink-bud mouth. "The salon is open."

"Okay, but just my hands. Been a while since I had a manicure."

Violet sat at one end of the sofa while Franky took a spot between them.

"Everything go okay here?" Bren raised his gaze to find Violet's fixed to his bare chest. He rubbed his mouth to hide his grin at the thought of being ogled. "Violet?"

"What? Oh, right. Yes! Fine. We found another tenant for Slugville, though I think it's turning into Slumlord Ville. Too many occupants in too small a space."

Franky made a sound of discontent. "They like being close together. Like family."

"What about you, Cat? Get any piano practice in?"

"Nope," his oldest said, but her gaze found Violet's, secrets in her eyes.

He caught a quick wink from Violet to Cat, which was mighty encouraging. Cat in a good mood and sharing something with Violet? A foreign warmth flooded his chest, and he didn't even mind that he was out of the loop. Feeling happy and relaxed, he waited to speak until Franky finished Violet's nails with a green polish.

"You guys had breakfast yet?" The girls were still in PJs, so it was possible.

"Nope," said Franky, then, with imploring eyes, asked, "Can we make an apple pie later?"

His heart soared. "Course we can, but go on and have some breakfast first. I'll join you in a second."

Once they were out of the room, he waited a moment, then pounced.

"Bren," Violet gasped as he pulled her into his lap. Her fluffy skirt was no match for his hands, which soon found home wrapped around the curves of Violet's amazing ass. She couldn't resist him or else she'd mess up her just-polished nails.

"Hi," he whispered against her ear, then added a nip.

Her low moan went straight to his dick. "Bren, did

you just send your kids to the kitchen so you can feel up the nanny?"

"Maybe."

"Uh, not cool." She scrambled off his lap and put a foot of frustration between them. "Did you see that someone posted a video of us on Facebook?"

Another restaurant customer had shot footage of them having a good time dancing away. Rebels PR had run with it: anything to prove he was a rehabilitated human.

"Is that a problem?"

"You said yourself we shouldn't confuse the kids."

"It was just a day out organized by the woman who looks after my girls."

"And now people will read into it."

"And that's bad because?"

"Come on, Bren. The hot athlete hooking up with the nanny? The multimillion-dollar pro in the cross-hairs of the gold digger with no marketable skills beyond her world-class ass?"

This wasn't what he'd expected when he woke up to a pedicure. "Violet, you are a woman of means. No one is going to think you're after me for my money. Christ, your share of the franchise has to be worth five times my contract. So what if you don't care about running it? Your worth isn't determined by what you contribute to the Rebels organization and its bottom line."

Her worth to him was immeasurable, and not just because of how amazing she was with the girls. He hazarded a guess as to what was going on here.

"I know you're worried about the surgery tomorrow."

She folded her arms, clearly uncomfortable. "Maybe a little."

"I'm going to ask Skylar to watch the girls so I can be with you."

Now she looked at him as if he'd grown three heads. "Why would you want to do that?"

"To be supportive."

"Bren, that's not necessary. Harper and Isobel are insisting on going with me. Cade, too, though I told him I've got this."

Jealousy flared. Ridiculous, perhaps, but Cade should not be the one holding her hand.

"I'd like to be there."

She grimaced. "You show up and people will start asking questions. Assigning motives."

"They can assign whatever motives they want."

"No, they can't, Bren. What's happening between us is great, but it doesn't extend to that kind of stuff. I want to keep it simple."

Simple? They'd moved far beyond simple. That last time at her cottage, he'd shared things with her that he'd never told a living soul. But he was seeing now that it was a one-way street. Violet wouldn't open up unless he unsealed her with a crowbar.

"I don't really do simple."

She went wide-eyed. "This is temporary. This job, you and me, my time in Chicago. All of it."

"Right, because you're just here while your one-third investment in the Rebels gets more valuable."

Hurt flashed in her eyes, and he immediately regretted his sharp words. "Violet, I—"

She gave the hand of *shut up*. "Right now, you have the trifecta: child care, laundry, and no-strings sex. Though I wouldn't count on that last one anytime soon. Don't complicate it." And then she flounced out of the room.

If there was anyone worth getting complicated for, it was this amazing woman who was doing her best to push him away.

"You really don't have to be here. I know you have stuff to do."

Violet watched as Harper fluffed a pillow for the seventieth time. It happened to be one of the firmer sofa pillows that were resistant to fluffing, but that made no odds to Harper. She bashed and shaped it to her will, then placed it in its original spot on Violet's sofa in the cottage.

"I'm happy to be here," Harper said in a voice that was a little high pitched.

"What's going on?"

"Other than the fact my sister had serious surgery this morning?"

"Outpatient surgery," Isobel muttered around a salted caramel from the stash Addison had brought by earlier. The procedure to remove Violet's lipoma had lasted thirty minutes and she'd been awake the entire time. So, the least dramatic surgery ever.

"I'm fine, Harper." She lifted her arm and pointed at the bandage that would stay on for a couple of days. "Now in a fat-free version."

"Well, your armpit is," Isobel said, barely looking up from a copy of *Sports Illustrated* with the Rebels on the cover. "As for the rest of you—"

"Leave my ass out of this," Violet said with a finger point.

Harper twitched her nose. "Look, we couldn't be there for you last time, so we just want to be sure we're doing all we can this time. Like a real family."

Isobel shared a mischievous look with Violet before announcing in the most deadpan tone ever, "Sure. Great job, Harper. Your pillow-fluffing abilities are without equal."

"Oh, shut it," Harper said, throwing the just-fluffed pillow at Isobel's head. She sat down and relaxed for the first time since this morning at the hospital. Faced with Harper in CEO mode, the doctor and her staff had been very afraid.

"I know you think I'm crazy, but when my mom was going through her health issues, I sometimes think I didn't do enough. I so wanted to be out of there." She looked off in the direction of Chase Manor, a couple of hundred feet from the room where they were sitting. Harper's mom had died of ovarian cancer when Harper was seventeen, so this was clearly a sore spot. "I don't want you thinking that all we Chase girls are good for is wine chugging, eighties movies marathons, and inappropriate ceramic sculptures. That we don't know how to do the important stuff."

"She knows, Harper," Isobel said, not quite as blasé as before. "But if you keep this level of nutjobbery up, she's going to be cutting and running before the season is over. Stop being so . . . you!"

Everyone laughed, even Harper, whose eyes had misted over. She knuckled the welling moisture away. "So, is that still the plan? You want to sell your share of the team to us and travel the world?"

Isobel was paying closer attention now, waiting on Violet's answer.

"The team means everything to you, but it doesn't have a similar pull for me. I don't contribute in the same way and I need to figure out what comes next."

Since her diagnosis, she'd been treating her life as a do-over. Trying new things, grabbing life by the balls, the Year of the V. Now that she was a woman of means, she could travel. Maybe get a degree in education. No more working in bars or low-rent tattoo parlors.

You're just here while your one-third investment in the Rebels gets more valuable.

"Not everyone has to work for the family business," Harper said. "And there are plenty of other reasons to stay."

"*Aye*, plenty," Isobel said with a wink.

Violet glared at her, then quickly moved to throw Harper off the scent and put her at ease. "Don't worry, you're not getting rid of me that easily. The peanut needs a cool aunt, don't you think? The kind who drops in unexpectedly from her world travels with crazy stories about swimming with dolphins and hooking up with hot hung guys on long train rides."

Harper sniffed at that.

"Oh, God, you're going to set her off again," Isobel groaned.

"What's this?" A deep voice sounded from the entrance to the living room. Moving closer, Remy placed a giant stockpot and two Whole Foods bags on the floor. "Minou, can I not leave you alone for a second? Every time I turn around, you have tears in your eyes."

"I'm fine! We're all fine!" Harper stood and threw her arms around her man. They stared at each other for a long moment, which was sort of embarrassing to watch.

Isobel coughed. "Cool it, sex fiends."

"Did someone call for a sex fiend?" Another bass was added to the mix, this one with a distinctly foreign flavor to it.

Isobel grinned at her boyfriend, Vadim, who had come in behind Remy. "Hey, Russian."

He bent over and kissed her chastely on the forehead. "You are right. We shall keep our shocking antics private. Best not to make others jealous of our wonderful sex life."

"Keep up your winning ways and there's a handie in it for you, babe. A BJ if you score more than once."

Violet rounded on Isobel, her mouth open in wonder. "You're holding out unless he wins?"

"Too right," Isobel said with a wicked grin. "A good coach works on the incentive model."

With an eye roll appropriate to his Russian-ness, Vadim abandoned his coach and kissed Violet on the cheek. "How is my future sister-in-law?"

The shocks, they kept on coming. "Your future sister-in-law is feeling great, but a little confused. What have I missed?"

All eyes turned to Isobel, who had developed a water-color bloom in her cheeks. "So he asked and I said . . . maybe."

"*Maybe?*" A chorus of horrified voices called out, except for Vadim, who looked remarkably unruffled.

"She wishes for the team to win the Cup first. Our relationship has always operated on incentives. This is no different." He took a seat on the sofa beside Violet. "And as I know we will win, I am calling you my future sister-in-law. Though you will always be my tattoo twin first."

Vadim and Violet spent most of their quality time together comparing their respective ink. It was good to have hobbies.

Remy narrowed his eyes at Petrov. "There's no certainty in play-off hockey, Russe. Take it from the guy who's lost three finals. And I sure as hell don't need you jinxing it with that kind of talk."

The team was flying out to LA in a couple of days, with the semifinals series tied at 3 all. So far, they had been playing like their lives, careers, and children's futures depended on it. No one could quite believe it, but it certainly made for great TV. The ratings were the best the NHL had seen in years, and one more win would send them to the Stanley Cup finals.

"We talking about Petrov's proposal again?" Cade walked in, followed by Dante. Damn, it was like Grand Central Station in here. The Texan cupped Violet's face and planted a sloppy kiss on her forehead. "How's that weight loss program workin' out, chica?"

She laughed and made a big to-do of wiping off his smooch. "Pretty good. And how come you know about Petrov's proposal and I don't? Some BFF you are."

"Hell, he's been yammerin' on about it for so long I figured the whole world and his uncle Jerome had heard about it." Cade slid onto the sofa on Violet's other side. "Move it, girl. Where's Lord St. James?"

Violet schooled her features to blank. "Watching the girls, I suppose."

"Thought maybe he'd be here wowing us all with his Ferris Bueller dance moves like in that Facebook video. The voice, though. Brutal." He delivered a smartass grin and she stuck out her tongue in return.

Dante's smile was far too knowing. "You hungry, Vasquez?"

"Starving. I think Remy might have brought something, though."

"Uh-oh," Cade muttered. "Dante *also* brought something. Ingredients for pasta puttanesca."

All attention shot to the chefs, watching as the two men sized each other up, kitchen masters about to throw down. This could get ugly real fast.

"DuPre," Dante said, all gravity.

"Moretti," Remy replied, equally serious.

Both were the same age, had been drafted the same

year, were formerly coworkers in Boston, and could destroy a room with a blue-eyed stare. While Dante had been out of the game for over ten years because of injury, he still dined off his reputation for never backing down.

The face-off continued for a good ten seconds until Violet finally said: "For God's sake, you're both pretty! Share my tiny kitchen, make all the food, and I guarantee you I will eat every last bite."

"Right answer, future sister-in-law," Remy said, and at everyone's bug-eyed expressions, he chuckled. "Now, *mes amis*, it's not a done deal yet—"

"Because you haven't asked!" Harper exclaimed.

Remy turned to her, his face filled with such love Violet's heart clamped hard.

"Last I checked you're a kick-ass, take-no-prisoners woman in charge *and* we're livin' in the twenty-first century where women are perfectly capable of making marriage proposals." At Harper's dropped jaw, he held up a hand. "But I'm a bit of a throwback and won't be standing for that kind of nonsense. *I'll* be doing the asking, and soon. I won't be placing any conditions on it, either, like winning the Cup and whatnot, and neither will you. My momma would never forgive me if I didn't make an honest woman out of you, minou."

"Marrying me to please his momma." Harper sighed. "Be still my heart."

Everyone laughed at that while Remy scooped up Harper and kissed her thoroughly.

Violet smiled at a winking Cade, a wobbly smile

quivering her lips. Every day she spent here, she fell deeper and deeper in love with this crew of people. Her sisters, the guys, the Sc—

Best not to go there.

He had offered to come with her to the surgery. More than offered. Insisted. And she'd shut him down because she didn't want to let him into this part of her life. Lines had been crossed, confidences exchanged, hearts engaged. Hers, for sure.

He'd called a couple of times to check in on how she was, and she'd played the coward and texted him back that she was *fine! Absolutely fine!* He knew she'd have a posse to take care of her. She wasn't his problem and all his energy had to be for his girls. She told herself this, was quite insistent. She admired his dedication, especially after her own experience without a father.

Yet, why did her heart ache as if *it* had been removed instead of that fatty underarm lump?

TWENTY-TWO

"Violet."

She jerked awake, and for a hellish moment thought she was back in Rusty's Biker Emporium in Reno. This reaction might have had something to do with the scary-looking beard leaning over her. Quickly, she sat up, realizing that she had fallen asleep on the sofa. Yep, that was drool dampening the plush pillow beneath her head.

Bearded Biker Dude looked annoyed, but she set that aside because he also looked hot. A smart blue button-down shirt contrasted nicely with a charcoal sports jacket and dark wash jeans. Some sort of styling goo had structured his hair.

"Bren?"

"You left the door open," he said sternly. "Anyone could have walked in."

"It just seemed easier. Everyone wants to visit, so why not let them in without me answering the door all the time?" She stretched, then winced at the tug to the two-day-old-and-still-healing wound under her arm. "What time is it?"

"Seven in the evening." He plunked down on the sofa beside her, his big body taking up a ton of space. "How are you?"

"A little sore, but just glad it's out. The doctor called this afternoon with the pathology results. Completely benign."

He exhaled and nodded, clasped her hand, and remained silent. The quiet stretched for a while—not unpleasant. She loved how easy it was with him. She usually felt a need to fill gaps, entertain the masses, be "on," but not with Bren.

"I'm sorry I got pushy the other day," he finally said. "About attending the surgery. I just don't like the idea of sitting around, not helping."

"You've helped." He had no idea how much. She was trying her best not to confuse either of them, and in the process, she might have come down on him too hard. "I should have let you hang with me, but I don't want anyone getting the wrong idea." *Especially me.*

He stared at her, into her. She suspected it would be best for her mental well-being to look away, but it seemed she had no idea what was good for her.

"If you're up for going out, I'd like to take you to dinner, Violet."

Dinner? Had he not heard a word she just said?

"It's only dinner, not a marriage proposal. While I'm crazy about my kids, right now I'd love some adult conversation with a funny, sexy, beautiful woman. And wouldn't you like to get away from everyone for a bit?"

He had a point. He had also called her funny, sexy, and beautiful. "Where are the girls?"

"With Skylar. I gave that Jeremy kid the stink eye for a good thirty seconds. Pretty sure he won't try anything."

"He's twelve."

"He's male."

She let it go, because Bren in protective papa-bear mode was both adorable and sexy.

"Current ensemble working for you?" She gestured to her oversized Rebels tee and tube socks. No need to gesture toward her three-days-without-washing hair and her lack of makeup. Best not to overwhelm him with *too* much hotness.

"It's working far too well."

"You silver-tongued devil." Heart thumping madly, she blinked at the Bren-grade intensity waving off him. "Can I shower?"

"Uh, please do."

He got a Harper-fluffed pillow in the face for that one.

━━━━⌐━━━━

Bren drove them to the West Loop in downtown Chicago, where they ended up in a fancy hipster restaurant called Smith & Jones. The Scot's hand on her hip guiding her through the dense crowd waiting for a table felt acutely possessive and wholly magnificent.

Murmurs of recognition buzzed around them, yet no one approached the unapproachable captain of the

Rebels. After Bren gave his name to the hostess, they were told their table would take a moment to be ready. In that several-second stretch, Bren drank her in.

Perhaps she shouldn't have worn this magenta jersey dress, but it was draped loosely enough so as not to aggravate her wound, and that looseness created a little gap in the cleavage area. Her date didn't seem to mind. His gaze was molten fire over her skin, taking an exacting inventory of her breasts, hips, thighs, all the way down to her high heels. While her fashion sense was considered "unique" according to Harper, tonight's outfit was conventionally sexy.

"Stop staring," she muttered.

Evidently encouraged by her self-consciousness, he dug his fingers into her waist. "Why?"

"People are taking notice. You're sort of famous, y'know?"

Those dominant fingers slid to her ass, a move hidden from the view of those around them. Bren's appreciation for her booty knew no end.

"You look gorgeous tonight, Violet."

She loved how her name sounded on his lips, like a mini aria. *Vi-oh-let.*

"And you look very pretty, too."

His smile reached all the way to his eyes, and he leaned in to graze his lips against her ear. "Maybe we should skip dinner. I spotted a dark alley near where we parked the car."

That sounded lovely and dangerous and she wasn't all that hungry anyway.

"Your table's ready!"

On their way to being seated, a surly, tatted badass in a chef's jacket saluted Bren from the kitchen's entrance. Bren saluted him right back. The place was packed to the gills, and soon they found themselves in a cozy spot far enough away from the bar to feel private. The perks of being a famous hockey player, she supposed.

Bren held out her chair. She might have swooned, which is why she sat quickly.

Once Bren had seated himself, a shadow entered her peripheral vision. She looked up, expecting a server, but was instead confronted with a movie-star-handsome man, about one notch above Moretti, which was saying something, because their GM was a gift to men and women the world over.

This guy sported a designer suit, flawless bone structure, and a charming smirk. Beside him stood a smiling pregnant woman with a shock of red-brown hair. Around her upper arms, tattooed Celtic bands celebrated—or venerated—the names SEAN and LOGAN.

"I'm sorry to interrupt," she gushed to Bren, taking Violet in with her blinding grin. "But I'm a huge fan and I just wanted to wish you guys luck in LA."

Bren stood, holding out his hand. "Mrs. Dempsey-Cooper, it's a pleasure to meet you. This is my—Violet."

Violet's heart jumped into her throat and barely stuck the landing. *My—Violet.*

"Oh, call me Alex," the woman said, shaking Violet's hand with a firm grip. "And this is my husband, Eli."

Violet recognized them now. The mayor and the

firefighter, a couple who had blown up the Internet a couple of years ago when *she* saved his life in a fire and *he* tanked a mayoral election to prove he loved her. To have someone adore you that much . . . Violet couldn't begin to imagine a guy making a sacrifice that major for her.

"Great to meet you. When are you due?"

"Two months and a week, give or take," Eli said, his pride evident. He slung an arm around his wife's hip. "And then it'll be a battle to keep her off the fire truck."

"It's where I'm meant to be." Alex smiled at Violet. "I expect you hear stuff like that all the time, being a woman in a male-dominated profession."

"My sisters hear it more. I'm not that involved with running the team." But she liked Alex's sentiment all the same. *It's where I'm meant to be.* Violet's contribution to the Rebels might be minimal, but she was starting to think she might have found her place.

"We'll let you get back to your evening," Eli said, tugging gently on his wife. "The whole town is rooting for you, Captain. Good luck."

Bren nodded again, and they both watched as the most perfect couple in the history of perfect couples walked away.

"You know their story?" Bren asked as he re-took his seat.

"I read all about it when it happened. The kind of tale that keeps a city enthralled." Sort of like a luckless NHL franchise run by three women, a gay guy, and a reformed alcoholic who were now on the cusp of the biggest moment of their lives.

The waiter stopped by and asked about drinks.

"Just water, thanks," Violet said.

"You'd like wine," Bren stated. "Unless you're still on pain meds."

"I'm not, but—" She wanted to be respectful of his struggle.

"She'll have a glass of Malbec."

The waiter nodded and left.

"How did you know that's my favorite wine?"

"I know."

The notion that this man had watched her long enough to file away her wine preferences took her breath away. But then Bren St. James had been stealing life-giving oxygen from the moment she saw him.

"And you don't need to think of me when you order a drink. I've been resisting temptation for a long time. A total of nine months, one week, three days, and seven hours, in fact, give or take a few minutes."

That didn't sound right. "I thought you were sober for almost a year."

"Aye, a year today."

Her chest flushed with pride. "Congratulations. That's quite an achievement."

"Thanks." He smiled, a little shyly, and she melted into a puddle in the seat.

"But if you're sober for a year, what did you mean about resisting temptation for nine months . . . ?"

"One week, three days, and seven hours? That refers to a different temptation. That commemorates the day I left rehab and happened to be in the Empty Net when three 'fans' decided I needed to hear their opinion on my shortcomings."

The day she came across him in that near bar fight.

The day she found out about Clifford's will.

The day she made a very unsubtle pass at Bren.

The temptation he spoke of was *her*.

And he'd counted down to the moment when he finally succumbed.

Luckily she didn't have to respond immediately, because the waiter appeared with her Malbec and launched into a recitation of the restaurant's specials. It all sounded amazing.

Once he'd left, she could have glossed over what Bren had said, but she didn't want to. It was too important and she was tired of eliding the big stuff.

"The day I met you, you'd just left rehab, and you ordered a drink. As a test?"

"Yes." He chuckled as if it was the most amusing thing in the world. At catching her serious expression, he stopped. "I can joke about it now. Back then, I wanted to see how far I'd come. I had no idea that the real temptation would appear before me in the guise of a woman." He said *woman* like it rhymed with *devil*.

"I'm not some biblical temptress."

His eyebrow disagreed.

"Okay, maybe a little. I mean, look at me." Preening a touch, she fluttered her eyelashes and drew his rough chuckle. "I just saw something I wanted. I didn't even know who you were until you started banging on about whether I recognized you. Then I just thought you were some overpaid, entitled asshole—who I happened to own, by the way."

Both of them met in that bar, at a crossroads in their lives, only he didn't respond to her overture.

"Seems my dick-raising powers were having an off day."

"I'd spent a couple of years making bad decisions, and fucking some stranger in a bar restroom wasn't really how I wanted to start over. Yet I'm guessing that this was how *you* wanted to start over."

"Perhaps. I'd just left the lawyer's office, where he told me I was part owner of the Rebels. Clifford had given me nothing but a few tuition checks when he was alive, but now he'd decided to throw me into the deep end with running his beloved team. I was going to sell, get out of there, run away, but I saw you. And—" What was she thinking, telling him all this?

"And?"

"I thought a quick, anonymous hookup would be a good way to exorcise some demons, I suppose. The first time since my surgery. Don't worry, I realize your reject-ing me wasn't personal."

Not even a hint of a smile. After a moment, he spoke, as if forced to summon the words from some deep, dank pit. "Violet, it was immensely personal."

"Okay, no need to drill it home."

"No, listen. Choosing not to screw an engaging and gorgeous woman I'd just met was a personal decision to respect you and myself. I had no legitimate hopes of seeing you again, but if it had happened, I wouldn't have wanted some quick rut in the bathroom of the Empty Net to be the abiding memory of how we first connected. Turning you down in that way was personal because sex for me, and I think for you, is very personal. Despite your pretending otherwise."

This isn't what she wanted to hear, yet somehow it was exactly what she *needed* to hear. Why couldn't Bren St. James keep things flirty and sexy? Why did everything with the Scot have to be intense to the nth degree?

She changed the subject. "So you knew Clifford. What was he like?" Out of the frying pan, perhaps, but something she could handle.

"Your sisters haven't told you?"

"I haven't asked them, to be honest. They each have their own biases. Harper hated him, Isobel loved him. Of course, Iz recognizes now that he was an asshole, but she worshipped him for a long time so it's hardest for her. She's incredibly conflicted."

"Cliff was the kind of man who produced polarizing opinions across the board. Great player, decent coach, terrible manager."

"And how did he fare as a man?"

He tore off a piece of bread in a basket. "Not the best. But it's hard to be a good man in this day and age."

So not true. Bren St. James was one of the best men she knew, his effort all the more astonishing given the struggle he went through every day.

"Why are you making excuses for him?"

"We all have faults. The man was an asshole, but he was still your father. I'll respect that, because without him you wouldn't be here." He followed this up with some top-notch eye-fucking of the Scottish variety. "When did you find out Cliff was your father?"

"When I was thirteen. My grandmother was ill and had just been moved into a nursing home. My mom was working double shifts at a diner just to make ends meet. But I was going to a private Catholic school and I started asking questions about how we could afford it. I'd visit my grandmother, and one day, she told me."

"You'd never asked your mom?"

"I had, but she always said he'd never wanted to know us. That part was true, but . . ."

"But?"

She inhaled a quick breath. "What I didn't realize was that my mother had known who he was the night she met him in Caesar's in Vegas. She'd targeted him. Saw a way out of her hand-to-mouth existence and got herself knocked up. On purpose."

Not unlike that story she'd heard from Skylar about Kendra. She assessed his expression, waiting for judgment. None came.

She rushed on. "He knew from Day One. Pre–Day One, actually. He agreed to child support, but for my schooling, he paid the bills directly to St. Ita's so my mom couldn't use it for something else."

"Once you knew who he was, what did you do?"

She smiled, loving that he understood she'd not be the kind of girl who sat on that kind of knowledge. "I wrote him a letter because I thought there was no way he wouldn't want to see me. If he paid for my schooling, it was because he wanted me raised a certain way. To give me the advantages befitting a daughter of Clifford Chase, and he was just biding his time until I was ready. Until I was molded to his liking."

Bren's eyes on her were as hot as a dragon's breath. She'd never told anyone this before. Not the whole story, straight through.

"I wanted to meet him. I wanted to know if I was like him. If I had his temper or his sense of humor. If he was the reason my eyes are green with little flecks of gold. I wanted—I—" She got stuck. She felt stuck.

He grasped her hand, rubbed a thumb along her pulse. Soothing. Inciting. "You wanted."

"Yes." Relief that he understood bolted through her. "I loved my mom, my gran, my aunts, but a piece of me needed to know. His lawyer called and said Clifford would come see me. While I waited for him to show up in a big black town car and whisk me away to afternoon tea, I did my research. I watched clips of his games. I even went to a hockey match—that's what I used to call them because I hadn't a clue—just so I could say I'd done that when we met. Isn't that nuts?"

Her voice had emerged high, unrecognizable, in an uncontrollable gush.

"I looked for pictures of his wives, and especially his daughters, online. These sisters I didn't know. These sisters I wanted to know."

She couldn't stop talking now. Bren said nothing while she babbled like a fool. She swiped at her eyes, unable to force out the hurtful truth.

Finally Bren spoke it for her: "He didn't show."

"No," she whispered, the shock of it still a slice through her heart. "Sounds like I was better off. How he treated Harper and Iz, the pressure they both lived under being his daughters—well, I had a lucky escape."

She told herself this every day. Clifford Chase had stayed away. *Lucky*. Her boobs were scooped out and replaced. *Lucky*. Denny had revealed his true colors and she'd kicked his Jag-driving ass to the curb. *Lucky*. These days, she made her own luck, and she didn't rely on anyone.

But she could so easily rely on someone. Her sisters. Her new friends.

This man.

How could she have let herself get caught up in this temporary life that felt more real and permanent than anything she'd ever experienced?

"He was a fool," Bren said. "About a lot of things, but mostly about his daughters. However, he made up for it with that will. Best thing he could have ever done."

"Forcing us to jump through hoops to run the team?"

"Bringing you all together. You stayed to get to know them."

No, she didn't. She stayed because Bren St. James piqued her interest that day in the Empty Net. Because he still drew her like a magnet to his metal.

And she would eventually leave for the same reason.

TWENTY-THREE

Harper threw a Memorial Day cookout every year, but it was usually held postseason and poorly attended by the players. Iz said that they were invariably sick to death of each other and their failure of a season.

But this year was different. The boys were Western Conference champions! Two nights ago, the Rebels had won game seven in LA. All the players and the WAGs were here, enjoying that moment when they were winners before the next stage when they might lose it all. The day after tomorrow, they would fly to Boston for the first game of the Stanley Cup finals.

Violet might not be a fan, but even she knew it was a huge deal. Throughout the early rounds, the Rebels were the underdogs, which was exactly how they liked it. From this point forward, there was no slipping under the radar. They'd proved they deserved to be here. Boston would be ready.

Under the big Congrats, Western Conference Champions sign strung between two oak trees (Cade and Erik had nearly broken their necks hanging it up), the party partied on. Large metal tongs in hand, Remy hovered over the Weber grill as big as a Cadillac, wearing an apron that said: Your Opinion Is Not Part of the Recipe. Love was in the air, happiness was all around. Even Gretzky tried to get in on the action, wooing Gordie Howe, the yappy little pom belonging to Mia, Vadim's sister. It felt like the official start of summer, like only good days lay ahead.

Near the large picnic table set up for the salads and burger fixings, Harper cast her gaze about frantically. Violet waved a hand in front of her. "What do you need, Fearless Leader?"

Big sis rolled her eyes, pretending she didn't like the moniker, but they all knew better. Harper was born to run this former shitshow of a team. The same might be said for the family.

"I need a spoon for this potato salad."

"On it."

Charged with her task, Violet walked into the kitchen at Chase Manor to find a very pretty sight: Cade and Dante in a lip-lock. They still hadn't seen her, and the big serving spoon was right there on the kitchen island . . . She reached for it, but a noise behind her put her on notice.

Franky stood there with her head cocked curiously, as if the boys were a couple of slugs in her care.

"Are they allowed to do that?" she asked Violet loudly.

"Sh—shoot!" Cade pulled away from Dante. "Didn't realize anyone was here."

"Clearly not," Violet said cheerfully, then to Franky, "They're allowed. Boys can kiss other boys."

Franky folded her arms. "I know that. I mean because Dante is everybody's boss."

Oh, good question. "Cade, care to explain the murky politics of workplace relationships to Franky here?"

"Well, Francesca"—he always called her that and it always made her smile—"sometimes bosses need to be kissed. Right, Vi?" He winked at her. She scratched her nose, giving him the middle finger. After seeing that Facebook video, he'd finally forced from her the truth of her ongoing fling with Bren. Needless to say, he was enjoying this information immensely.

"So, honey, you need something?" Violet asked Franky.

"I just came in to get my backpack." She headed off to another room in the house.

Cade shook his head. "It's a different world."

Dante had remained silent this entire time, but now he leaned in and kissed Cade's lips lightly. "Later." Passing her by, he said, "Vasquez."

"Moretti," she said with mock gravity to equal his. "Here, do me a favor and take this spoon out to Harper."

They both watched him leave and join Harper outside. "So, sneaking away for stolen kisses, Alamo?"

Cade smiled. "Dante's an ass grabber, so we figure we should keep that for special."

She didn't smile back.

"Vi, I've already told you how we're handling this. Most everyone on the team knows or suspects, so it's not really a secret. We just don't want to shove it in everyone's faces."

She still didn't like it. It felt disrespectful. "Don't tell me you wouldn't want to have him claim you in front of everyone."

"He did. The day I went public, he kissed me in the Rebels' front office!"

"And then everyone was sworn to secrecy until *he's* ready to talk about it."

Cade crossed his arms. "What's this about? Yeah, I know you care and I know you're nosy—a pretty lethal combo—but I also know that you're not the kind of person to dictate how other people conduct their sex lives."

She squirmed, aware that she was projecting her own past hurt on Cade's situation. "I just don't like secrets, especially ones that have the capacity to make people feel disrespected or unloved or small. You've come so far these past few months and I don't want to see your wings clipped at this stage."

Cade pulled her into his arms. "Thank you."

"But you've got this?"

"I do. All the same, thank you."

Still holding each other, they went back to looking out the window. Bren stood off to the side, a Coke in his hand, nodding at something Vadim was explaining with dramatic hand gestures. He still managed to keep one eye on Franky, who was on slug watch in Chase Manor's flower beds.

"Made any travel plans yet?"

"What?"

"That's what you said you wanted to do," Cade continued. "As soon as the season was over, you were heading out, around the world, and no hot Scot was going to get in your way."

She narrowed her eyes. "Stop fishing."

He clutched his chest dramatically. "Wouldn't dream of it! I mean, it's not like you ever stick your nose into my business. Just curious about your plans."

"You think they involve a hot Scot?"

"I think he hasn't taken his eyes off you in the past nine months and he's not going to let you go easily."

Did Bren want her in that way, a more permanent part of his life? She assessed the scene in the yard, all these people loving and laughing and living. Maybe she could do this. Accept the love that people wanted to give her.

She sought safer territory. "Is Dante pissed because Remy's doing all the cooking?"

"Yep. But he brought a vat of pasta salad to save face."

"Hey, why you hiding in here?"

Violet jumped at the sound of Bren's voice as he stepped into the kitchen, promptly spilling half a glass of white wine down the front of her Bitch Please T-shirt. "Shit!"

"Sorry, love, didn't mean to startle you." He took in the situation. "Are you hiding in here to have a drink?"

"Of course not—no—" She threw up her hands. "Okay,

yes! I'm secretly imbibing because I'm aiming for solidarity and failing miserably."

This woman. "Vi, I've told you that you don't have to do that. I would never have you change the habits of a lifetime—"

"Hey!"

He grinned. "You don't have to sneak off to have an adult beverage because your boyfriend is an alcoholic. I've tasted alcohol on your beautiful lips before and it didn't turn me into a raging hulk. Were you planning on not kissing me tonight?"

"No," she grumbled. "I thought I'd gargle so you never knew."

"I remember that trick. There was a time I was as expert in brands of mouthwash as I was in whiskey." He wrapped his arms around her.

"You used the B-word," she said.

"Beverage?"

"Boyfriend."

He had. "Just popped out of my mouth, all natural like. How did it sound?"

"I—I don't know."

He remained silent, leaving her to think on it. Violet's mind tended to run a mile a minute and she often needed time to hash things out.

"Let's not rush anything," she finally said. "Take it slow."

He wrapped his hand around hers and dragged her through the kitchen and down a hallway until they reached a door that led to the laundry room.

"Bren, we can't—"

"But we can." He closed the door and pinned her against it, his hardness finding the perfect welcome against all her softness. His hand slid up the back of her thighs, one finger brushing over the thin scrap of material between her legs. "This slow enough?"

She dropped her forehead to his shoulder and closed her eyes, trusting that he would alert her if someone crashed the party. "Slow . . . enough?"

"You said we should take it slow."

Her ass in his hands was a miracle. Her mouth against his was divine. He should question this hot burn of lust, how it inevitably led a man to damnation, but the heaven of her kiss was crowding out all other considerations.

Her hand cupped his cock, the heel of it rubbing hard against his growing erection. He liked to think he had more stamina now that he'd been getting some semiregularly—but with Violet, everything was so urgent. So needy.

He wasn't sure if it was lust driving them or something else that smacked of quiet desperation, a realization that their time was counting down to a conclusion. One he would not like. He might be a champion at the end, but it would mean nothing without her in his life.

She fisted his T-shirt. "Bren, I need—"

"I got what you need, *mo chroí*." My heart. That's what she was and that's what she owned. He could bargain with her. *Stay. Be mine. I'll worship you with everything I have. My mouth, my body, my soul.*

It was either the worst or the best time to initiate this.

He decided it was the worst. Maybe his dick was running the show. More likely, his heart was afraid of what it would hear. That she might not want him.

"Turn around, baby. Show me that ass."

He whipped her away from him and dragged her hips forward. She placed her hands on the wall while he took a moment to appreciate her form. That high, well-rounded ass, the cleft between that he wanted to drive into deep and true. A slide of his fingers under her skirt put him back in familiar country.

She moaned, a little loudly. He placed his palm across her mouth and leaned in over her shoulder. "Maybe this is a bad idea. 'Cause you like to scream and I like to hear it."

"I ca—" Something muffled.

He released his hand. "What?"

"I can be quiet," she rasped.

"If you can't, someone might hear." He continued to stroke through that soft, receptive flesh between her thighs, drawing new moisture that made the slide so slick and hot.

She grabbed his hand and placed it over her mouth. "Do it. Please."

This was crazy and dangerous, but Violet made him like this. Reckless and wild. He'd thought it was the worst of himself coming to the fore, the slippery slope to Bad Bren, but he realized now that it was the best. Violet made him want to be a better man, one who was good enough to hold her.

He would fight to keep her. Burying his body inside her would be a good start.

He unzipped and released his cock, already primed and seeking her wet heat. She was swiveling her hips, teasing him, begging him to take her. Securing the condom took a few seconds longer than he would have liked, but then it was done and he was sliding into her tight, hot channel.

Jesus. She gripped and pulsed the moment he entered and screamed against his hand. She was already coming, milking him to bring him up to speed. But he could last a little longer and coax another orgasm from her.

He moved his lips to her ear. "Couldn't wait, huh? That greedy pussy of yours is already taking its due before I've had a chance to make it better for you?"

Slamming hard into her, he sucked at her neck. "Going to fuck you harder now and you're going to take everything I've got to give you. You're going to beg me for more and then you're going to make me beg."

"Oh," she moaned. "Oh." And then nothing but their ragged breaths, their booming heartbeats. Nothing but them.

"Love it when you go all quiet. That's when I know you're close. You're right there on the edge."

She was panting now, and then her legs were buckling, and she bit down on his hand as she fell apart in his arms.

"Dios mío!" The words were raspy, barely grated out, as he thrust into her over and over. With every pump, his heart responded with *this, this, this*. On the descent, he felt like nothing would ever be the same again.

He hugged her tight to his body, cradling her close while he sought the right words to win her. "Violet, I'm not a big talker. I don't have one iota of charm and I rarely know what to say when I need to say it. What I said before about being your boyfriend, it might have sounded like a slipup, but it's what's on my mind. In— in my heart. I know you have things you want to do, places you want to visit, a big inheritance you want to blow.

"But when you're ready, I'll be here. Waiting with my girls for the one person who made us whole again. Who gives me hope and makes me smile."

Rather than wait for her to second-guess him or say something he couldn't bear to hear, he zipped up, covered her exposed rear, and left her to think about what he'd just said.

TWENTY-FOUR

Bren couldn't remember the last time he'd felt so happy. Playing the best stretch of his career was helping, though having his girls here was the prime reason.

Then there was Violet. The woman made him feel like a god. Her concern at keeping him on the straight and narrow touched him beyond belief. He liked to think he was strong enough to resist the taste of wine on her lips—and while it had tasted good, she tasted better. She always would. He needed her to know where he stood. Had he come on too strong? Perhaps, but this was too important for indecisiveness. Violet should know his intentions toward her were serious.

He looked around at his men, his daughters, his family, both blood and ice. He was in a good place.

Someone nudged him, and he peered down to find Harper peering up, her hand shading her eyes. "You seem to get taller every year."

"And you seem to get shorter."

"Watch it, St. James."

"Yes, boss."

A few notes on the guitar filled the air. Remy liked to play, and no doubt he was getting ready to serenade his woman. "He's going to go nuts when your kid is born."

"I know," she said, her voice heavy with emotion. "He'll be a great dad."

Bren had no doubt. Sure, Remy would make mistakes, but nothing like the shitstorm Bren had caused to rain down on his own head. Married too young, trying to please the wrong woman, show the world he was a big shot. The intervening years had taught him many lessons, not least of which was that all his problems amounted to a big pile of nothing if he couldn't do right by his daughters.

"Don't hurt her."

Bren blinked at Harper's words. Pretending ignorance wasn't his style, so he didn't even bother.

"I'm in love with her, Harper."

"Well, we all are." He turned to find her sniffing and wiping her eyes. "I mean, how could anyone not be crazy about her? She's a breath of fresh air, the life force this stultified family needed. She seems to think that because she doesn't have an official job with the Rebels that she isn't valuable to us but . . . I don't think Isobel and I would be where we are without her putting us straight. She's like Clifford in that respect, which she'd hate to hear. Crashing in and blowing things sky high, only unlike with Dad, we're left reminded of how truly blessed we are."

That was Violet: party crasher, bringer of blessings, before *poof!* she was gone.

But not if Bren could help it.

Harper shook her head. "Look what Remy's demon spawn has done to me. Changed my personality so now I'm just a vomitorium of emotion."

Bren pulled her close to his side. "The baby's revealing your true personality. Softhearted to the core."

"Oh, shut up. And you'd better not say a word about this to Violet. I have a reputation to maintain."

He kissed her forehead. "Your secret's safe with me, boss."

On the trail of those first few guitar chords, a small, quiet voice started up—a small, quiet, female voice.

"I took my love, I took it down; climbed a mountain and I turned around . . ."

Bren's head whipped around in surprise. That was his Caitriona, singing and playing Stevie Nicks's "Landslide" on the guitar.

Holding his phone screen in front of her, Remy murmured instructions about which notes came next. They must have been looking at sheet music. She stumbled a little, shook her head in frustration, but she didn't give up.

Everyone had stopped to look at Bren's beautiful daughter lighting up the world with her talent. Cade and Erik were bobbing their heads. Violet stood over at the kitchen entrance with Franky, gamely holding a slug jar. She caught his eye and winked. Was this another miracle she'd performed?

After a couple of stops and starts, and two verses later, Caitriona halted and blushed to everyone's cheers. Bren walked over to his daughter and scooped her up.

"Dad! Put me down!"

So maybe she was too old to be held, but she would never be too old to be loved or hugged to death.

"You've been holding out on me, Cat. Had no idea you had that in you."

"I'm not very good. I need to practice more." She squirmed in his grip.

"Aye, we all do." Finally, he put her down.

She smiled up at him, and he rejoiced in the knowledge that his daughter was back instead of the scowl monster who'd shown up six weeks ago.

His youngest appeared at his side. "Whatcha think about your sister?"

Franky held up a slug in response. "Clifford liked it."

He almost choked. "Clifford?" He lowered his voice. "Probably don't want to call him that. Clifford was the name of Violet's dad. Harper's and Isobel's, too."

"Oh, I know," Franky said, mischief in her voice. "Violet said he had slug tendencies."

"She's not wrong," Harper said, walking by.

"The slug can't be all bad," Bren said, still not quite at ease with the name selection. "Sounds like he has good taste in music."

Caitriona rolled her eyes. "Great. A slug for my number one fan."

"Got to start somewhere, sprite. And he's your number two fan. I'm top dog."

"Thanks, Dad." She smiled shyly, then her face

crumpled as her gaze slipped to some point behind him. Both his daughters beelined for a tall, willowy figure standing at the side entrance to the backyard.

Kendra.

"My babies!"

Bren watched as his ex-wife gathered into her arms the daughters she'd abandoned and hugged them tight. As if she hadn't seen them for weeks.

Oh, right. She hadn't. Who the hell did she think she was showing up unannounced like this?

"You've grown so much!" Kendra gushed, her smile only cracking slightly when Franky held up Clifford the Slug for inspection. Kendra had never been a fan of Franky's outdoor pursuits.

Shock had cemented his feet; now his blood flow reactivated him and sent him flying into the fray. He placed a hand on each of his daughters' shoulders and made his claim.

"Kendra, you never call. You never write."

She knew him well enough to understand his tone of quiet, restrained, white-hot fury.

"Bren, you're looking good. I always thought a playoff beard would suit you."

A little dig about how he'd never gotten this far—a bone of contention during their marriage. A journeyman NHLer wasn't what Kendra had in mind when she said *I do*. Each year he didn't make it to the postseason had been another chip away at the foundation of their wedded bliss. She'd expected great things: endorsements, championship rings, to be queen of the WAGs. He couldn't blame her for her disappointment.

But he could blame her for the stunt she had pulled six weeks ago.

She turned her attention back to the girls. "So guess what I have for you both? *Hamilton* tickets!"

Caitriona clutched her mom's hand. "Really?" The hope in her voice broke his heart in half.

"Day after tomorrow," Kendra said.

"We need to talk, Kendra."

His ex-wife raised her gaze, a poisonous sweetness in her smile. "I know."

Exhibiting perfect timing, Violet appeared. "Hey, girls, might be time for ice cream."

Kendra flicked her hair over her shoulder, took one look at Violet, and immediately dismissed her. Bren had seen her do that to women before—only a certain type pinged Kendra's radar, and Violet wasn't it.

Still, Bren didn't appreciate Kendra's disrespect. "Thanks, Violet. As you've probably guessed, this is my daughters' mother."

"Right," Violet said, sort of clipped.

"Oh, so you're the mystery daughter, Clifford's secret love child."

"Kendra," Bren warned. "Violet's been looking after your children while you were"—*at a fucking spa*—"not well."

Kendra didn't take it for the criticism it was. "Thank

you for doing that. I hope you were paid well. Not that you'd need to be, because one-third ownership of a hockey franchise has to be quite lucrative."

Violet could have uttered a sassy comeback, but because she was all class, she played it cool for his daughters' sake.

"Girls, let's give your mom and dad a few minutes to catch up."

Franky peered up through her glasses at Kendra, then turned to him. "Are we going back to Atlanta?"

Bren couldn't tell if her query was out of yearning or dread, but he knew one thing: that would happen over his dead body.

"We're going to talk about everything, sprite."

Then he cupped his ex-wife's arm and drew her around the side of the house.

"Ooh, baby, I love it when you get rough." Kendra giggled, a sound he had no doubt lingered on the air so everyone at the barbecue could hear.

"What the hell are you doing here?"

He got a better look at her, and he hated to say it: she looked good. But then again, a month and a half of yoga, meditation, and finding-her-fucking-self does that to a woman. Gives her a glow.

She smiled. "Still my bad-tempered brute. And now you're my winning, bad-tempered brute." She threw her arms around him.

He unhooked her hands. "Guess you can overlook all my faults when I'm in the finals, huh?"

"Now, don't be like that. Neither of us is perfect."

"You can't just show up like this, Kendra. The girls have been through enough."

"Yes, Bren, they have."

He didn't like that tone. That's how Kendra sounded when she was planning something. It also reeked of playing the victim, and while he wasn't buying that, a flurry of dread rippled through him all the same.

"What do you want, Kendra?"

"I want to reconnect with my family." She lay her fingertips on his chest, then flattened her palm. "*All* of my family."

No fucking way. "What about Drew?"

"He's not the father of my children."

"Dumped your skinny ass, did he?"

"Baby, you think I'm skinny?" She giggled. He felt ill.

"This isn't happening, Kendra. I've talked to my lawyer and I have a good case for sole custody."

"You tell him everything? Because you might want to share some of the stunts you pulled. Give him all the facts."

That hint—hell, full-flavored mouthful—of a threat washed over him.

His hand fumbling with the ignition, the slot impossible to find. Sobs echoing in the car. Dropped keys. Feeling for them on the floor. There!

"Go home, Kendra. Drew's been good to you. I haven't."

Her face turned as hard as glass. "I want to take the girls to see a show on Tuesday. I thought you could join us."

"No can do." As if he'd let them go with her unsupervised. "I'll be in Boston getting ready for the first game on Wednesday. Any further discussion or requests for visitation can go through my lawyer."

"You haven't exactly been a model father."

He moved in close, noting how her eyes flared.

"I screwed up. My drinking was out of control, put a terrible strain on you, maybe destroyed whatever chance we had." He was being kind. True, his alcoholism made him a terror to live with, but he and Kendra did not fit. He'd happily take all the blame if it got him what he wanted.

"And now things are better. You're sober, you're playing better than you've ever been. We're good together."

His winning turned her on, but where would she be during the bad times?

When he didn't answer, her expression changed. "Don't make me fight dirty, Bren."

"You come at me and I will cut you down, Kendra. We've both fucked up, but you did it last, and now the girls need stability."

"With a nanny? With that inked-up punk girl, hated by her father so much he refused to acknowledge her for years?"

"She's been a better mother to those girls than you."

Kendra's eyes flew wide in recognition. "The nanny, Bren? A little clichéd, don't you think?"

That was him, a walking cliché. "See yourself out, Kendra."

Heading back into the gathering, he was aware of

every eye on him, but all he could think of right now was his daughters. He found them in the kitchen, their dark heads close together. In times of adversity, they seemed to put aside their differences and find common ground, just like now, comforting each other. As sisters should. Violet and Isobel were arranging tubs of ice cream on the counter along with toppings, those little chocolate sprinkles and . . . chopped nuts.

By the time Bren reached the counter, Violet had already whipped them away.

Isobel's mouth fell open. "Oh hell, I'm so sorry! It's just that Vad loves nuts on his ice cream."

Violet winked. "Bet he does. And it's okay. No harm done." She shot a searching look at Bren, one that asked if everything was okay.

He had no answer for her, none at all.

TWENTY-FIVE

Violet grabbed her overnight bag and started packing for her stay at Bren's. The team was flying out this afternoon for the first two games in Boston and she was back to the role she'd been hired for: nanny to his girls.

As for the role she'd been unconsciously aspiring to? *Liar, nothing unconscious about it.* The role of Bren's woman was currently open again, it seemed.

Her surly Scot had decided to check out.

After Kendra's appearance at the barbecue, he'd reverted to early Bren—the guy who was unable to communicate, who lived so deep in his head that nothing could find voice. He had to have known his ex would make an appearance sometime, so Violet was at a loss to explain why her showing up *now* should have thrown him so much.

The only conclusion she could draw was that they had unfinished business.

They might no longer be married, but it already felt like Violet was the third wheel. The other woman. Her own mother, for God's sake! And invariably, the fate of the other woman was bye-bye, watch to be sure that booty doesn't get hit by the door on the way out.

This is why she didn't want to get involved. And now, that idiot Scotsman had made her fall in love with him then shut down at the first sign of trouble. She was trying not to travel this road riddled with doubts, but if Bren refused to talk to her about it, what was she supposed to think?

She checked her phone. Already late.

On opening the door to the cottage, she got the surprise of her life: Kendra in the California girl flesh.

"Got a minute?" Kendra asked.

"Not really. I'm running late."

"This won't take long." Without waiting for an invitation, she passed by Violet and dumped her oversized purse on the kitchen table. She looked around, then did the most annoying thing ever: ran a finger over the back of a chair as if checking for dust before taking a seat.

Sighing, Violet placed her own bag down and closed the door behind her.

"How can I help?"

"Can we talk, woman to woman?"

"Sure."

Kendra looked like she was choosing her words carefully, when really she had to have her speech prepared. "Your being here confuses my girls. They like you and that makes it difficult for them. They think they're being disloyal if they're nice to you around me."

"It doesn't have to be one or the other. They know the difference. You're their mother."

Kendra cocked her head. "I'm not sure Bren does, though. He's pretty infatuated with you. Of course, he used to look at me like that."

Violet examined her nails, the ones she was digging into her palm to stop herself from shaking. "What do you want, Kendra?"

"Bren's lawyer got in touch with mine to tell me he's shooting for sole custody." She stood and walked to the sink. Her fingers gripped the edge. "I—I don't know what he's told you about me. Probably painted me as a heartless witch, right?"

"He hasn't spoken much about you at all. He's too respectful to badmouth you." She'd heard everything about Kendra from other sources. Would it have killed the man to bitch about her even a little? But then it was another reason why she was crazy about him. He was decent to the core and respectful of his daughters' mother.

"That sounds like Bren. It's why I fell in love with him in the first place—he's such a good guy, you know." She wiped an invisible tear from her eye and turned back to Violet. "I see that goodness in my girls. They're the best of both of us and we owe it to them to give our marriage another shot."

"So why aren't you telling him this?" *Could it be he can't stand the sight of you?*

"He's angry with me now, but he'll come around. He knows how badly he screwed up during our marriage and he wants to make amends. That's what they call it in AA, isn't it? He needs to apologize for what he did, and once that happens, we can rebuild."

Violet had had enough. "Like I said, this is between you and Bren. Now I really need to go."

"Yes, you do. Out of Bren's life so we can figure out the next steps without any noise."

The odds were good that Kendra would happily tolerate the noise of an arena cheering for the Rebels as Stanley Cup champions.

"Good luck with that," Violet said cheerfully.

The woman still refused to move. All this protesting!

"Let me give you some advice," Kendra said, a hard glitter in her eyes. "You won't be enough for him. Underneath that stalwart exterior is a man who needs constant validation. That's why he married me, so he could tell the world he'd arrived. He'd made it out of his scratchy beginnings, not because he could use a stick on ice, but because a goddess looked on him with favor. It's why he bought that house. It's why he cried when Caitriona was born. I made his life complete. I gave it meaning. And when I took that away he was a wreck. He's hanging on by a thread and I can snip it at any moment or double knot it to give him hope. You won't be enough for him because there are a million girls like you. There's only one me."

"Well, I won't dispute your last point, Kendra. I've never met a woman like you, so congratulations, you're a real winner there."

Kendra's smile was the fakest thing Violet had ever seen.

"I know all about you. How Clifford Chase didn't

want you, how he only included you in the will to screw with Harper. I understand why homing in on a ready-made family is so appealing when your own is so lacking. You remember what it was like growing up in a one-parent household. Would you wish that on anyone? Would you wish it on my girls?"

"There are lots of different ways to make a family. No one says it has to be perfect." Look what she had with her sisters. Perfect it was not, but it was real.

"You're right. Perfection is impossible. But that's just it: we're an imperfect family. We have problems, but there's nothing we can't overcome with therapy and a boatload of apologies for Bren's behavior."

Okay, she'd bite. "What happened? Did he leave the toilet seat up?"

"He didn't tell you?" There was a malevolent glee to her tone that put Violet on edge.

"He's pulled so many stunts, it's hard to say which one you're getting at."

"How about the one where he drove his daughters while he was drunk?"

Dios mío. Not what she'd expected at all, but was it really so surprising? Bren wore his guilt like a shroud. It would only be over something of this magnitude.

"Yep, he could have killed them. That's what sent him into rehab in the end. Not the threat of losing his contract, but what he could have done to his girls. He's always adored them more than anything."

She sounded jealous of her own flesh and blood. What a shrew.

So it wasn't the most savory information, but Violet knew Bren was a good guy. He'd fucked up but he'd turned it around.

"I could have told the lawyer," Kendra went on. "Used it to deny him any access whatsoever, but I'm not heartless."

Oh yeah, this woman was all heart. But laced in her tone was a threat: *she could have used it. She'd happily do so to get her way.*

"He's moved on." He'd told Violet he'd wait for her, for the one person who made him and his girls whole again. She'd felt his heart beat more wildly as he promised them a future. So he was acting like he'd forgotten how to string two words together, but that would change. Violet could get through to him.

"Yes, he might think that. Now. But we'll always be tied together by the girls. There's no denying this magic we created together, these two beautiful little humans." She almost sounded . . . poetic.

So what? Violet had never been a fan of poetry.

Facts were what mattered. Bren's hands on Vi's ass, his mouth on her breasts, his breath against her lips. That moment when he slipped inside her body and his expression registered surprise at how good she felt. Every time.

And then there were her dumb jokes. His heartfelt promises. The place she'd carved with him, his family, and her sisters. These were tangibles she could sink into.

Bren belonged to *her*, and Violet refused to go down. "I'm going to fight you for him."

It was out of her mouth so fast and with such passion that Violet shocked even herself. Kendra's eyes flew wide on hearing it.

"You have no idea what you're getting into, chica," Kendra said.

Chica? Oh, this piece of work was messing with the wrong Boricua.

"Bring it, girl."

TWENTY-SIX

Fifty million reasons came to mind why Bren should not be in a Boston hotel bar, but the one reason he should be rose above all those negatives: they'd won game one of the Stanley Motherfucking Cup finals on away ice. One more game in Beantown the night after tomorrow, then back to Chicago. If they swept the first four games, they could win the whole bloody thing at home.

Wouldn't that be something? Lifting the Cup with his girls looking on.

Petrov, who had just bought drinks for the entire bar, set a soda before Bren and threw a tattooed arm around his shoulder. "Captain, you played—what is it you say? A blinder?"

"*Da*, Russian, I did. We all did."

"The return of your wife has not affected your game. This is good."

He wouldn't say that exactly. He'd talked to his lawyer, who still thought he had a good case, given Kendra's behavior these past six weeks. But Bren hadn't been exactly honest about his own bad behavior. He'd never even revealed it during his drunkalog.

Your "drunkalog" is the story of what happened when you were still drinking and fucking up. Recovering alcoholics usually shared parts of it in group therapy sessions in rehab or during AA meetings. Talking about the stunts you pulled, the pain you caused, the lows you sank to. Then you talked about your recovery.

The most entertaining drunkalogs involved acute embarrassment and brushes with your own mortality. Extra points for allusions to public nakedness, philosophical chats with leprechauns, or a bout with homelessness. Putting the people you loved the most in peril might make for a compelling story in AA, but it sure as shit was not something Bren wanted out there. Not when it could be used against him, lose him everything.

He knew what Kendra wanted. To play at happy families, pretend their problems were just the regular ones every married couple went through. She was willing to overlook everything he'd done—everything she'd done—because he was now on a winning side.

She could have shown up as soon as he won the finals, but she was clearly crafting the optics. It wouldn't look good if she waited until after he had the championship ring. Popping up now meant she could be present when he crossed the finish line. When he lifted his girls into the arms of a champion, Kendra intended to be there, too. Unease cramped his gut.

Not. A. Chance.

A hand on his shoulder drew him out of his fugue.

Remy clinked a beer bottle against his soda glass and nodded at Vadim.

"Mes amis, there's no one I'd rather be making this journey with."

"You gonna get emotional, brother?"

He wiped a fake tear from his eye. "No cryin' yet, but there will be the night we win. And I won't be ashamed of it, either. Just praying we can finish it in Chicago."

Vadim nodded. "All the Chase women should be present, *da*?"

True, and especially Harper. That dynamo had steered this fucked-up ship away from the rocks out to open sea and should be on hand to see her dream come true.

However, there was only one Chase female Bren wanted to talk to this very minute. When Violet had come over yesterday to stay with the kids, she'd seemed a little off. He put it down to his own bad mood in the wake of Kendra's arrival rubbing off on everyone else.

"So, when are you going to make it official with Violet?"

Bren shot Vadim a look. "What makes you say that?"

The Russian looked past him to Remy, who shook his head in amusement. "There is cagey, Captain," Vadim said, "and there is ridiculous. This woman is all you have thought about for months. When she comes into the locker room, you cannot take your eyes off her. When she speaks to one of your teammates, you plan fifty ways to murder him. Eliminate the pretense, claim your woman properly, and do not leave her in any doubt as to your intentions."

Faced with such clear-cut advice, Bren gave a mental shudder. The usual doubts were creeping back in. If he told her what he'd done, how low he'd sunk, would she stand by him? "She has plans that don't involve me."

"Change her mind," Remy said. "Give her a reason to stay."

It wasn't as simple as that, and with the return of Kendra, he felt like he was back on a medieval torture rack, one specially designed to pull his body and soul in a million directions. If he thought Violet might truly want to make a go of this, he'd put his heart on the line for her. But she was also young and had her whole life ahead of her. Perhaps it was better to give a wild creature space to run free than to try to tie it down.

In a few minutes, he'd slip away and call her. He needed that smart mouth setting him straight, that husky voice making him hard, her dirty promises encouraging him over the edge. But more than that, he needed her to give him a sign she was on his side for the long haul.

His phone vibrated in his pocket and his heart fell at seeing the identity of the caller.

"Gotta take this," he told Remy and Vadim.

He answered, asking Bill Carson, his lawyer, to hold on while he found a quieter spot to talk. That quieter spot happened to be outside in the hotel's lobby.

"What's up?"

"Nice win, Bren. You guys played great."

"Thanks. It was a good night." But he had a feeling it was about to go downhill, because no lawyer called at eleven fifteen in the evening with good news.

"Kendra's been in touch through her lawyer."

She didn't waste any time. He thought she'd put the screws on him first before she went for the legal option. "And you said I had a good case."

"I would have, but she seems to be under the impression that you're screwing the nanny. The nanny with no child-care qualifications whatsoever who looks like she walked out of a biker bar."

Anger flared, swift and sharp. "What I do in my—"

"Private life? Is that what you're going to say? Because there's no such thing in a custody battle. I told you to keep your nose clean and not get into trouble. I told you not to give Kendra a single reason to be able to target you. Are you telling me you couldn't find some hot Swedish au pair with a child education degree?"

Jesus, you'd swear Sweden's only exports were hockey players, Absolut, and nannies.

"There were extenuating circumstances. Violet stepped in to help when I needed her."

"Was that before or after you decided to indulge your early midlife crisis and bang the help? And I'm only saying what her lawyer is going to come at you with."

Bren could make his own case. "She's great with my kids. They love her and I—I trust her with them." *I trust her with my heart.*

"Enough to risk losing them?"

Bren let himself into the house at 4 a.m. and laid his forehead against the wall.

What a nightmare, starting with the series. Won one, lost one, and his lack of focus had cost them last night. On the flight home, he'd snarled at anyone who came near him, knowing he was fit company for none.

But there *was* someone who would accept him and his faults, who would whisper sweet nothings and the promise of oblivion. He headed to the kitchen and opened the cupboard that stored the olive oil and rice.

His trusty friend Johnnie Walker Double Black stared back at him. *Uisce beatha*, water of life. He didn't have to unscrew the cap to recall its heady scent, the peaty, oaky flavor he loved so much. He didn't have to unscrew the cap at all, but he did, and poured a dram into a lowball glass.

He rounded the kitchen counter where his daughters would have their breakfast in a few hours, where he'd roll out the pastry for apple pie, and took a seat at the table. Undercabinet lighting shone an eerie glow, shrouding his actions in secrecy. In shame.

Ah, but the whisky had never looked more beautiful, its amber a beacon claiming to hold the answer to his problems. The familiar scent tickled his senses and made his blood rage with a need that never dimmed. His finger circled the lip of the glass, part of the ritual. The first step toward pleasure and pain.

"Dad," he heard in a soft voice behind him.

He turned to see Caitriona in Hello Kitty PJs, her dark hair a little wild, her eyes a little wilder.

"Hello, sprite."

Her gaze flicked to the glass, then back to him. She approached him like she would a wounded animal, all compassion, no fear. He waited for tears, recrimination, anything, but was rewarded instead with her arms circling his neck from behind, her chin on his shoulder.

"Sorry you lost the last game."

"I could've played better."

"Yeah, but it's a team sport."

Wise girl. It *was* a team sport, and he was lucky to have his brothers picking up the slack. Coming back from Boston with the series tied was better than losing both away games. And how blessed was he to have his daughters filling his gaps? Team St. James.

"How'd you get to be so smart?"

"Books," she said.

He smiled against her arm and inhaled her sweet scent. "Everything okay here?"

"Mom didn't come to see us again. I thought . . . well, I thought she might want to when you weren't around."

He'd instructed her lawyers through his that she couldn't just turn up for a visit without warning, but he wondered how his daughters had taken it.

"I'm sorry for all the confusion. We still need to work things out properly."

The half-light illuminated her skepticism as she rounded his shoulder to face him. "It's not fair," she whispered.

"No, it's not," he replied, not sure what wasn't fair, but in no doubt that something wasn't.

"She—she can't just show up and think everything's okay. That all's forgiven."

"She's still your mom. And we're going to work something out that's fair for everyone."

"I want to live with you and Franky and Violet. That's what's fair for everyone."

His tongue was too thick to speak. Somehow, he managed, "I want you all here as well."

She hugged him tighter at that and he absorbed her strength and love, used it to fuel his veins, unblock the pathways to his heart, fill his soul. Whiskey couldn't fix him, but the love of his people might. He stood and picked his daughter up, holding her to his body while he returned her to bed.

"I love you, Dad."

"Love you, too, Cat."

He dropped a kiss on her forehead and left her to return to the Land of Nod.

The drink waited below on the kitchen table and the door to Violet's room was ajar. Never had he needed to see her so much, to touch her and ensure that she was still here, part of his family.

Part of him.

He slipped inside her room and closed the door behind him. A quick strip, a thief's slide under the covers. There was no ambient light, so it took his eyes a few moments to adjust to the dark. She lay on her back, her forearm over her eyes. He could just about make out the sliver of skin between her tank top and her panties. Heat radiated off her and he bent close to inhale the skin at her abdomen.

Then lower.

His mouth watered, the memory of how she tasted flooding it. He needed that again.

He needed her.

Running a finger along the border of her panties, he kissed the skin he'd primed. She stirred and said one word: "Bren."

It was enough.

Violet's body was on fire, every nerve ending aflame with unrelenting sensation. Her eyes creaked open, her gaze unavoidably drawn to the apex of her thighs.

Her man was licking her to paradise.

Oh, God. Her thighs fell open, and she couldn't help the hip swivel that begged him to hurry, *lick*, hurry, *eat*, hurry, *fuuuuck* . . .

His strong hands spread her thighs wider so her knees touched the bed, then they scooped under her ass and raised her for maximum tongue delivery. The build happened so fast that the orgasm surprised her, making her body vibrate like a tuning fork, shaking loose every thought in her head.

Except one: inside me now.

He was panting against her wet center, his breaths hot, stoking the embers of another rise to an even higher peak. This time, together.

She reached for him and . . . tugged his beard.

"Ow!"

"Shit, sorry." But it still made her laugh.

"You will be." He loomed over her, terrifyingly sexy in the dark, but a flash of white revealed he saw the humor in the situation. Without preamble, he slipped right in, her barely sated flesh giving no resistance.

No longer in that twilight between sleep and wakefulness, all her senses sparked to life with this hulking man inside her. He clasped one outsized hand to her ass and used it to leverage himself deeper, to the root.

"Violet," he rasped out. "Baby, I need you. So bad."

This was what it was like to feel wanted. Needed. Integral to this man's life and soul.

She'd meant what she said to Kendra. She would fight for him. He was in her blood, curling through it like smoke and sin. She would stand with him while he defended his family. She would love him without reservation. All in.

Their bodies moved in sync, each long stroke and deep, liquid pull pushing her up, up, up. She dug her nails into his ass, clasped him tight to let him know with actions what words could not express.

Mine. Yours. Ours.

Take all I have.

Treat this gift well because I don't bestow it lightly.

The moment built, a rise she couldn't stop, would never have wanted to. Biting down on his shoulder, she screamed his name while her heart and lungs and cells flew apart.

Seconds later, his body rattled and emptied into her. A minute passed. Then another. She held on, suddenly overcome with irrational fear that seemed to blossom right out of the lingering twitches of her orgasm.

It's too good. It's too right. You don't deserve this.

He rolled away, rolled off the condom—she hadn't even thought to check, but thankfully he'd thought of protection for them both—and dropped it onto the floor.

"Welcome home," she whispered, drawing his laugh.

"Not sure what came over me. I only meant to check if you were okay, and then the next thing I knew—"

"Your face was accidentally buried between my thighs? Hey, shit happens."

He laughed again. Making him happy was the headiest narcotic. Enough light filtered in around the edges of the blinds for her to see his rough-hewn jaw, his crooked nose, his heavy-lidded eyes. His mouth's smiling curve.

What Kendra had told her would gnaw at Violet if they didn't get it all out in the open. There'd be no festering secrets, not with her history as a forgotten daughter.

"Kendra came to see me at the cottage."

"She what?"

He'd turned to her, his breathing quick, his eyes shining lights in the dark.

She flipped the switch on the lamp. "She tried to convince me you'd be better off without me. When that didn't work, she dropped her bombshell. About what you apparently did with the girls when you were drunk. You drove?"

His blue eyes darkened to pinpricks. Oh no. That's what she was afraid of.

"Did that happen?"

"Not exactly."

"So, what exactly?"

He lay back down, his arm over his forehead, his eyes on the ceiling. "I was angry with her. Another fight about the usual shit—how I'd not given her the life she deserved, something more glamorous. How trapped she felt. She wanted me to trade to a better team, as if I had a choice in the matter. She threatened to take the kids. That was always her ace—she knew I wouldn't care if she left, but if she took them, I'd move heaven and earth to hold on to them. I—" He stopped, covered his eyes with his arm. Hiding his shame.

Her skin tightened with dread. "What, Bren?"

"I told the kids to get in the car, we were leaving. But as soon as I realized my condition, I put a stop to it."

"So you didn't drive drunk with your kids?"

He turned to her, his eyes as wild as a madman's. "I—I drove to the end of the drive. A hundred and sixteen feet. The girls were sobbing, telling me to stop. To take them home. Kendra came after me with a hockey stick. Bashed the side of the car."

Wow. Good old Kendra.

"I didn't turn out onto the road, into traffic, but I came close. It's the most shameful thing I've ever done, Vi. It was a turning point for me, made me realize how far I'd sunk."

"You gave up custody because of how close you came

Kate Meader

to hurting them. Because you felt guilty and she used it to her advantage."

"I gave up custody because I was failing as a father. As a human fucking being. I had a lot to work on to make myself whole again. To make myself worthy of my kids and . . . of a good woman."

She inhaled sharply, the breath stabbing her lungs. Was she that good woman? She wanted to be, badly enough to taste it, even with the pain of his revelation. She was that far gone.

He went on. "I needed rehab. But even with what happened with my kids, I still thought I could pull it together myself. Only when I showed up at a game drunk did I realize I couldn't do it alone. Harper gave me a shot and I've been working every day to restore her faith and to earn my kids' forgiveness."

"They've forgiven you, Bren. They adore you. But Kendra is still going to use this against you."

"I know."

The two small words sat between them, sending a shiver skittering down her spine. Not a nice one, either.

"I don't want her in my life, but I have to play it cool. Figure out the best way to ensure she doesn't use what she has against me."

"You didn't hurt them." It was so unfair, but then life was unfair.

Bren blew out a breath. "But I did. I came close to doing something catastrophic, and every day I have to live with that. My lawyer says my case is still strong, though, as long as we're just pitting my bad behavior against her bad behavior. My word against hers. As long as I don't do anything dumb in the meantime."

"Like what? Sleep with the nanny?"

It was a joke, meant to relieve the mud-thick tension, but he didn't respond. No, that wasn't quite right. His silence was the response. A whole conversation of big, fat, ominous agreement.

She sat up, her brain trying to understand what he had yet to voice aloud. "Your lawyer said that?"

"He did. Said I need to hire qualified child care."

She gasped out a laugh, the sound shrill in the night. "That's what I told you in the first place. And now you're—fuck, are you *firing* me?" The farcical nature of the situation popped up, did a Benny Hill circuit of the room, and punched her in the throat. Here she was being canned from a job she wasn't qualified for and had never even wanted!

"Violet, I can never thank you enough for stepping in when I needed you, but I have to do what's best for my girls. I can't risk it. Not now." He leaned his arms on his knees, still gloriously naked, the bastard. "This doesn't change what's happening between you and me."

Now hold up, mister. "You mean your lawyer thinks I'm not good enough to watch your girls, but I'm okay for what? A fling?" *Or you think that?*

His eyes darkened to volcanic depths. "Don't twist it. This is purely a legal strategy to make my case stronger."

"And if this doesn't change what's happening between us, then what's next? Do we go back to secret rendezvous? Hookups while the kids are with the real nanny? Your dirty little secret while you present Butter-Wouldn't-Melt Dad to the world and some judge?"

"They're my kids, Violet."

She knew that. She'd never expected to be number one in his life, but she sure as hell wouldn't be shoved back into the closet with the tuition receipts from St. Ita's.

All her life, she'd told herself that her needs were minimal when it came to men. No dad in the picture? She didn't need one. Bred by her mother to score a jack-pot? Her mom and aunts had loved her the best they could. She had friends and good people in her life, so why would she need a man to complete her? Especially one who didn't need her.

"Then you should be with your kids."

"You and I are separate from that."

"You can't have it both ways, Bren. If I'm considered a threat to your children's well-being, then I can't exist on the fringes like some tropical storm that may or may not make landfall." There was Violet as afterthought, and then there was Violet as a handy vessel for Bren to sink into when he needed to bury all that tension.

The magnitude of that conclusion slapped her hard. "You knew this and yet you still came in here and woke me up with your tongue buried inside me. You knew you were going to tell me I wasn't good enough for your kids—*for legal reasons*—yet you still got your rocks off be-cause hell, at least I'm good for something?"

"Violet—"

She cut him off. "A while back, you said you didn't have the bandwidth to give me 100 percent and I said I was fine with that, that I only needed the tiniest sliver of your time."

She almost laughed bitterly at that patent lie she'd told herself because it would seem she'd been faking that all along. She needed the love of a man who thought this pink-haired, tatted-up, vino-swilling chica was worth 100 percent of his love. Who would fight for her to be in his life.

But Bren was a parent first. He was doing the right thing in removing any barriers to winning his custody fight, even when the primary barrier was her. She couldn't fault him for it, but she had to retain some semblance of self-respect.

She threw back the covers and grabbed her clothes from where she'd slung them over a chair. "This was never supposed to be more than a casual thing, us playing out the hot dad and nanny cliché. Something to relieve the stress you were going through with the playoffs and my drama in the wake of that health scare."

"Relieve the stress? Are you fucking kidding me?"

"Keep your voice down. Think of the girls."

He shot up in the bed, pulling his sweats on with an angry jerk. "Do you really think this is just about stress relief, Violet? Do you think I'm that much of an asshole?"

"No." She was just lashing out, not herself at all. She understood it had meant something to him for a while, but now she felt dirty. Expedient. "You didn't want me as your nanny until I was in the right place at the right time with Franky. You didn't want to sleep with me until I gave you the sad eyes when I found out I wasn't going to die. With each game we get closer to the win, the pressure mounts and I'm here. Va-Va-Voom Violet. Geographically convenient."

He grabbed her arm and pulled her down under him.

"Does this feel geographically convenient?" His back-in-action erection pushed against her core, eliciting a moan.

"You hadn't been with anyone for over a year," she panted, her body straining both toward and away from the man who owned her completely. "Then you started getting some regularly. Who'd say no to that?"

"So any woman will do?"

She reached for his face, stroked his craggy beauty. "This wasn't supposed to happen, Nessie. We were supposed to enjoy each other and move on. You always knew I'd be gone soon, only now with Kendra back and your life so complicated, it's better to make a clean break."

He still loomed over her, her fierce, grumpy Bren. "You think this break can be clean? You think we can just turn off what's happening between us? I've wanted you from the minute I saw you in that bar, Violet." He slipped his fingers inside her panties, and her body switched on at his rough touch. "No one's gonna do you this good, Violet. No one's gonna make you feel like this. I know because no one makes me feel like you do. I can't be the only one caught up in us."

She gasped at his words, at his touch, at his *everything*.

But she knew what it was like to want a dad, to cry in his absence, to need the comfort of those strong arms telling you everything would be okay. Bren's girls had gone through so much, and she wouldn't dream of endangering their futures with their father. He needed space to fix his life.

She would have fought for him if he gave any inkling that he'd fight for her. For what was inside, not just the great ass and straight-from-a-catalog rack.

Pushing his hand away from her center, she slipped out from under him. Then she grabbed her overnight bag, not caring that she was probably leaving half her belongings behind. Underwear, toiletries, her shriveled, useless heart.

At the door, she stood and turned to find him holding himself taut, a Scottish beast about to strike.

"Violet, this isn't finished."

She blinked away a tear but kept her fist clenched at her side.

"Win the Cup, Bren. Love your daughters. Sort your life out. No one is rooting for you harder than me. Truly."

Then she shut the door quietly behind her so as not to wake the girls.

TWENTY-SEVEN

"Hey, it's me!" Isobel's voice echoed from the kitchen.

"In here," Violet called back. Damn, prepare for awkward. She'd hoped to stop by Chase Manor first, then Vadim's house, where Isobel now lived, and make a quick surgical excision.

Iz walked in, arced her gaze over the strewn-about clothes and half-filled suitcase, and twitched her nose. "Going somewhere?"

"Thought I'd visit my mom in San Juan."

"We're only two games into the finals with a possible five to go. Don't you want to wait until it's over?"

It already is. Violet grabbed a bustier and stuffed it into her case. "Look, Iz, you know I said I'd stick around until you guys made the play-offs, and then I had the nanny gig, but really, you have it from here."

Middle Child sat on the bed and picked up a cowboy boot. Dropped it. "Does this have anything to do with a blond, blue-eyed piece of work whose name rhymes with Bendra?"

"No. Okay, sort of. They have unfinished business.

I don't want to be in the way of that." Bren might not have intended to hurt her when he said her nanny services were no longer required, but he had. Deeply. "With me in the picture, it just confuses everyone."

"Is that what Bren said?"

"Sort of."

"You don't sound so sure. In fact, it sounds like the only one confused here is you, Vi. And what about us? Are you just giving up on us?"

Violet placed a hand on her hip and dialed up her best cheer. "This isn't the last time you'll see me, Iz! I'll be back looking for my cut as soon as the Rebels win the Cup, when my third will be worth a fortune. Better work on raising the funds to buy me out or start tapping your Russian billionaire almost-fiancé."

Isobel didn't smile and Violet felt like the bitch she knew she was projecting. But she'd never fit in, not really, and their connection was forced by circumstance. She hadn't even stayed for them in the first place. She'd stayed for *him*. The minute she saw Bren St. James fending off those haters in the Empty Net, she'd crashed.

So what if every day since, she'd become more embedded in the fabric of this family? So what if she loved her sisters and they loved her? How could she look at them, hear a word about hockey, go to a family cookout, and not be confronted with the evidence of her loss?

She rubbed at a knot of pain pulsing beneath her breastbone.

"Well, at least I can help you pack," Isobel muttered.

They worked side by side, though it went slowly because Isobel insisted on picking up every single piece of clothing, holding it to the mirror, and asking, "Would this look good on me?"

After a few minutes, she said in a quiet voice, "You're not in this for the money, Violet."

"You think I stayed to help you out? To help you fulfill the terms of the will? You're wrong."

"Then why?"

"It—it doesn't matter."

"Oh, I think it does," the voice of a new arrival said from the entrance to the bedroom. Harper stood at the door, all five feet one and a half inches in full-on battle mode.

Violet glared at Isobel. "You called her?"

"Hell yeah, I called her. No way are you leaving without completing your exit interview with the boss."

Oh, for fucking out loud. Harper moved closer and in such a stealthy manner that Violet didn't even realize what was happening until the petite blonde had taken Violet's hand and splayed it over where the new life was growing inside her.

"You're not getting off the hook that easily. Now I know it's too early to feel the baby kicking, but she knows you're here. She knows you're waiting to play Stevie Nicks tunes and teach her how to swear in Spanish and be generally inappropriate. Every girl needs a crazy aunt, and let's face it, Isobel is far too reasonable to fit the bill."

What was it with these women? They needed to be doused with an iced cold vat of truth water.

"Harper, I've been lying to you from the beginning. My mom—she planned it all along. Saw Clifford in Vegas. Targeted him. Made sure there was an empty net so that puck could go all the way."

Her sisters stared at her, their expressions ranging from hurt to confused, and Violet's heart shattered for the second time in twenty-four hours. She was a rotten human being and it was about time they figured it out.

Isobel broke the silence. "I've always suspected you've known more about hockey than you let on."

"Did you not hear what I said? This has been a shakedown twenty-four years in the making!"

Harper gave her arm a condescending pat. "Listen to me, *mi hermanita*. So your mom saw an opportunity and sent you to collect—how is that your fault? Do you think we care that this is what brought you into our lives? Clifford owed you. *We* owed you. Now maybe you'll sort things out with Bren, maybe not. But there's no confusion about how *we* feel about you. It's very likely that if we weren't actually related and we met on the street, we probably wouldn't have found a single thing in common. We're all very different, but it's to our advantage, because we each bring something unique to this family. Somehow, these past nine months we've given birth to something."

"We have?"

Isobel stepped in and slipped an arm around Violet's waist. "A holy trinity of such power and awesomeness that nothing—not the press, NHL brass, fanboy haters, crappy exes, bad memories, and awkward sister bonding nights—can break it."

"Damn straight," Harper said approvingly. "We'll let you go and visit your mom because we recognize that you need to get away from everything hockey. We'll fill in the huge, yawning void you'll leave for the moment, but I refuse to accept that this is something more permanent. Your niece needs you. Your sisters need you. And the Rebels need you."

"Could you be any more of a manipulative bitch, Harper?"

"I haven't even started." Her big sister grinned through tears and gathered her into a hug. All this strength in such a tiny package. How her father had underestimated her. How he had underestimated them all.

Violet pulled back, swiping at her eyes. "You keep calling the peanut 'she' as if you're so sure."

Harper laughed. "Remy has four sisters, I have two, and we need a new generation to take over the team. Only a girl could do it, don't you think?"

She wasn't wrong. Besides, if Harper Chase decreed it, who would dare to mess with her plans?

The house felt hollow. Stuffed with furniture and books and slugs, but it was missing something—a piece of Bren's soul. His insides felt jagged, like he was going through detox and his heart was screaming at him to feed it what it craved.

A shot of Violet.

"Dad!"

He faced Cat, realizing that she'd been trying to get his attention from the other side of the kitchen counter.

"What, sprite?"

"Do you think I'll be able to play Remy's guitar at Harper's house?"

"Sure, assuming he's left it there."

She stuffed a notebook into her backpack. "I'm writing a song and I think it would be easier if I could play along."

He tried to focus on parenting. His job. What he was made for. "We can go shopping for a guitar tomorrow, if you like. Maybe Remy can help, because he knows all about them."

"That'd be awesome."

He eyed his youngest daughter, who had just come in from the garden. "No slugs over at Harper's, Franky. We need to be respectful of our host."

"I'm going to free them all."

"You are?"

"Yeah. It's getting kind of crowded in Slugville."

She didn't elaborate—very unlike Franky. Then she leaned on the counter like she wanted to tell him a secret. "Dad, did Violet leave because of us?" He knew when Caitriona didn't say the question was dumb that it was weighing on her mind as well.

"Nope. She just missed her mom and wanted to go visit her." He hadn't told them that Violet wouldn't be their nanny again. They'd had enough upheaval, and

326   Kate Meader

once the finals were done, he'd be available for them full-time.

"And will Mom be coming to live with us again?"

Not on your life. "No, love. We're both happier apart, but we'll be sorting it all out very soon."

"So Violet just needed a break from us," Franky continued. "Like you when you went away. And Mom."

He closed his eyes. When he opened them again, Franky was peering at him with those wide, wise saucers.

"Gimme a hug, sprite."

She threw her thin little arms around his neck. "I never needed a break from you, baby girl. I needed a break from myself."

Cat watched them closely, her mouth set in a grim line. Finally, she asked, "Are you going to get scary again now that Violet's gone?"

He inhaled sharply, the pain of what he'd put his girls through redoubling with the fast beat of Franky's little heart.

"No more scary Dad. And I'm going to work things out so you see both me and Mom. If that's what you want."

Franky drew back and shared a glance with Cat. "We've discussed it and . . . we'd like to stay with you most of the time. And Gretzky."

Gretzky barked at the sound of his name, while Bren's heart expanded so much his chest hurt. For a year, he'd been cultivating new habits. The habit of self-respect, of fatherhood, of teamwork, of pride. Even if the Cup eluded him, he'd still had his most successful season to date—not because of hockey, but because his daughters had forgiven him.

Damn, but he missed Violet.

He missed the life she'd sparked in him, the man who was a better person for knowing her. He swiped away a tear, not sure if it was for what he'd won or what he'd lost.

"Dad, don't cry," Franky said, gazing on him with her usual scientific curiosity.

"Just something in my eye, love." He cupped their beautiful faces. "Now, go take his lordship out for a potty break before we head over to Harper's."

His gorgeous family trooped out, leaving him to finish an important task. He opened the cupboard above the sink and pulled out the bottle of Johnnie Walker. It had given him false courage and nothing but trouble. It had unearthed his ugliness and brought his demons out to play.

He would always want it, but he sure as hell didn't need it.

He unscrewed the cap and watched as the amber liquid spilled its deceptive promises down the drain. If Violet had been here, he suspected she would've been proud.

TWENTY-EIGHT

Violet shook hands with Dr. Nielson, a lot more at ease now than when she'd walked into the woman's office forty-five minutes ago. No doubt the doc saw all sorts crossing her threshold, especially on a campus as big as Vanderbilt, but Violet had still taken the precaution of toning down her Violetness. A long-sleeved blouse and knee-length skirt covered up most of her ink. Gone were her weathered Lucchese cowboy boots, and in their place she wore strappy black sandals. Perfectly conforming. Harper would've shed hormonal tears of pride.

The pink streaks in her hair had stayed, though. She had to maintain some link with her wild child credentials, after all.

"I hope after our chat that you feel Vanderbilt might be right for you, Violet," Dr. Nielson said with a warm smile. "A substantial segment of our student population is considered mature. Not everyone can be attending keggers."

Violet chuckled at how the word *keggers* sounded coming from Dr. Nielson, who had to be in her late fifties.

"Hard to believe twenty-four years old is considered mature around here," Violet said. Around anywhere. The campus was officially in the summer semester, most of the undergrads on break, but on her way in to meet with the program director, Violet had passed by several small groups lounging around the quad. All of them looked like babies, the perfect fodder to wither under the force of her smart mouth and life experience.

"We like a nice mix of students in the early childhood education program," Dr. Nielson was saying. "Getting a few years under your belt, especially in an environment where you supervise children in a professional capacity, can often be as valuable as traditional grades. You have an interesting backstory that gives you compassion and empathy, great qualities to have in our future educators, especially when our charges are so young. Your youthful attitude would help you fit in." Her knowing grin activated the fine lines around her kind gray eyes. "You have my contact information, Violet. Let me know if I can answer any more questions about the program."

"Thanks, Dr. Nielson. I will."

Violet headed out into the Nashville sunshine and tipped her face to the sky, shaking her arms out to get loose after sitting still for so long. What a beautiful day. For the past three days, she'd been taking college tours, something she'd never had a chance to do. She'd missed out, but that didn't mean she couldn't catch up now. First stop had been the University of Texas at Austin, where her usual fashion sense fit right in. Tomorrow, she'd head to NYU to see if the hustle and bustle of the big city suited her. She had her eye on a couple of programs in Illinois, but she didn't want to think about those just yet. The wound was still too raw, thoughts of Bren like a fingernail scraping across it.

She'd spent a few days with her mom in Bayamón, just outside San Juan's city center. Although she was thrilled to have her there, Louisa's first question on arrival was: *Where's the money?* The second: *What bastard put this frown on your face?* Money and men, as inextricable for her mother as ever.

The ache in her heart was surely a normal response after a painful excision. She'd gone through character-building surgery before. This would be no different.

Her phone vibrated and she pulled it out of her cross-body bag, expecting Iz or Harper or even Cade, who had been checking in every day with game scores as if the Internet was unavailable outside Chicago. The finals were tied at two-all because those dumb Rebel lugs couldn't make it easy on themselves.

Her phone blared brightly with a FaceTime call from Hell's Highlander himself.

Heart in her throat, she sank to a nearby bench in the quad, smoothed her hair, and hit the answer button. Franky's big blue eyes, the exact shade of her dad's, blinked rapidly behind her glasses.

"Hi, Violet!"

"Hey, Franks! Is everything okay?"

She'd called them the day after leaving Bren to let them know she'd be visiting her mom. They'd been ac-

cepting, but they knew something was up. On seeing
Franky's serious little face now after what seemed like
forever, Violet felt her dumb old heart leap outside her
body and crash against the screen.

"I've decided to give the slugs a vacation," Franky
said, as if they were just picking up a conversation they'd
recently left off. "I'm putting them back in the garden."

"Oh, cool," Violet said, but Franky was no longer listening, having already started Operation Slug Repatria-
tion. Propped up against a rock with a straight-on shot
of Franky, the phone recorded each lucky winner accepting an all-expenses paid vacay to the St. James backyard undergrowth. The ceremony was set to a funeral
dirge for piano, a strange choice for what should have
been a joyous occasion for the slugs. Cat must have put
aside her dislike for the instrument to collaborate with
her sister. Knowing that did Violet's heart good.

Eight minutes and five slugs later, Violet had tears
streaming down her face. For a bunch of slimy gastropod mollusks? Really?

Now both Cat and Franky smiled back at her, making her heart morph into goo.

"When are you coming home?" Cat asked, a little
rudely. So like her father.

Home. That cliché about home not being a place but
a feeling had never seemed more apt. Violet knew deep
down where she belonged.

With him. With these girls. With your sisters and the Rebels.

"I—I'm not sure. I'm traveling and—"

"Who you talkin' to, sprites?"

Bren.

Her thumb moved instinctively to sever the connection. No one would question a dropped call, yet she couldn't bring herself to do it. Just knowing they were linked in this tenuous way sent her heart soaring.

"It's Violet," Franky said, as though it were the most normal thing in the world.

Bren grunted something. No surprises there. No surprise, either, that he didn't put his bearded beauty on screen. He probably wanted this awkwardness to be over with as soon as possible.

She'd make it easy on him. "Girls, it was great to talk to you, but I should get going."

They waved goodbye and blew kisses and told her they missed her, and she swiped at her tears like a sap. The phone shifted and Bren came into view.

Her heart did backflips at the sight of him, then sank like a stone because he hadn't changed. At all. Shouldn't he look different? *She* felt like a completely different person, and surely that was reflected (negatively) on her outside. Why wasn't the beautiful bastard suffering?

"Hello." He adjusted the screen to portrait view. "Didn't know they had my phone."

"I thought it was you calling."

"It's a wonder you answered."

She sat up straighter. "I'm not going to ignore you, Bren."

"Aye. You've never done that, have you?"

What did that mean? Was he implying she'd thrown

herself at him? Before she could pitch a fit, he asked, "Are you in Puerto Rico?"

"I was, but now I'm in Nashville. Vanderbilt, actually. I'm—I'm visiting colleges with early childhood education programs." She hadn't told anyone where she was or what she was doing, but she knew Bren would understand. He'd never doubted she had more to her.

"Vanderbilt? That's great, Violet." His smile gave her life. "You'd be perfect at that."

"I don't know," she said, her old doubts checking in to say hello. "It's just something I've been thinking about, and working with the girls made me realize that corrupting young minds is where my true talent lies. *And* I have all these quality jokes that need an audience!"

He chuckled, but didn't follow up with a comment. Typical Bren. She wished he could just let it all out. Scream at her about his ex, his sobriety, his life. After all, she wanted to yell, to blame anyone and everyone for the pain she was enduring.

For a moment, she thought the screen was stuck because he was so damn still.

"How are things?" she asked nervously. "Is Addison close to popping? Is Remy still driving everyone nuts with baby talk? Why haven't you won the Cup yet and made me rich beyond my wildest dreams?"

Bren laughed, and then he proceeded to fill her in. She already knew most everything he told her, but she still loved hearing about these people who'd carved their initials into the bark of her heart. Mostly, she loved hearing his voice. She'd always had, even when he barely spoke a word to her.

Maybe they could get through this. Be friends. She couldn't imagine not having him or the girls in her life, yet tears clotted her throat at the idea of half measures with this man she wanted body and soul. She'd thought her problem was that she was a commitment phobe, but it turned out she was a commitment junkie. She wanted love that was unapologetic, unrelenting, unreserved. Love with no conditions. But she knew his girls *had* to come first.

She loved him for it.

The reason this couldn't work was the very reason she adored Bren St. James. *Thanks, Grade A Bitch of a Universe.*

Though she hadn't said a word, he picked up on her melancholy. "I'm sorry, Violet."

"Bren, you don't have to—"

"I do. You deserve the best, baby. I once said you were a gift because you appeared in my life at a certain time. The right time. Like an angel with a mission to make me—my girls better. I meant that. You're a woman without equal. I don't think I could have gotten through these past couple of months without you."

Just as she couldn't have done it without him. He was there for her when she needed him, right until he stopped needing her.

"I should go," she rasped. "I have to catch a flight."

"Where next?"

"New York!" *I'm going places!* "I have an appointment with the program director tomorrow morning."

"They'd be lucky to have you."

"I know." It had taken her a while to realize this. People were fortunate to know her, to have her in their lives. Anyone who couldn't appreciate that could take a hike.

"Just win the damn Cup already, Bren."

He smiled, a heartbreaker of a grin that made her feel both hopeless and hopeful at the same time.

"Good luck, Violet Vasquez. Go forth and be victorious."

He didn't sign off, just stared at her with that trademark St. James intensity like he was trying to memorize her. With a shaky finger, she ended it. Again.

An incoming message chimed in on the screen from Remy: *In Petrov's suite on 15. Don't make me come down there.*

Bren would much rather stay in his Boston hotel room, wallowing in his misery, but Remy would eventually stop in to haul his ass out. Two minutes later, he knocked on Vadim's door, which was opened almost immediately by a grinning Cade.

"About time, Highlander. Your girls good?"

"Aye." He stepped in, surprised at seeing that the contingent was smaller than usual. Besides Cade, just Remy, Erik, Ford, and Vadim.

"Where's the rest?"

"Figured we'd keep it quiet. By invitation only."

Remy pulled a bottle of Coke out of an ice bucket and passed it to him.

Bren nodded his thanks. He was grateful that it wasn't some noisy affair, yet there was something a little expectant about the way his brothers were looking at him. And make no mistake, everyone was looking at him.

"If this is some kind of intervention, I'm not interested."

Cade smirked. "Pretty sure that's what every interventionee says."

Bren took a seat on the end of the nearest sofa. "What's happening in my personal life is not impacting my game. You've seen how I'm playing."

"Bren, Bren, Bren." Remy squeezed his shoulder. "Like that's going to stop us from interfering. I seem to recall you having no problem getting all up in my business when I had a few problems with my beautiful lady."

"And you were the first person on the team I came out to," Cade said.

"Which I didn't ask for. You blurted it out because you were at the end of your rope. I was geographically convenient." A label he hated. The label Violet had assigned to herself.

Cade patted his arm. "There's no such thing. There are only people who step up and people who don't. You offered to be there when I told my dad the truth, and you sat with me in that press conference when I told the world. Stop denying your awesomeness."

Annoyed, Bren shook his head and turned to Ford. "What have I ever done for you, Callaghan?"

Their right-winger considered this. "Some pretty good passing in that last game." Eyes to the ceiling, then a big, dopey grin. "Yeah, that's about it. Makes you the best in my book."

Bren's eye roll took him next to Erik. "What about you, Fish?"

"You ruined my chance to be with Violet."

This was more like it. Someone with a grudge, who wouldn't want any part of this ridiculous bromance shit.

"Sorry about that," Bren muttered halfheartedly. Like he could possibly regret a single moment with Violet.

"But now she is free again and I can take my shot," Erik said cheerfully. "So, we're good, Captain."

Bren merely glared at Erik, but it had no effect. It was like the Swede's mouth was surgically curved upward.

Vadim stood from the sofa. As usual he was shirtless, but no one questioned it because the guy was a Russian supermodel and it was assumed this made him more comfortable.

"It's decided. We all think our captain is worth saving from his own worst impulses."

"Wait a second, Petrov," Bren said. "I barely know you and we're sure as shit not buddies. You've got no horse in this race."

Vadim muttered something in Russian, which Cade nodded at despite the fact that he couldn't possibly know a lick of the language. "If Violet is unhappy, then this has an impact on my Bella. On all our women, because they are close, these sisters. Also, I am prepared to lend my vast experience in the workings of women. I, more than anyone, understand how they will happily remove your heart, hold it bloodied and pulped to the sky, and offer it in sacrifice to whichever gods they pray to."

Jesus wept. "Does Isobel seriously put up with this shite?"

"She has accused me of drama on occasion. I have no idea why."

Over the resulting laughter, Vadim continued. "What I am saying, Captain, is that these trials are often a necessary test. Just like the finals are a test of how solid the bonds are between the men on a team. Are we strong enough to win the next two games and win the Cup? Are we strong enough to do what is necessary to win the hearts of the women and men"—he gestured at Cade—"who make us worthy?"

Bren had thought that after a year of sobriety, he could handle anything, even listening to this BS spewing from Petrov. Nothing would stand in the way of a meaningful life with his daughters and his drive to make it to the top of his sport. Redemption in the eyes of his girls, his team, and the fans.

In walked Violet.

No. In *boomed* Violet.

He had failed her. He wasn't brave enough to risk losing his daughters again, not while Kendra held this sword over his head.

"I'm not worthy of Violet. I doubt I ever could be." He looked up at his friends, none of them as amused as before. "I let her down."

"*Dites-nous tout,*" Remy said quietly. Tell us everything.

He did, including his shameful behavior when he almost hurt his girls and how it would forever haunt him.

Heart sinking with every word ripped from him, he waited for their disgust. Last year, he'd shown up drunk before a game in the dying days of the season and was immediately suspended. It was the night after he'd hit rock bottom, and how do you think he celebrated? By getting shitfaced.

Cade and Erik were the only men present who had witnessed that, but everyone else knew. Word of Bren's suspension and mandate by management to get dry had spread faster than Petrov's slap shot. He didn't do it for his team. He didn't do it for himself. He did it for his girls.

"What did the lawyer say?" Remy asked, his face a mask of concern.

"That if Kendra brings it up, I risk losing all access. We've got her bad behavior over the past two months, but it's not criminal. And if we win the Cup, she'll be gunning for me. Maybe even—shit, wanting to get back together now that I'm the winner she signed on for all those years ago. That's not happening."

"Don't worry, Highlander, we'll throw the game if it keeps you out of Kendra's clutches."

Everyone glared at Cade, who'd uttered that piece of junk.

"Uh, kidding. Look, this whole thing is basically Kendra's word against yours. She didn't report it."

"I won't lie about it. I won't say I didn't do that."

"It is honorable," said Vadim.

"No, it's stupid. What about Violet?" Cade's voice was as hard as glass.

"She knows why I can't commit to her fully, but . . ." He trailed off.

"But what?" Ford asked.

"She didn't fight. I expected she'd have ideas on how to counter this, but she just assumed I couldn't come up with a solution. She gave up." And now she was looking at degree programs in fucking Nashville and New York. Torn between happiness that she was embracing her future and misery that it didn't involve him, he'd barely managed to hold it together on that phone call with her this morning.

"She's got it in her head she's not good enough," Cade continued, "when we all know it's the other way around and she's the best thing to ever happen to you. You should be fighting this together, telling Kendra where she can shove her accusation. I reckon you're both total idiots."

Everyone went silent, thinking on what had just been said.

Finally, Remy spoke. "Maybe you should come clean."

"With Violet?"

"With the world."

Bren stared at him. "Tell everyone what a fuck-up I am?" That was exactly what he was trying to avoid.

His entire universe had collapsed when he realized how close he'd come to endangering the people who were most precious to him. It was bad enough the media, fans, and his team knew he couldn't hold his liquor. He'd fessed up to his teammates, but he doubted everyone else would be so forgiving.

Remy had a curious look on his face, like he wanted to say something but would prefer Bren work it out playing charades.

Tick. Tock.

Cade made some weird noise that sounded like *aha!* "You *did* say you wouldn't lie about it if Kendra accused you."

"Right, but I'd rather it not come out at all."

The Cajun rubbed his beard. "But if it did, people wouldn't approve. Lots of people."

"Da!" Vadim had the same look on his face as when he'd scored twice in game one. Was Bren the only person here who didn't understand what the hell was going on? "In fact, Captain, I'd say a revelation like that might have a very negative impact on your career."

Recognition seeped into his consciousness slowly, building to a full-scale lightbulb-over-his-head moment.

Yes . . . it . . . would.

His heart was beating a hundred miles a minute. It was a gamble, but if he wanted to restart his life, then he had to go big in order to go home.

Because home would be nothing without *all* his girls.

TWENTY-NINE

Stanley Cup Finals, Game Seven
Chicago Rebels at Boston Cougars

Violet was a masochist.

That could be the only explanation for why she was at a hockey game ten days after leaving Chicago. Harper and Iz had bugged her with texts and calls every day, and begged her to return in case all their dreams came true tonight. Hers, too, given that the franchise would be worth more if the Rebels were crowned champions. The series was tied at 3–3, and now the Rebels had to win game seven in enemy territory.

Mercenary considerations aside, she knew why she was really here: that other C-word, closure. Time to act like a big girl. She might never live in Chicago again, but she'd want to see her niece—she wasn't an unfeeling monster. There would be visits and family gatherings, at which other team members would no doubt be present. Bren. Maybe with Kendra . . .

No, that was unlikely. Not once had he ever indicated a reconciliation was in their future. But he would eventually find someone. Someone who would complement the image he needed to present to the world.

Heading to the visitors' executive box to meet her sisters, she stopped when something crashed into her.

"Franky!"

Franky peered up, raised her hands slightly as if going for a hug, then changed her mind. A brief twist of hurt flashed over her face.

"Hey, kiddo! Where did you come from?"

In answer, Caitriona exited from one of the sky-boxes, two doors down from the owners' one. "Hey, Violet," she said with a shy smile.

"You missed the last game," Franky accused. "Dad scored the goal to keep us in!"

"I saw that. I had to go see my mom in Puerto Rico. I missed her."

Franky nodded in understanding, Violet instantly forgiven. "That's okay. You're here now."

"We missed you," Caitriona said.

Violet's heart checked, especially hearing that from Cat, who wasn't given to unprompted displays of emotion. "I missed you guys, too. So, uh, could I have a hug?"

The girls shared a glance, then Cat, for once, took the lead. Violet held them both close, wishing things could be different.

She had to ask, though she suspected she knew because of where they'd emerged from. "Is your mom here?"

Caitriona thumbed over her shoulder. "Yeah, she's in there."

"And things are good?"

"She's better," Franky said, suddenly the least informative child on the planet. "We have to go to the bathroom. We don't want to miss the beginning."

"Okay! See you guys later." She watched them head to the restroom, looking out for each other like sisters should. At the last moment, Franky turned.

"Hey, Violet, where does Batman go to the bathroom?"

Tears thickening her throat, Violet managed to croak out, "I don't know. Where?"

"The batroom!"

Cat rolled her eyes and dragged her sister away. With one last look at the entrance to the skybox they'd just left, Violet headed to the owners' suite, and put her head around the door.

"Hey, Rebelistas."

"Vi!" Harper jumped up and hugged her tight. Amazingly, she'd increased in baby girth in the past ten days. "How was your trip? Mom okay? Your aunts?"

"Fine. Good. The same." Violet smiled on seeing Isobel, who walked over from the buffet and squeezed her until she could barely breathe.

"About time, sis. I thought you were going to miss the start of the game."

Dante stood near the window, suited up as usual, a scotch in his hand. He placed it down and walked over, surprising the hell out of her when he wrapped her in his big bear embrace.

"Welcome back, Vasquez. Your snark and general inappropriateness were sorely missed. Apologies, I don't have any of that Chivas junk you usually drink."

"The pricy junk will do."

Releasing her, Dante poured a couple of drinks, handed them off, then turned to her oldest sister. "Harper, I've no doubt you have something to say. You always do."

"You betcha, Moretti." She sipped from a glass of sparkling water. "This is it, team. I was going to say that I can't believe we made it, but well, I can. Because with this crew, anything is possible. We're not a normal family. We're screwed up, we're a little broken, but together we're stronger."

Isobel grinned. "No matter what happens tonight—"

"Don't say there's always next year," Dante said with a groan.

"I was going to say that we've proven the bastards wrong. We've proven Clifford wrong. And that's almost as good as winning the Cup."

"Almost," Harper said, clearly unconvinced, which made them all laugh.

Dante downed the rest of his drink in one shot. "Okay, puck drops in a few. I suspect I won't be able to speak to any of you for the next ninety minutes without hissing, so I'm going to go throw up and then I'll see you on the other side." He left the box and yes, they all checked him out. Then they looked at each other and giggled, just like old times.

"I don't know why I'm here," Violet murmured.

"You're here to fight." Harper stepped close and squeezed her arm. "I'm feeling some déjà vu here, ladies. Game night, a future on the line, love for the taking—"

"Hormones gone wild," Isobel muttered with a wink at Violet.

"Maybe," Harper said. "Maybe it's just this crazy roller coaster of a season. Together we've overcome a lot of obstacles."

"With wine," Violet said.

"I miss wine!" they all said in unison.

Chuckling, Harper linked Violet's arm while Isobel took ahold of her other one and practically dragged her over to the glass. She felt like she was being led to the edge of a volcanic crater. Her knees were on the verge of folding, but her sisters kept her upright with a strength only Chase women could possess.

The warm-up was in the final stages. After Bren's great performance in game six—and she'd watched every pass, penalty, and goal—there could be no doubt that he'd feature prominently tonight. Her eyes frantically searched until they found him.

O Captain! My captain!

"Don't Stop" by the Mac came on, a classic crowd pleaser. Bren was right, it was overplayed, but it was also perfect, because at that moment, he looked up and their gazes connected. He waved. And Violet moved her hand back and forth like a crazy person until she realized that most likely he was waving at his daughters a couple of boxes over.

She couldn't tell if he smiled at her. She couldn't remember what his smile looked like at all. How could she have forgotten?

He did another circuit of the ice, punctuating it with

a second glance upward. This time, he placed a fist on his chest and gave three short taps. When his hand came away, she saw it.

A pink ribbon, the kind that people wear to support breast cancer awareness. Even stranger, he wasn't the only one. Cade zipped by heading for the blue zone, an unmissable flash of pink on his chest. Remy, too.

All the players were wearing one. She turned back to the box to find Harper affixing hers.

"What's going on?"

Isobel smiled. "Charity begins at home, sis. It was Bren's idea."

Harper's eyes remained on the rink. Her kingdom. "A donation equivalent to tonight's gate will go to breast cancer research. In the name of the Rebels."

"But that has to be—"

"A couple of million," Isobel said. "Give or take." The lapel of her tracksuit had a ribbon on it.

"You bitches, are you seriously trying to make me cry?"

Isobel laughed. "You? Pretty sure your tear ducts are glued shut."

Not anymore. Not now. Finally, she broke.

"She's—she's—here," she said between spectacularly ugly sobs. "His—wife."

"His ex-wife," Harper said. "And he's down there, but he's not thinking about her."

"He's thinking about his daughters and he's thinking about you," Isobel said. "You're going to have to learn to deal with her. If you want a relationship with him, with those girls, then you have to learn how to co-exist. It'll be messy, but hey, look where you come from. You're a Chase. When has it ever been anything else?"

"I don't know if he still wants me. If he ever really wanted me."

"I already told him I'd cut him if he hurt you." Harper's mouth tipped up. "Now I know he did, so I reserve the right to beat him to a bloody pulp after tonight's game. But I think he needed to figure some stuff out. You both did. Athletes are intense guys, but they're not always the sharpest blades on the ice. Bren's a man. He can't be expected to get it right the first time."

How lucky she was to be part of this family. She'd never thought she'd be grateful to Clifford Chase for anything beyond a Catholic private school education and the one-third ownership he'd given her in the Rebels. *Love fierce* had always been her motto. Violet needed to love deeply and be deeply loved. She hadn't expected it with these girls. She hadn't expected it with anyone.

"Thanks," she said quietly to both her sisters. "Seriously." Then she offered a silent prayer of gratitude to Clifford Chase—great player, so-so manager, terrible father, all-around asshole.

The reason Violet was as strong and amazing as she was.

A captain's band meant something. Responsibility, leadership, rock-solid strength. And Bren needed every one of those traits to be working at 110 percent when they entered the third period tied at two-all.

Petrov had scored a sniper shot in the first period to even up the score. When they fell behind in the second, Remy managed to level two minutes before they entered the last break, a minor miracle because he was playing on the right wing with Ford off the roster. Baby Callaghan had decided to pick the most important day of the postseason to make his entrance.

But finals games weren't won on the ice in the third period—they were won in the heart. At that point, skills didn't matter. Stats were worth shit. Passion was the only benchmark.

The woman who represented Bren's was here.

She'd waved at him during the warm-up, but then every time he looked up while he was sitting on the bench, there was no sign of her. He saw his girls, though, their hands spread wide on the glass. He heard their shouts of encouragement in his head above the screams in the arena.

Had Violet left? He refused to entertain the notion that she might not be here afterward, win or lose.

Four minutes left in the period. Boston was getting cagey, relying on their shaky defense and doing a lot of passing back in their zone. No one wanted to fuck up when they were so close to getting to overtime.

Three minutes, ten.

Coach called the final time-out and the team huddled. "No one get fancy out there, because if they score now, I will murder each and every one of you fuckers in your sleep."

Nervous laughter greeted that and died quickly when Coach maintained his balls-shriveling glare.

"Petrov, that was really directed at you. I know you like to take chances, but not now. Not until we make it to overtime."

"At which point we're looking at first to score, Coach," Remy said. "And it's over."

"Yeah, but we get a few minutes to breathe first. Regroup. Everyone here is fuck-tired, but I don't want any sloppy moves in the last couple of minutes of regulation. Get us into overtime, got it?"

The crew mumbled its affirmation.

Back on the ice, Bren gripped Remy's arm. "You see an opening, you take it, okay?"

"Hell, yeah."

He saluted Petrov on the skate-by, then did a figure eight that took in his D-men, Cade and Kazinsky, and Jorgenson in goal. "You're a wall back here," he said to Alamo. "Nothing gets by you."

"Aye, Captain," Cade said with a wink and a shit-eating grin.

Boston had possession, but was obviously under the same orders from their bench: hold on to the puck and don't make any sudden moves that might result in dispossession. But they also had three guys under twenty-five on the forward line, players with fresher legs than the Rebels. Sure, Chicago had Petrov, a relative baby at twenty-seven, but combined they were looking at fifteen years plus on the age of those Cougar pins.

Chicago might not have much left come overtime.

Two minutes, forty-five.

One of the Boston defenseman, Billy Stroger, had history with the Rebels. History that involved physical abuse of Harper years ago and the eventual beat-down by Remy in a January regular season game. So far, they'd kept the trash talk and shoving to a minimum, but now Stroger took it upon himself to get all up in Remy's grille. Words were exchanged, and whatever occurred, Stroger came out of it fuming.

One minute, thirty.

During the next play, Stroger made a mistake: his pass to his teammate fell short.

Remy pounced. Not only had Stroger left it hanging, he'd also left an alley a mile wide up the right lane—the lane that Remy was now streaking through on his way to the goal. Petrov had already cut left, and Bren hung a few feet behind, waiting for Remy's pass.

He scooted it across to Petrov, who had a better shot at goal from the left, and with the instincts of a killer, the Russian drove it to the top shelf, only to have it deflected by the Boston tender.

The rebounded puck landed right at Bren's feet.

They say that at the moment of death, your life's important moments flash through your mind. The highs, the lows, the ones that defined you and made you a man. No one ever told him that it would happen at other times, such as in a moment of rebirth.

Holding a wrinkly baby Cat for the first time.

Hearing a precocious ten-month-old Franky say "Dada."

Feeling the warmth of Violet's smile the day she found out she was still cancer-free.

Now he could add one more:

Watching as the puck slid through the pocket.

He knew it had made it before the buzzer sounded, before the crowd roared, before Remy crashed into him, screaming, "Yesss!"

Puck luck had found Bren at last.

Forty seconds.

Now they would be cagey.

Boston threw everything into it, including their goalie, leaving an empty net. But every Rebel stayed back and defended what was theirs. Trap-pass. Trap-pass. Trap—*buzz*.

It was over.

THIRTY

The entire arena exploded in pande-fucking-monium.

Bren whipped around, frantically seeking out his girls. Harper was already here, crashing into Remy's arms before he fell to his knees and kissed the child swelling her belly, whispering something over and over in French.

Petrov was practically humping Isobel against the Plexi. She had her legs wrapped around his waist and her lips suctioned to his face. Even Cade and Dante were getting in on the act—about time those two offered a little PDA to the soap opera–hungry masses.

Still no sign of his girls.

He skated over to Harper. "Where are they?"

She looked over her shoulder. "They were right behind me. Where have—oh, there they are!"

And then he saw them, running down the tunnel, their beautiful faces shining back at him. Kendra walked behind them slowly with Drew beside her, but that was okay. Bren held no ill will toward him, and they had to figure out how to get along eventually.

Fuck, they'd won.

"Dad!" Franky yelled, and crashed into his out-stretched arms. Cat joined in and twined herself around his neck.

"You won!" she screamed in his ear. "I knew you would."

"Glad one of us did," he said, laughing.

Over their heads, he shook hands with Drew and met his ex-wife's eyes. "Thanks for coming to the game."

A week ago, he'd flown to Atlanta, and against the advice of his lawyer, met with her one-on-one to tell her how their daughters' custody would be handled from here on out. She'd fumed and railed and called him names, but he had her over a barrel, and she knew it.

She wouldn't be the wife of this NHL champion, but he expected she'd land on her feet. Kendra was a survivor.

"Dad, Violet's here," Franky said. "We saw her up in the box."

He stood, his mind crazed with missing her. With needing to see her and touch her and hold her close.

He had to find her.

A large palm landed on his shoulder and he turned to see Remy. "Come on, mon capitaine. You're needed for the Cup presentation."

Kendra smiled at him over their daughters' heads. "I've got them."

The next ten minutes were a blur. The commissioner spoke and a few other suits said their piece and then there she was, brought down on the red carpet by NHL brass wearing white gloves: the Stanley Cup. All shined up and ready for their greedy mitts.

It was his right as captain to raise it first, and as he skated to the pedestal where they'd placed it, his mind rewound to everything that had happened this year. Rehab, divorce, hell away from his girls, getting them back, making it to the play-offs against all odds.

Violet.

She was here somewhere in the building. She wouldn't come to the final game of the season to support her family and leave without a word. She'd want to see it through.

He scanned the faces of his teammates, his coworkers, his soul brothers and sisters. They'd put up with his shit, and he couldn't have done this without them. The commissioner congratulated the team and called out his name, but he was already skating back to his circle of truth before he'd laid a finger on the hardware.

"Remy," he said to his friend, who had his arms wrapped around Harper. "I'd carry your woman and child, but I reckon you'd feel safer doing it yourself."

"Captain, you have a trophy to lift," Harper said, gesturing behind him.

"Aye, but not alone."

Remy smiled in understanding. "C'mon, minou." He lifted her heels a few inches off the ice, and holding her tight, skated over to the pedestal with Bren following him.

"What the hell? Remy, put me down!"

"Yes, boss."

The commish, who had never exactly approved of a woman-owned team, looked on in semidisgust, but the man had to admit Harper Chase had done a helluva lot more for the Rebels—and hockey in general—than her old man had.

Usual form was for the commissioner to hand it off to the captain, but there was nothing usual about this Cinderella run to the finals and all the way to the winner's circle. Bren took Harper's hand, squeezed it, and placed it on the Cup.

"Thank you, Harper. For everything."

"You bastard," she said with a watery sniff. "You know how hormonal I am." She lifted the Cup a few inches off the pedestal.

"Good enough," he muttered, then he took over and raised it above his head. Damn, the fucker was heavy, but it was a weight he could handle. One he'd longed for. To raucous cheers—and a few boos because there were still some shitheads who hated him—he skated a couple of rings before passing it off to Remy.

"Merci, mon ami," the Cajun said before he whooped and hollered like a little kid.

Tears streamed down Harper's face as she watched her man achieve his life's goal, or one of them, anyway.

"Is she still here?" he asked her.

Harper nodded, smiling through the tears. "She came back."

"For her family."

"For *all* her family." Harper grasped his arms, but as she was short, even in heels, she could only reach his elbows. "While I'm glad I didn't can your ass last year, Bren, if you don't tell my sister you love her, I will trade you out at the first available opportunity."

He had no doubt she'd do it, too.

But Bren didn't need threats from Harper Chase-soon-to-be-DuPre. He just needed Violet.

Alamo now had the Cup and was howling his head off while Dante looked on indulgently. This could take a while, so it was a good thing Bren had something better to do.

He had the hardware. Now for the true prize.

―――――――

At the far end of the tunnel the noise was deafening, yet Violet could still hear her pounding heart above it all as she paced outside the locker room.

Go out there. Go tell him you love him. Do it dramatically in front of a million people.

That's what Harper had done in the full-blown view of the sports media. Isobel, too, with the team looking on as she told Petrov what a fool she'd been. Cade had come out during a press conference, for himself and his man. Dante had since claimed him right back.

All these emotionally stunted people of her acquaintance had somehow managed to get their heads out of their asses and tell the people they loved that they . . . well, loved them! And here she was, wandering backstage at the Cougars' arena after the team she owned had *won the Stanley freakin' Cup.*

Just do it. Year of the V, girl. Where V stands for Vagina, Victory, and . . .

"Violet."

Oh, thank God. She turned to greet a bearded god. God himself, maybe, if the Almighty was Scottish and grouchy and beautiful.

"You won."

"I did. *We* did." He motioned between them.

She shook her head, suddenly shy. "I didn't do anything."

"You sure about that? Violet Vasquez, the mixer, the troublemaker, the bringer of fun? The woman who questions the status quo and pushes everyone on this team and in this family to do better? To *be* better. You're underestimating your contribution to the Rebels." He paused, then added a gruff, "To my happiness."

"Of course you're happy. You just won the Stanley Cup!"

"Doesn't mean much without you, Vi." His brow lined, his mouth skewed. "That night I told you what the lawyer said, what he'd advised, I was being torn apart. To come so far and to get so close to them again—I couldn't think beyond that to a point where I could have everything I wanted. Cat, Franky, you—this life I imagined with us all. Fighting for my girls is something I'd only recently learned. Fighting for myself and for us was something I still needed to learn, and baby, I'm sorry I didn't make that clear."

She widened her eyes to stave off the tears. "This

isn't all on you, Bren. I—I panicked at the first sign of trouble. I didn't want you to regret fighting for me. I had a hard time believing I was worth it, so I didn't grab on to that sexy beard and pull you close. I could have told you I had your back, that we'd work it out together. Instead I convinced myself that walking away was doing you a favor. And when you didn't stop me, I felt vindicated in every preconception I had about how men—how people—can't be trusted. I thought I had a lucky escape not knowing my father, that none of those hurts he'd inflicted on Harper and Isobel could touch me. Shows what I know. I'm even more screwed up than them!"

"No, you're not. Well, maybe a little, but you're this family's heart, with the blood of your sisters pumping through its chambers."

She liked that. Not Clifford's blood, but something more elemental. A feminine power she shared with the Chase women.

He stood about three feet away from her, balancing on his skates, but with the grace of a cat and the solidity of a mountain.

She took a step toward their future.

So did he.

"I was worried about my girls, about what Kendra could do to rip them from my arms. But I'm not going to let her get in the way of me living my life. Of this life I want to build with my daughters. With the woman I adore. I wasn't ready for you, Violet. I wasn't fully formed. You need a man who will give you 100 percent

of his focus, who will treat you like the queen you are.
It took me time to become that man. He stands before
you."

And this guy thought he had no words! Her heart
leaped in all-consuming joy, before checking ever so
slightly. Didn't they still have a Kendra-sized problem?
"You'd risk her going public with what happened?"

"I've already hit rock bottom. There are no more lay-
ers of hell to visit. If she wants to dig deeper and find
one I don't know exists, then she can go ahead. I'm not
going to run from this, even if it means confessing my
mistake to the world to get a jump on her."

Another step from him.

One more from her.

"So I told her as much."

"You—you'd tell everyone what happened?"

"I'd be honest. Tell my side. And while I might not be
charged with a crime, I would be tainted, and that stink
of scandal could result in me losing it all. The Rebels
wouldn't re-sign me. No other team would touch me."

Oh my God. She saw it now. "You lose. She loses. No
more alimony, no more anything."

His smile was wry. "She could be the rich ex-wife of a
Cup-winner or the poor ex-wife of a washed-up drunk."

"But—but the Rebels would have stood by you once
they heard your side of the story. I would have made
sure of it."

"She doesn't know that. She can't have it both ways.
She can't paint me as a villain and expect no consequences for her own life. I did something I'm finding

it hard to forgive myself for, but if I have my girls, I can work on it. I can work on anything."

She was so proud of him for coming to this realization. Love was the ultimate battle and the future was so worth fighting for.

He was barely inches from her now. "Thing is, I called her bluff. But I'd have gone through with it in a heartbeat and taken my chances in court. I know I have people on my side, an amazing support system with my team and my friends, and I hope that includes my woman. I need it to include my woman. Because I might have my daughters, but there'll always be a hole that only one person can fill. I've been asking forgiveness for over a year, trying to make amends to everyone I've hurt, and I'll do it for the rest of my life if it means you'll spend it with me. Will you stand with me while I fight for my girls, Violet? For *all* my girls?"

"Yes."

"Then why are you over there and I'm over here?"

They were mere inches apart, but he was right: it felt like a giant chasm still existed between them. "I don't know!"

"C'mere, lass." His chest heaved, releasing what must have been a pent-up breath, and he gripped her face with both hands. His mouth sought hers, such hunger, such joy in it, and she gasped in relief.

He wanted her.

He would fight for her.

She would claw the heart out of anyone who tried to come between them.

"I love you, Bren," she said when he let her up for air.

"Aye, well, I love you more, my valiant, vibrant, victorious Violet."

And then he kissed her again so she couldn't argue with him, as if his loving her more was even possible.

It wasn't, and one day she'd tell him. For now, she'd climb her Scot like a tree and cling for dear, dear life.

EPILOGUE

Thirteen months later . . .

"Nervous, *mon frère?*"

Bren squinted at Remy, wondering if he'd made a mistake in giving him this incredibly important job.

"I wasn't until you brought it up." After all, he'd done this before, not that his previous experience set a good precedent. For his first wedding, he'd thrown up in the bathroom beforehand when he saw that four hundred people had filled the church in Brentwood, California, most of them guests of his then-fiancée's family.

He looked out over today's more intimate gathering on the grounds of Chase Manor on the shores of Lake Michigan. The floral-covered bower was set in a semi-shaded spot halfway between the cedar-and-stone mansion and the cottage where he'd made love to Violet as much as his raging libido allowed. His teammates, their wives, and a few close friends gazed back at him. Kevin, his sponsor, had actually brought a date, and while she looked great, he still looked like shit. Even Kendra was here, still with Drew, who'd had a good enough season on the gridiron to keep her interest. The girls would spend a month with them after the wedding so he and his bride could have a little time to themselves to christen all the surfaces of the house.

"Thanks for standing up with me," Bren said to Remy, meaning more than just today.

"Figured I owe you after you did the same for me. Besides, what else have I got to do now that I'm retired?" He thought for a second. "S'pose I could open a business planning bachelor parties in my hometown."

The New Orleans stag party *had* been a pretty righteous blowout, even for a man who didn't touch a drop. "Think you have your hands full at home."

"Yeah, I do," Remy said with great feeling as his eyes zeroed in on Amelie and Giselle, his twins, now close to eight months old and currently in a double bassinet under the care of one of Remy's sisters—Josette? Martine? The man had four, and Bren still couldn't keep track of who was whom, even after he had spent last Thanksgiving in New Orleans with them. Remy'd kept his promise to Harper to retire when the Rebels won the Cup last year, though there was no missing that envious look in his eye when the team made it all the way to the finals for the second year running, this past month gone. They'd fallen to the New York Spartans in a heartbreaker of a game seven, a loss that wasn't made easier by the fact that they were the defending champions.

Winning the Cup just once wouldn't be enough, but the Chase sisters had proved that their first two years of leadership weren't a fluke. They had more championships in them.

Vadim stood on Bren's other side, pulling at his collar. "Perhaps we should text them. There is a good chance I will melt before we get to the vows."

"I know covering up is tough for you, Petrov, so I'm very grateful you've made the sacrifice."

"Anything for my captain," Vadim added with a salute and another tug of his collar.

The final member of Bren's wedding party walked their way. Dante had become a good friend in the last year, and now he placed a hand on Bren's shoulder. "I have to warn you that if you had ovaries they would probably be exploding in approximately three, two, one..."

"Sweet, wonderful you..."

The opening strains of Fleetwood Mac's "You Make Loving Fun" started, chosen by both Bren and Violet in lieu of something more traditional. All eyes shot to the end of the aisle, and Bren's man ovaries went *kaboom!* at the sight of Franky and Caitriona walking toward them in pretty blue dresses, bearing small bouquets. They looked so grown up, and his heart tripped at the sight of their beautiful, incredible, unique selves grinning broadly at him. He'd given his blessing to a (temporary) streak of pink in their hair to honor the woman of the day, and somehow that one concession had made him dad of the year.

Next came Harper and Isobel, polar opposites in appearance and personality, but united by something stronger than sisterhood. Survival. Harper was pregnant again and going through a less traumatic time

than her first go-around. Smiling at their men, they
took their place on the other side of the celebrant.

Gretzky trotted a couple of feet behind them, his
black coat groomed to a blinding shine, the most obe-
dient Bren had ever seen him—*and* he spoke too soon,
because the dumb mutt spotted Bren and charged him
with mucky paws.

"Down, boy."

"Which is what Violet will be saying later on tonight," Vadim commented as he took charge of the dog
with a few commands in Russian.

About to growl his displeasure at Vadim's cheap
shot, Bren halted, because it appeared that Petrov might
be onto something.

Here comes the smokin' bride.

She'd gone with white, but that was about as traditional as Violet "Va-Va-Voom" Vasquez would ever get
on her wedding day. In the July sun, her vibrant tattoos
and cocoa skin gleamed above her strapless gown, the
jewels on its bodice winking in the sun. The dress fell to
midcalf, giving everyone an excellent view of her navy-
green tartan cowboy boots.

St. James tartan, that is, which matched the kilt
worn by Cade, who was giving her away, and which was
also worn by every man in the wedding party, including the groom. Apparently, he'd lost a bet, the details
of which were hazy. Whatever. Violet's wish was Bren's
command.

Last summer after they won the Cup, he had taken
his family to Scotland, and on the shores of Loch Ness,

fell to one knee and asked this woman to allow him to love, cherish, and sing to her tunelessly for all the days he had left on this earth. On her screech of "Yes!" the calm surface of the lake broke, the resulting ripple caught by an early morning ray of sun.

Nessie approved. Both of them.

Today, she didn't dawdle, but then that was Violet, a woman born to march in, mix up, and make the world her own. Only this time she wouldn't be pulling a Mary Poppins and going *poof!* with her flying umbrella. No, Violet Vasquez would remain earthbound with Bren, giving him heaven in every moment.

Cade left her off with a kiss on her cheek and a wink at Bren—was it too late to punch him?—before taking his spot beside Harper and Isobel.

Bren's woman studied him from head to toe, taking in his argyle jacket, full-dress sporran, knee socks, and gillie brogues. The kilt pin, usually shaped like a sword, had been custom made in the form of a hockey stick—a gift from Harper for the entire wedding party.

Violet sighed her approval. "Looking good, Nessie."

"Looking better, Vi."

Their stupid grins rivaled the sun above their heads. Her happiness was his, and with his career winding down and hers starting up, he figured they had a good balance that would bode well for marital harmony and his daughters' teen years. Don't get him wrong—he was dreading the moment one of his girls brought a guy home on a date. But Violet would have her early child-hood education degree from Loyola University in Chicago by then and would likely have advice on how to handle it. He suspected he wouldn't be allowed to deck any potential suitors or chase them off the property with a blade. More's the pity.

The music faded. The celebrant opened his mouth. Violet held up a hand.

"I'm sorry, but could I say a couple of words before we get into the nitty-gritty?"

Bren rubbed his jaw. "Will these words leave me crying and/or jilted by the end of them?"

"Jilted? Oh no, you're not getting out of it that easily, St. James. But I can't guarantee tear-free." She waved in front of her face, her eyes already misting over. "I'll make it quick, I promise."

She clasped his hand, squeezing it for strength, and faced their guests.

"I just wanted to thank you all for being here and say a few words to the people who made me their person. Rebels, every single one of you are champions and I love you all." She pivoted to the wedding party. "Cade, you're the brother I never knew I wanted, and those months as your fake girlfriend while becoming your actual best friend will stay forever in my heart."

Cade winked and mouthed *I love you.*

She went on. "Dante, you're undoubtedly the hottest guy I've ever seen in real life." To the groomsmen, she added, "Sorry, boys, we all agree." A quick visual survey of the women present confirmed the general consensus on this. Even his Cat nodded! "But you're not just a pretty face. You've also been an amazing friend to me, all the more special because I wasn't always such an amazing friend to you."

Dante kissed his fingertips Italian-style and gestured with his hand toward her.

"Mami," she said, turning to her mom in the first row, seated with two of Violet's aunts. "You worked so hard to raise me, making sure I never went without even when you did. I'm so glad you're here. *Te quiero mucho.*" I love you.

Her mother sniffed loudly, which set off the aunts and most of the guests. Louisa clutched at her chest and nodded her love right back.

"Girls!" Violet reached for Cat and Franky, who wrapped themselves around her. "Thank you for sharing your dad with me. What you're giving me is the most awesome gift imaginable."

"We don't mind," Franky said.

"Yeah, it gets him out of our hair," Cat deadpanned, drawing laughs from the crowd.

"Uh, what did we say about propping up your dad's ego?" She kissed the tops of their precious heads. "Just pretend it's tough to have to share."

Her gaze fell on her sisters, and words seemed to fail her—but this was Violet, so not for long. "Harper's usually the one for big speeches, and no one can harangue, guilt, or manipulate like she can with a few words. I can't possibly do justice to my feelings for you two amazing women, but I'm going to try. You had no reason to accept me into this family, a million reasons why it would be easier to ignore me. I've been looking for something, a life with purpose, and you gave it to me, no questions asked. There've been times when I wanted to strangle you both. I expect that instinct won't disappear because you're incredibly stubborn and a pain in my ass. But the love is there wrapped up in this holy trinity of power and awesomeness. Yes, I stole that one from Iz. I love you guys." She swiped at her eyes and raised a fist to the sky. "Not yet, god of happy tears!"

At last, she turned her attention to Bren with a splay of her fingers over his chest, soothing the *th-thunk* of the heart that beat madly for her.

"My beautiful, grumpy Scot, thank you for being patient. Then, today, and for the rest of our lives." She didn't explain the *then*, though they both knew what she meant. Nine months, one week, three days, and seven hours, give or take a few minutes, from the moment he first saw her in the Empty Net to the moment his body found peace inside hers. "Thank you for loving every part of me. For seeing who I am and who I want to be. For turning the Year of the V into a lifetime of love."

She leaned up on the toes of her cowboy boots and he met her halfway to accept her kiss. He should be thanking her, but he had no words, only his mouth and arms and body to worship her with. When their lips parted, he tried to tell her with his eyes how grateful he was that she had found him and hooked him.

"I know, Nessie." She understood, but then this woman knew the rocky contours of his heart better than anyone. Eyes bright with joyful tears, she turned to the more-than-patient celebrant.

"Okay, Padre. Let's do this."

ACKNOWLEDGMENTS

What a glorious ride we've had with the Chicago Rebels. This has been such a fun series to write and I hope it's been an equally fun series to read! Thanks to all of you who followed me from the firehouse to the ice rink.

To the team at Pocket Books, especially Kate Dresser, my editor; Molly Gregory, who kept me on track and answered all my dumb questions; and eagle-eyed copy-editor Faren Bachelis, who fixed all my dangling modifiers with the patience of a saint (I think I figured it out by this last book!), thanks so much. My gratitude also extends to Melissa, Abby, Hannah, Marla, Lauren, Jean-Anne, and Liz for making every book release a pleasure.

I'll admit that while I like hockey, I'm more of a tennis fan—don't hate on me, guys! So I needed a little help with the ins and outs of the sport, especially with the business side of things. Thanks to Kelly Jamieson for filling the gaps and for taking me to my first hockey game in Chicago. Go Hawks!

Now, you might have noticed that this series featured several characters with sexy accents, some of whom actually spoke in their native tongues. Thanks to Lana Kart for her help with Russian and Samantha Roldán for her assistance with Puerto Rican food and culture, and Spanish phrasing. All mistakes are mine, of course.

Finally, to my romance family and my actual family, thanks for the mountains of support you've heaped on me. Like Bren in *Hooked on You*, there's not a day that goes by when I don't count myself blessed to have such amazing people in my life.